THE WOLF OF TEBRON

THE WOLF OF TEBRON

A FAIRY TALE BY

C. S. LAKIN

LIVING INK BOOKS

Writing Worth Reading

The Wolf of Tebron
Volume 1 in The Gates of Heaven® series

Copyright © 2010 by C. S. Lakin
Published by Living Ink Books, an imprint of
AMG Publishers, Inc.
6815 Shallowford Rd.
Chattanooga, Tennessee 37421

ISBN 13: 978-0-89957-877-4
First Printing—June 2010

THE GATES OF HEAVEN is a registered trademark of AMG Publishers.

Cover designed by Chris Garborg at Garborg Design, Savage, Minnesota, and Megan Erin Miller.

Cover Illustration by Gary Lippincott
(http://www.garylippincott.com/).

Interior design and typesetting by Reider Publishing Services, West Hollywood, California.

Edited and proofread by Rich Cairnes, Christy Graeber, and Rick Steele.

Various quotations throughout this book are from *Mere Christianity* by C. S. Lewis, © C. S. Lewis Pte. Ltd., 1942, 1943, 1944, 1952. Extracts reprinted by permission.

Printed in the United States of America
15 14 13 12 11   –V– 7 6 5 4 3 2

"Some day you will be old enough
to start reading fairy tales again."

C. S. LEWIS

In Memoriam –
Gilbert and Clive: May your words light the way home
for millions more . . .

And to –
Megan and Amara, whose creative imaginations
spill into my writing

PROLOGUE

EXHAUSTED AND battle-weary, the wizard chose his footsteps carefully amid the sharp granite crags. Daylight barely seeped through the dark shroud of morning; a few renegade stars dotted the horizon. The sentinels of mountain that hugged the vale were bathed in a lavender hue, their peaks pointing toward heaven in seeming supplication. Leaves, curled and crisp, frosted over with icing, crunched under his boots as he squeezed his way through cracks and crevices, fatigue making him stumble. Cold air burned his throat as he panted. He paused to catch his breath. From the cliff outcropping he could make out his lone cottage burrowed under a ledge of rock, a wisp of smoke from a leftover fire rising and twisting slowly in the chill air.

The wizard tugged his woolen cloak tighter around his neck. His silver hair, matted and leaf-ridden from days of fighting, fell around his face, stuck to his damp cheeks. His scabbard banged rhythmically against his leg—the one without the long gash, bound and oozing blood. His feet throbbed in their boots, the toes numb. But, his wounds disturbed him less than the ache in his heart. For this had been just one of many fierce battles against a force intent on annihilating all the wizard held dear.

He squeezed his eyes shut, and across the stream of time he could see the wake of endless conflict, stretching back beyond his mind's reach. And in its wake death, pain, and suffering. He sighed

· 1 ·

deeply. Only a little farther and he would slip into warmth, peel off his filthy clothes, heat water for tea and bath, and fall into Rhianne's arms. Later he would assess their losses; later he would mourn his fallen companions. He brushed the visions of the slain and the wounded out of his thoughts. Those were weighty burdens he could not now carry in his heart if he hoped to make his way home.

He stopped suddenly. A gnawing sense of doom thumped against his chest, caught in his steamy breath. His throat clenched shut. He felt a pallor spread across his face. Without turning, he knew what pursued him.

Running as fast as his bruised body allowed, he skipped down sheer walls of slate and landed hard, ignoring screams of pain, pushing fear aside with all his might, willing himself to muster some scant reserve of strength.

It came first as a chill on his neck. Then, a cacophony like a myriad of squealing bats with thrumming wings sounded overhead, heading toward his home. Blackness thick as mud engulfed pale morning light; even the stars were swallowed up in pitch. As he ran, dark funnels swirled in a frenzy, with a piercing hiss and the sound of a million claws ripping through silence, tearing his protection spell into shreds, his resolve into panic.

His cottage vanished before him into a void. Blindly, he fumbled for a door he knew should be there, threw it open, and ran to his bed where Rhianne lay asleep in peaceful ignorance. Rafters creaked and groaned from the weight of the invasion. Frost raced across floorboards, scurried up the cracks in the walls. The wizard gagged from an evil so caustic that his throat stung.

Slogging through the thick gloom with outstretched arms, he cast scraps of words that he frantically gathered around him, remnants of the tightly woven spell draped over her. But they were torn to pieces, useless. His jagged words siphoned into the roar of the storm. And he had no name by which to call this malevolence, to draw its attention away from his wife. In horror, he watched impotently as Rhianne thrashed, flailed, fists pummeling the air, the distance between them uncrossable.

Harnessing magic, the wizard hacked through the void and fell onto pillows, finding no one. He screamed in anguish, stumbled backward, then glanced to his left. Black wisps regrouped, gathered force, and headed down the hallway with purpose.

Pale light seeped out from under the nursery door. There was still hope! Fueled by anger and desperation, the wizard outran the evil, sliced through it with sharp focus, and burst into the corner room, still warmly illuminated and undisturbed. He threw himself over the cradle, weaving a new spell as the chill surged into the room. As blackness enveloped him and his sight failed, he repeated his incantation over and over, his love, his joy giving him strands of power with which to fabricate a membrane, clear and gelatinous, to encase the young child. His ears rang from the shrieking and tearing of air around him, but he kept his eyes and heart on his son. The membrane wrapped him, the boy, and the cradle in a cocoon of thick light: pale, weak, but holding. All he could do now was lay there, his body limp, his heart oh, so heavy—and wait.

Finally, with a shudder, the house settled. Not daring to look up, the wizard sensed the blackness lift, disperse, and seep out of the room. He felt more than heard the calmness of dawn return to his mountain. Below him, his son fidgeted, hot under blankets and his father's sweating body. The wizard lifted himself off the cradle and reached in to pick up his child. He looked into the gray eyes that laughed back in innocent delight. A small hand grabbed two worn fingers and yanked. Mindlessly, he stroked his son's curls, caressed his cheek. He removed his cloak, feeling his age and the burden of his defeat. The room thawed and warmth returned. Quiet settled like a warm current, with Rhianne's absence more palpable than her presence ever was.

The wizard wept.

Holding the child, he sat in the rocker, beautifully carved of alpine cedar, Rhianne's favorite chair. Heavy sobs shook his chest as hot tears dripped onto his son's nose. The baby tugged on the silver beard with chubby fingers. Through the window a weak sun was rising over the crags, splintering light in all directions and illuminating a day that had no business dawning.

After rocking the baby back to sleep, he lowered him into the cradle and ambled down the hall to the front stoop of his cottage. Cold morning air assailed him and for a moment he stood there, immobile. Resolve came slowly but deliberately, until it faced him down like another indefatigable foe.

Anya. Anya. In his mind he crystallized an image of the thick, lumbering bear. He saw her sleepy, curled up in her musty den piled with cypress branches and tufts of dead autumn grass. *Anya!* He poked her with his thoughts and she twitched, annoyed. Finally, she stretched her large bulk, hung her head, and arched her back. It took her a moment before she understood.

Coming, my lord . . . sleepy . . . what?

The wizard prodded her. *Please, Anya, make haste!* He felt her grow more alert now, recognizing her den and sniffing the morning air. She shook her massive bulk, tossing off dirt and debris. Snips of questions flitted through her head, which the wizard ignored. Explanations could wait. He went back into his cottage and rummaged through a large trunk by the door. Pulling out a cloth satchel, he began stuffing food, clothes, blankets, toys. When finished, he sat on the stoop and waited.

Soon, he could make out the brown shape climbing up the ridge in a steady, methodical rhythm. Anya's bulk swayed from side to side as she took deliberate steps with her giant paws, wending her way around ponderous boulders and cautiously fording small creeks. When she arrived at the cottage, the wizard buried his face in her neck, rubbed her small ears.

My lord, how may I serve you? She made a clumsy bow, as good as a bear can manage. The wizard found a smile.

My sweet girl, I need your help. It is no longer safe for the child to remain here. I cannot remain, either. I had hoped this day would not come; come it has. He paused, then took a deep breath. *I have to find a way to rescue Rhianne and the others. Where I am going, the child cannot come.*

The bear lowered her head and nuzzled the wizard's palm. *My lord, I will take the child. I will take him to the woods of Tebron.*

Yes. He will be safe there until I can retrieve him. The wizard stroked her silky coat. *I am eternally grateful, my friend.*

The wizard attached the satchel to the bear with a linen sash, tying it across her back and securing it with metal hasps. He went into the nursery and gathered up his son, then fastened him to the bear's warm chest, against her heart, with a long panel of curtain yanked down from the kitchen window. When all was secure, he ducked his head under Anya's snout and kissed his dozing son on the crown of his head. Anya suppressed a yawn, shook sleepiness from her head.

He is precious to me; take good care of him.

Lord, he is precious to me too. Do not trouble your heart. I have kept many cubs from peril.

With a tender, reluctant pat he sent Anya on her way, watching as she cautiously padded down the rock faces to the canyon below. He did not loose his gaze until her body diminished to a small, brown speck against green fields, the sun high in the sky, and bird songs returned again to the bushes beside his home.

Far beyond the green meadows, green even in winter from the mild winds and flowing creeks tumbling out of Logan Valley, the mighty trees of Tebron Wood rose stately and crowded against the towering cliffs behind them. And beyond that, the wizard could make out the tiny cottages nestled in the hillside encircling Tebron, with the ribbon of cart road winding down, down, out of the isolated village toward the rest of the world.

• PART ONE •
THE LUNATIC MOON

ONE

A DARK BIRD, no more than a shadow, circled over-head. Joran looked up into a night in which stars refused to show. Although his clothes were dry, he saw he was immersed in water, the wind bobbing him roughly across the surface of the sea like a skimming rock. Waves caught in timeless repetition, trapped by the Moon's whimsy, slapped a distant shore as she tugged at them to lull her to sleep. The Moon glared her defiant and harsh light down upon him as the bird snipped at her hair, pulling threads of gossamer, like pulling worms from soil. Joran watched, fascinated, as the bird spread the strands of light across the expanse of water, a diaphanous blanket. The ocean then turned into a million shards of glass, reflecting broken bits of the Moon in a shimmer so bright Joran had to avert his gaze.

Imposing sandstone cliffs loomed up before him, crumbling, laced with erratic ribbons of pebbles. Obsidian rocks with jagged teeth barricaded the shore, with sea lions draped like discarded blankets, their barking puncturing the silence of the night. Joran stared up the steep wall of sand; eons of erosion had carved deep fissures into the cliff, chiseled by the Moon's persistence and single-mindedness. Waves carelessly tossed him onto the beach; he tumbled to a stop at the base of the cliff. He stood and looked around, realizing he had been here before.

Stretching perilously above him was a sand castle—a structure of stones, grit, and broken shell melded together. One window, as if dug out of sand, faced the sea and seemed composed of tumbled sea glass, misty and frosted—whether from salt spray or cold, Joran couldn't tell. Bleeding heart vines trailed like a messy braid of hair down the cracks of the cliff from the castle atop the bluff.

In slow motion, Joran reached one hand over another, grasping vines that surprisingly held his weight. Digging toes into the side of the hill, he edged his way up, swaying and righting himself, seeking purchase in the loose, uncooperative sand. He heard the Moon chuckle behind him. Anxiety grew the higher he climbed, until Joran's woolen tunic sagged from a heavy sweat. The wind kicked up, sending a chill through his limbs, sending the bird reeling and screeching. His clammy hands slipped along the vines, ripping deep-pink heart-shaped flowers to litter the beach below.

Determined, Joran dug his nails into a ledge and pulled himself up, breathing hard. Finally, he lay perched on the bluff, next to the sand castle, which leaned precariously toward the sea, as if yearning to fall in. Here the clamor of the waves grew to a deafening roar—almost as loud as the pounding of his heart. Gripped with an unwarranted fear of falling, Joran forced himself to stand. He hastily stepped back from the dizzying edge and approached the castle.

Joran breathed onto the window as he scoured it with his hand. He pressed close to the sea glass, aching to see in. The Moon laughed and slipped behind a cloud, and Joran rubbed harder, strained his eyes. His emotions tumbled, like rocks caught in the riptide; fear rolled over anger, anger toppled hurt. Night wheeled around him at a frantic pace, and Joran felt his world giving way under his feet. His hand stuck to the glass, fingers stuck to each finger in reflection, and Joran gasped.

Her face, just inches from the glass, stared vacantly at him. She was encased in ice, embedded in time, and her plea reached Joran's ears, a cry caught in midthroat, tinged with fear. Cracks in the ice spread around her face, and as Joran tried to pull his hand free, the cracks deepened and lengthened. The eyes staring back at him betrayed panic. Joran pulled harder. Finally, with a shock of pain as flesh tore from his fingers, Joran broke away and fell back, releasing a spray of icy water, broken pieces of glass smacking his face and neck. His feet pedaled uselessly under him as he plunged off the bluff and fell, screaming, toward the beach below.

Joran's eyes lurched open at the thud against the window. He abruptly sat up in a tangle of covers and straw, cool morning sun spilling through the glass. He squeezed his eyes and rubbed his throbbing head. Where was he? The familiarity of the barn loft, smells of hay and goat, helped him piece himself back together. It was Tuesday. He was sleeping in the barn again. And as the nightmare returned in wisps, he scowled. Why was he plagued with these images every night?

His thoughts were interrupted by a high-pitched moan that seemed to echo his own.

Ooh! Achin' head! Ow!

Joran, puzzled, looked around him, lifted blankets, and then—remembering the thud—unlatched the transom and peered out. A tiny frych, in brilliant emerald with a ruby head, lay on the dirt by the barn door. He could hear the goat in the back stall calling to him.

What was that? You slept late again. My udder is about to burst.

Joran found his pants and put them on, pulling strands of straw out of his pockets. *A bird hit the window. Sorry, I'm coming.* He climbed down the ladder and laced up his boots. He shook his head, trying to chase away the shards of nightmare that lingered. His body felt stiff from the uncomfortable and disturbed sleep. Now he was late for work—again.

Anger filled his heart, a feeling growing more familiar each day. Charris's face came to mind, her wavy long hair, her sage green eyes and thick lashes. Joran forced the image aside, striking the air, as if that somehow helped. His heart hurt, thick in his chest, a crushing weight, an anvil breaking his ribs. He threw open the barn door and a blast of cold wind assaulted him. Clouds gathered in the north, over the woods—thick, dark clouds heavy with snow. He heard a flock of songbirds welcoming the morning and smelled winter on the air. Joran shivered with cold but he didn't care. The gloominess fit his mood.

Joran reached down and picked up the frych. The little bird's head wobbled in a struggle to face Joran.

What hit? Who? A singsong voice.

I'm Joran. You seemed to have crashed into my barn. Can you move your head?

The frych turned her head from side to side. *Hurts. But okay. I think. But, ow!*

I have no time for this, Joran mused. He carried the bird into the barn, dumped out a wooden nail box and bedded it with straw. He placed the bird in the box and patted her gently. *Okay. No flying for you today. Here's some chicken feed and a soft place to rest. I will check on you later, when I get back. I'll put a dish of water next to the box, here.*

Oh. Thanks. Okay. Will stay here. The little bird settled down peacefully into the straw and pressed her eyes closed.

Joran smirked; he knew just how the frych felt. Distracted, he milked the goat, drank some of the musty milk with a chunk of stale oat bread and a block of cheese. He packed a sparse lunch in his sack and let the goat out into the yard where Charris's horse was pastured. The goat muttered her thanks between bites of grass.

Smelled that wolf again. When's Charris coming home? She's a better milker than you . . . softer hands . . .

Joran ignored the old goat. He looked up at the rolling meadow behind his cottage to the sharp-toothed ridge outlined against the sky. He scanned for the familiar shape, the lone hunter pacing steadily, or sometimes as still as a statue. Often, Joran could sense the wolf staring at him—but more likely his goat drew the wolf's attention. He had never lost any livestock to the wolf, but he heard tales from his neighbors of missing chickens, geese, cats. Sure, he was too far away to mindspeak with him, but Joran wondered if a creature like that would even stoop to converse with a human. Well, however curious, he certainly wasn't going to try to get close enough to find out. Today, he saw no wolf, but Joran knew he was out there, somewhere.

Joran's gaze traveled back to his cottage. Since Charris left he'd taken to sleeping in the barn loft. He knew he was being stupid—abandoning a warm feather bed and a toasty hearth for the damp, smelly loft. But, he couldn't bring himself to sleep in *their* bed; even walking into the house assaulted him with memories of Charris. He could smell her scent in the rooms, and there were her clothes and drawings, and spices in the kitchen. Everything in that house stirred anger and pain, so he stayed away.

After washing up and shaving at the pump, Joran dunked his head in the wooden trough and rubbed it dry with a towel. He flattened down his curly hair, smoothed his wrinkled clothes, and felt barely human. It would have to do. He slung his pack over his shoulder and headed down the dirt lane that led to the cart road.

Mounds of recent snow lay piled along the sides of the road, and the bare branches of alder and aspen reached out like needy arms. Fueled by agitation, Joran picked up speed and began to trot down the road. It wasn't until he got to the old Baylor farm that he slowed to catch his breath. Bile rose in his mouth as he surveyed the homestead with its small creek running through the field. A derelict waterwheel turned slowly next to a dilapidated hay shed. A small cottage with rotting steps leaned against the barn, paint peeled away long ago. He searched with his eyes, struggling between wanting to find someone there and dreading he would.

Joran fumed and quickened his pace, pounding the ground beneath him with intent. As he rounded the bend and crossed the bridge that forded the creek, he looked up, sensing something. On the hill, atop a brushy butte, stood the wolf. Joran halted.

Joran had seen wolves on occasion, heard them baying on warm autumn nights. But this one was unlike any other. His thick silver coat gleamed in the light, reflecting hues that made his image waver, like a mirage. His haunches were huge, his paws massive. And he always displayed a keen gaze, almost a knowing manner, in the way he often watched Joran through the seasons.

In Joran's earliest memories paced the wolf. Joran did not know how long a wolf's years were, but this one was at least twenty cycles. This one, for some reason, did not fear being seen by humans, and, Joran guessed, showed an interest in the affairs of men. Joran felt the wolf's gaze upon him. *What are you thinking, my mystery wolf? Do you laugh at us and our failures?*

Joran turned from the wolf and picked up his pace again. *Failures.* Joran cringed thinking what would happen once the entire village found out about Charris. He was kidding himself imagining he could keep up a charade in a town where everyone knew your business before you did. But he had to live here, work here. He knew his brothers would pry. The Weavers' Guild would inquire why Charris had stopped coming. He hadn't even thought up any good excuses—if any could be called good. There was nothing good about her leaving. Where was the good in *good-bye?*

Field turned to forest as Joran marched down the road. Flakes of snow landed on his coat, stuck in his eyelashes. The woods flanked him on either side of the road, tall trees with their tops in the heavens, and trunks so thick it would take ten men to circle one of them. He had lived in the village most of his life, but it was the forest of Tebron that had always beckoned to him from his earliest memories.

While his childhood friends had run about town, playing stickball in the streets and building forts in the narrow alleyways, Joran would disappear into the thickness of trees, embracing the solitude that resonated with his heart. For some reason he felt more a part of the woods than of the bustle of human society, and he thought perhaps that was why he had developed such a kinship and communication with animals. He spent many peaceful hours just sitting quietly, observing the birds as they chatted to one another, watching the little denizens of the woods—the foxes, the hedgehogs, the badgers—amble past him, burrowing and snuffling for grubs. But today he barely gave the forest a glance. They were solitary trees standing in judgment of him. He hung his head and sped up—and nearly collided with the goose woman.

"Take a care there, little cub."

Joran, startled, stopped. The tiny stocky woman looked up, straining her neck to study Joran's face. A patterned scarf bound her hair, and in her gnarled hand she gripped a staff of burlwood that was topped with a knob rubbed smooth from years of use. Geese honked around her, wandering in mindless circles, waiting for coaxing. Joran recognized her from the marketplace, where she often displayed her crate of enormous oblong eggs. He was surprised to see her walking along the road.

As if hearing his thoughts, she spoke, her voice gravelly and deep. "We live up there." She gestured into the forest where the ancient trees hugged the hillside. "We saw you coming."

The woman walked around Joran, stepping much like her geese in a jerky, halting manner. She wore oversized shoes made of wood, and her threadbare smock hung straight to her ankles. She reached into the pouch around her waist and pulled out a handful of feed, then scattered it on the ground, which set off loud honking and a bluster of goose movement.

Joran sidestepped the squabbling birds and nodded respectfully to the woman. "I apologize for not seeing you. I'm late for work, though. I apprentice with Elder Tabor, the blacksmith . . ."

"Yes, we often see you there." The old woman blocked his path and gripped his arm tightly. Joran stopped. "We see your dreams." Grabbing his collar, she pulled him down to meet her gaze. "You have taken her and trapped her, you have."

Joran abruptly pulled back. He felt a shiver dance across his neck, and hugged his cloak tighter. Geese surrounded him, hemmed him in. What was she carrying on about?

"Little cub, don't you understand? You must save her before the sand slips through the glass. You must loose the three keys and open the lock. You will have no peace unless you do this." The woman gazed up at him, her rheumy eyes flitting and darting. Joran smelled rancid breath and rotting teeth. He drew back, disgusted.

Joran pried her knobby fingers from his cloak. "You must be crazy, old woman. I have no idea what you are talking about." He pushed through the maze of geese and readjusted the sack on his back, watching her eyes laugh at him. This woman was loonier than his mother! What was she going on about—"three keys" and "sand through the glass"?

The woman called after him as he hurried down the road. "It is you who have trapped her. Between Moon and tide. Anger burns cold, but it will leave only ashes."

Joran covered his ears to shut out her words. What did that old fool know? How could she see his dreams? Was she talking about Charris? And how would she know anything about him or his life?

Joran quickened his pace, trying to focus on the day's work ahead. But as he neared the village, her warning rattled around in his head like the stones in his dreams, tumbling in waves, rolling and colliding, leaving him no peace.

TWO

JORAN TURNED the hickory handle on the bellows, forcing in air and fanning the forge's flames. Next to him on the anvil were the makings of iron horseshoes. The gelding pawed impatiently. Joran wiped his grimy hands on his leather apron and swabbed the sweat on his forehead with his sleeve. The smell of horse and burnt hooves filled his nostrils.

Can you hurry? My stomach is grumbling and I'm missing pasture time.

Joran reached back behind the row of tongs and punches for a handful of hay. He stuffed some into a net bag hanging by the horse, who tucked his nose into the treat without a word of thanks.

I can get done faster if you stop all that fidgeting! Joran grabbed the back hock and pressed a shoe against the hoof. He lowered the foot and, using tongs, thrust the iron into the fire. The bellows creaked and whooshed air as Joran cranked it again, then removed the glowing orange shoe and tempered it with a hammer.

Although the forged burned Joran's face, the coldness of the day seeped into his clothes and chilled his bones. He stamped his feet to warm his legs, kicking up dust. Scattered around him in the open stall were axles, traps, parts of cart yokes—most in need of repair, some unfixable. Bells jingled as carriages passed him on the street, but he ignored the waves of his neighbors. As usual, the morning air was redolent with the aroma of smoking sausages from the butcher's down the lane, and warm yeasty bread rising at the bakery. His stomach grumbled in complaint over his measly portion of breakfast.

As he pounded the shoe, Elder Tabor waddled over to him, placed a hand on his shoulder. Joran kept hammering, concentrating on his task.

"You seem out of sorts today, lad."

Joran glanced at his mentor. Tabor's ruddy face sported huge cheeks that looked stuffed with cabbages. His twisty moustache flopped down the sides of his pudgy lips. Years of facing the hot forge had etched dark red creases around his eyes. But Tabor's encouraging smile found its way out from under all that, a smile that had comforted Joran countless times. He watched Joran work, as he often did, with an air of pride and a dash of approval.

Joran held the shoe in the vise grips, then placed it on the horse's hoof for another fit; the hot metal hissed and steamed. After dunking the shoe in the slack bucket, he pulled iron nails from his pouch and stuck them between his teeth. As he nailed shoe to hoof, he tried to think of what to say. He had been apprenticing with Elder Tabor for four years now, since the week his father had been killed by a falling tree. The kind smith knew him well, and cared for him as if he were his adopted child. He knew Tabor sensed his distress, and as much as he wanted to share his heart, to talk to someone, Joran just couldn't. At least Tabor didn't nag, and never mentioned his tardiness, either. But the last few days had made his distraction apparent, as the pile of work grew around him. He owed Tabor some explanation.

"I'm sorry, Elder Tabor. I haven't been sleeping well."

"Are you sick, lad? Everything all right at home with the wife?"

Joran cringed. "Charris is off visiting family."

Elder Tabor whistled. "This time of year? That's a perilous journey, to Wolcreek Vale, what with the rivers swollen. Last winter you remember that lumber rig got swept away when the bridge gave out." He reached into a large bin and sorted through scraps of metal.

Joran rasped the hoof with a large file, avoiding Tabor's gaze. "She went with the delivery carriage. They travel that road every week."

"Yes, well. I still don't see what was so important to warrant a trip right after last week's storms." Tabor shook his head from side to side, making his jowls shake. "Maybe a family emergency, eh?"

Joran knew Tabor was gently prying, but wasn't going to say any more. He untied the horse from the post and turned to his employer. "I need to return him to Jareth's. I'll be right back to finish the axle over there."

"Joran, lad," Tabor called to him, fishing a long iron rod out of the bin. "Take some time off if you need it. All right?" He put a rough, chubby hand on Joran's shoulder, resting it there.

"I'll think about it. Thanks."

Joran pulled a soft leather hat over his ears and walked down the rough cobbles of the village street, leading the gelding with his newly shod hooves clacking on the stones. Not many people walked the streets as the fat flakes of snow fell. Joran passed shops nestled together, displaying goods behind their warmly lit windows. Wooden signs hung from archways announcing poultry, linens, and cheese. And down at the far end of the lane was the large cloth mill.

His village of Tebron was known for its woven works. Here, many of the local women worked on looms, passing shuttles back and forth, making images of horses, birds, and flames appear inch by inch to grace the windows, beds, and bodies of nobles and their ladies as far away as Sherbourne. Often, he would stop by at lunch hour to visit with Charris, bringing her scones from the bakery, warm and dripping with butter. Today, however, like the last few days, there would be no stopping at the bakery, or the mill. There would be no warm kisses, no watching Charris's eyes sparkle with laughter, no tickling or smoothing her hair. There would be no Charris. No more.

Joran seethed again; his anger flared like his forge—red-hot and consuming. Maybe in time he would get over her. Maybe in time he would forget that he ever loved her. Joran laughed bitterly. What love? Their love was a joke, a sham! And he was the joke. At least he had been able to hurry her off to Wolcreek without notice, before watching eyes and loose tongues could make a worse mess of his life. Despite her protestations, her dismay, he had insisted she pack and leave that night, and he did not even hold her hand as he hurried her down the road to the delivery station. When he left her sitting on the hard bench in the foyer, he didn't look back. He didn't want to see her tears or listen to the silkiness of her voice. He barely had enough resolve to do it; he couldn't risk feeling remorse. *It was the* right *thing to do!* he reminded himself unconvincingly.

As he rounded the corner at the Crow's Tavern, Callen called out to him. Joran's brother headed his way, with a large axe slung over his shoulder and his woolen cap down over his ears. Callen was like Joran's other two brothers—tall, dark hair and eyes, bronze skin that kept the summer sun trapped all year long. His father, Oreb, had boasted a full, black beard, thick as a hedgehog's coat and neatly trimmed around his neck. His mother, Shyra, had an exotic look; her large black eyes and heavy eyebrows gave her an air of intrigue. Their families had come from Ethryn in the far south, where the sun was hot most of the year and crops constantly dried up from unrelenting droughts. In prior years, villagers from the north and south kingdoms rarely mixed, but economies of need forced many northward seeking employment. Oreb and Shyra were only two of many darker-skinned who migrated to this wooded and fertile region to raise a family.

Joran's town was a mix of culture and tongue—the more fair-haired families, with their rough and broken speech, their informal manners and easy ways had long roots in Tebron, whereas the darker, more serious folk, with their soft-spoken, deliberate speech and curious habits, had to find a way to fit into the rhythms of Tebron life. Joran had been told of the numerous conflicts that came fast on the heels of the first influx of immigrants, but now, after a new generation had been born and reared—fair and dark together—the town had settled down like a hen content on her nest.

Joran, though, stood out like a mistaken brushstroke in contrast to his brothers—light brown curls, unruly and tangled. Fair skin, long-fingered hands that seemed too delicate for a man. When they were small, his brothers found amusement in hefting his lean, lightweight body over their heads to spin him around like a whirligig beetle. Joran had been the object of jest his whole life: His manly brothers teased him about his "girlish" looks. Neighbors coddled him, his mother babied him—he being the youngest—but after his father died he was mostly ignored.

Maylon had married, and Felas, the eldest, enjoyed his attractive status as eligible bachelor. Where Callen and Felas continued in forestry without Oreb, Maylon took to fishing, preferring the dreaminess of rivers to the hardness of wood. Of all three brothers, Joran found Callen the most creative and easiest to talk with. He carved beautiful buttons and staff handles from the dark burlwood he removed from trees he felled. Joran and Callen spent many hours designing patterns for wood and iron, and theirs was an easy comradeship, but right now he didn't need to run into his brother. Joran could never hide his feelings well, and Callen could always tell when something upset Joran.

"Hey, Jor," Callen said, coming to him with open arms. Joran embraced his brother and forced a smile. "Where're you off to?"

"I'm returning a horse. How about you? Working at Ryner's Grove again?"

"For the morning. Then we have a load of logs to take to the dock. Whew, am I going to be sore tonight!" Callen shook snow off his cap. "I hope the sky clears. Makes the road all slushy." He frowned and scrutinized Joran. "Where've you been the last few days? You didn't make it to Sunday dinner. Somewhere I heard Charris went back to Wolcreek. Is that true?"

"She left on Friday. Something came up." Joran averted his eyes, fumbled with the horse's halter.

"Nothing serious I hope. Are her parents all right?"

Joran hedged. "I'm not sure."

"Mother's been upset. You should go see her. She asks about you."

Callen pointed down the street. "Here comes Felas. Come to dinner tonight." It was more a command than a request.

Felas strode up to them; even his walk had purpose and conviction. His strong jaw, broad neck, and laughing eyes bespoke his role as head of the family. Felas took charge with authority, but Joran saw how his brother's joking was often read as insensitivity. Rather than maintain the family home, Felas chose to take the room over the tavern; he didn't want a big house. Or his mother, who went with it. Fortunately, Maylon and Malka were happy to live there with Shyra, caring for her, and watching that she didn't wander away. With two small children, they were always on the watch, anyway.

Felas slapped Joran on the back. "Hey, there's the little brother. Steal someone's horse?" Felas stroked the gelding's nose.

The horse snorted. *He smells funny.*

Joran smirked. *That's his special . . . ointment. To attract females.*

The horse rolled his eyes. Joran could tell from his expression that he thought Felas was sadly misinformed about the laws of attraction.

"It said something to you, didn't it? About me." Felas scrunched his face at the horse. "What did it say?"

Joran laughed. "Ask him yourself, if you care that much about a horse's opinion."

Felas cuffed Joran gently on the side of his head. "You know I can't hear them talk. It's a good thing too. Must be just a bunch of mindless chatter. Would drive me batty!"

"You can't hear them because you don't *want* to. You have to care."

Callen interjected, "*I* care, but it still doesn't work. Only my cat speaks to me, and that's only when he demands to be fed. Then he makes sure I hear him. Otherwise he completely ignores me."

"Cats are like that. You won't get much out of them," Joran said.

Felas jabbed Callen in the arm: "Don't you remember, Callen, when Joran used to work the woods with us? That one time we had to stop until he could pry that bee hive off the tree and move it somewhere safe?"

"You were about to drop it and crush the whole hive," Joran said.

"Yeah, well, it set us back a half-day's work."

"Hey, Felas," Callen said, poking him back. "Don't laugh. Joran got honey from that hive for over a year, and no one else could get near it."

Felas huffed. "Well, it's a good thing we don't all hear animals like Joran. All the deer would be pleading for their lives; the fish would cry, 'Please, throw me back in the river!' We would all starve to death out of guilt!" Callen joined Felas in laughter but Joran remained sullen.

His brothers knew that was why he gave up working in the woods, and fishing with Maylon. He had to find a trade where he wasn't distracted by animal distress. Every time a tree fell, an osprey's nest was dislodged, a marmot's or badger's burrow was smashed. Deer and rabbits grew agitated at the disruption in their quiet lives. And although fish were unable to voice in words, they more than made up for their lack of language with their pitiful gasps. So forging iron seemed an attractive profession. Putting up with an impatient horse or two was manageable.

And Felas was wrong—Joran wasn't bombarded with endless chatter; he only heard animals when they made a point of speaking to him. His attempts at eavesdropping on conversations between creatures never yielded him success—only stern looks of annoyance. He did think it odd, though, that most animals *wanted* to speak with him, whereas they bluntly ignored the rest of the villagers. At least, that was how it appeared to him. Maybe he just found it easier to talk with animals than with people. Animals were more straightforward, more honest. They didn't lie or betray you the way humans did.

With a sigh, Joran waved his brothers off and continued on to Jareth's, where he unlatched the gate and deposited the horse. With a twinge of guilt, he looked down the street to his family home, where Maylon and Malka took care of his mother. Joran could tell Malka had been diligent in the garden—hollyhocks rose up alongside the door with their crimson blooms, and foxglove and buttery columbine still thrived in the early onset of winter. She had made the place less gloomy, more cheerful, since moving in. Maybe if he made an appearance, his family would forget about him for a few days.

Dutifully, he trudged down the road and knocked on the door of the imposing hewn-beam house. He wouldn't stay long, with work pressing.

Malka pulled the heavy door open, juggling a baby on one hip and holding a spool of twine in her hand. Her honey hair fell in a heap around her shoulders and her pale cheeks flushed pink. The baby fussed and buried his head into her blouse. Malka's face lit up upon seeing her brother-in-law.

"Joran! Ooh, you're letting a mess of cold air in! Come inside and I'll brew you some tea." Malka pulled him by his coat and shut the door behind him. Joran shook snow off his hat and hung the coat on a hook by the hearth where a fire blazed and filled the living room with wonderful heat. Yards of fishing net draped over chairs, across tables, along the wood-planked floor where Bela played with her toys. Malka set the baby down alongside his older sister, who grabbed him and tugged him into her lap. Soon, Bela had him wrapped up in fishing net like a tangled sturgeon, causing him to gurgle and shriek in delight.

"He's teething, so don't be alarmed if he screams like a cornered rumphog from time to time." Malka lifted nets and wormed her way into the kitchen. Joran noticed his mother sitting by the kitchen window, staring out into the yard. "I'm just gettin' your mum some soup—want any?"

Joran shook his head. "Tea's fine. I was returning a horse down the street, so thought I'd stop and say hi. I can't stay long."

Malka pushed more net to the floor, clearing a chair by the fire. She poured from the metal pot on the hearth into a mug. "Well, here's tea. Warm you some and then you can go." Joran sipped and nodded toward his mother. "How is she?"

Malka shrugged. "Same. Had a cold for a few days but seems better, that way. Been asking for you some." Malka urged him with her eyes. "Go on, then. It'd be good for you to talk to her. Bela!"

Malka ran over to her daughter, who decided her baby brother would make a good cushion now that he was all wrapped up in net. While Malka pried Bela off and untangled the baby, Joran went into the kitchen and sat next to his mother. He noticed Malka had braided his mother's long black hair and dressed her in a warm smock, with one of Charris's shawls across her shoulders— the one with the lapis firebird entwined in maple leaves of gold and bronze. He had always marveled at the intricate detail woven into her shawls. Joran scowled. Just another reminder of Charris—reminders that assaulted him wherever he went. Joran reached over and took his mother's hands in his; they felt cool and soft.

"Hello, Mother. It's Joran. You look so nice today." Joran waited to see if Shyra recognized him, but she kept her gaze focused out the window.

"Someone was supposed to prune those fruit trees before winter," Shyra said. "Look, it's snowing now. I told him there won't be apples unless the branches get pruned." She tipped her head to one side and her eyes closed. Malka came back in and filled a bowl with warm soup from the stove. She set it on the table.

"Mum, here's soup, Mum." Malka gently shook Shyra's shoulder. Shyra searched with her eyes until she found the face the words came from.

"Did you prune those apple trees yet?" she asked.

"They were done weeks ago. Don't you worry, Mum, this spring we'll have plenty of Big Beauties, you'll see." Malka handed Shyra the spoon and watched to make sure her mother-in-law found her mouth with it. She looked over at Joran and shrugged. "Every day she asks about those fruit trees." Malka went back into the living room and fetched the baby. She brought him into the kitchen and placed him in a woven basket of birch, then set him by the window where he could stare out at the sky. Joran watched the baby, then glanced at his mother as she mindlessly sipped her soup.

"Mum, I have to go back to work." Slowly, Shyra turned her head and cocked it, reminding Joran of the little frych in the wood box in his barn.

Shyra nodded at the baby. "Your basket. You go in there. With the eggs." She looked at him. "Joran." She spoke with intent. She hadn't said his name in months and the word pierced like a sharp knife in his gut.

Joran wondered what she was talking about. That had been his baby basket, but why was she mentioning eggs? Joran sighed. After his father had been crushed by the tree, Shyra became disconsolate with grief. Months of crying wore her away, eroded her, so that, finally, when there were no more tears, there was not much of anything else, either. She would stop in the middle of cooking breakfast and wander down the lane waving a wooden spoon, smoke filling the house behind her. She would forget to put on her clothes and neighbors would find her out in the driving rain in her undergarments, looking for apples to pick.

She and Oreb had lived alone in the big house after all the boys grew up, but the four brothers conferred and agreed the house would eventually swallow her up if she remained alone. Maylon and Malka's small cottage grew even smaller with the arrival of the new baby, amid the copious nets. Malka had always tended a large family—it suited her to care for Shyra.

Joran could not see moving back home now that he had been on his own. And although he loved his mother, he had never felt close to her. A frown formed on his face as he watched his mother stare out at the orchard.

He had grown up in a family of affection and support, yet he felt as if he had watched his life from the sidelines. As his brothers played and joked and grew tall and strong, Joran had been a spectator, trying to insert himself into their games, their discussions, their vocations. They probably never noticed how hard he tried to belong and how often he felt alienated. He was different somehow—not just because he spoke with animals, but in a way more essential; even when at home, he never felt comfortable. More like a foreigner who paid close attention to learn the customs and behaviors of a strange land.

Shyra interrupted his thoughts. "Joran." His eyebrows raised at a second mention of his name. She pointed at the baby fussing in the basket. "Where are the eggs?"

Eggs? Joran stood and stretched. Every muscle ached. He kissed his mother on the forehead and took his mug to the wash basin. Malka wiped the counter with a wet rag. She stopped and touched Joran's sleeve.

"People are talking, Jor." She fumbled with the rag thoughtfully. "They say you sent Charris away."

Joran stiffened. He lowered his eyes, then went over to the hearth and picked up his cloak, which steamed from the fire's heat. The musty wool smell filled his nostrils. "She's visiting family. Went back on Friday."

Malka wiped her hands and came over to Joran. "Not what I heard. Just this morn the delivery carriage sent back word she never arrived in Wolcreek. Joran—what is going on?"

"Never arrived?" Joran panicked and his skin crawled. "She should have been there Saturday morn. Who told you this?"

"Cinder at the bakery. She's from the Vale too. The deliveryman made some comment to her early this morning when dropping off packages. Charris got on the coach Friday night, he told her, but never arrived in Wolcreek. No one at the Vale was expecting her; not a soul had seen her." Malka paused. "So, did she plan another stop?"

Joran's heart raced. "I have to go." He put on his cloak and yanked open the door; a blast of cold wind assaulted him. Malka looked at him with concern. "Joran, what is going on?"

"I'm not sure. But I'll find out." Joran slammed the door behind him and hurried up the street to the blacksmith stall. Elder Tabor was heating a long rod in the forge, pulling and stretching it with grips. He stopped when he saw Joran rush in under the beams.

"Joran, lad, what's the matter?"

"I need to take the day off. Something's come up."

"Can I help?" Tabor pursed his lips, waiting for a reply.

Joran looked down the street. Today, few stalls were set up in the marketplace. What could he do? No one here would know Charris's whereabouts. His mind returned to his earlier encounter with the old woman and her geese. Her warnings about the sand slipping away, the three keys. How he had trapped Charris in his dreams. He turned to Tabor. "Have you seen the goose woman today? Did she come to market?"

Elder Tabor shook his head. "Haven't seen her. Why on earth're you looking for her, lad?"

Joran rushed off without answering, leaving Tabor frowning. *Where could Charris be? Would she have gotten off at another stop along the route to Wolcreek?* Except for the scattered farms in Logan Valley, there were no towns along the way, only delivery stations. Remote junctions with roads that led east and west to barren lands.

Joran thought back to the night he had confronted her. The tears in her eyes, Charris wiping her face with her sleeve. All his attempts to pry the truth from her failed. As he relived the argument, his blood boiled. As painful as it was, he had wanted to hear the details, wanted to know just what she hid from him and why. Didn't she still love him? Wasn't he the man she vowed to honor and abide with? Despite Charris's denials, Joran could tell she was lying. She had to be!

Finally, taking no more, Joran had ordered her to pack a bag. Go see your family for a while. Go think over your marriage vows. She had tried to take Joran's hand, but he'd pushed her away. "Why are you doing this to me? I love you!" she begged him, falling to her knees and crying. Joran had hardened his heart. He wanted more than anything to believe she still loved him. But he would not listen to lies!

As Joran raced up the cobbles to the cart road leading out of town, he thought back to the day he met Charris. She had come to his town for a weavers' gathering at the Guild. Her village bought fabric and clothing from Tebron, as they had no guild of their own. Wolcreek wanted a mill, but weavers needed to be trained. Charris came not just to attend the gathering, but to seek apprenticeship. The oldest of five daughters living in a crowded home, she yearned to find a new, unfettered life.

Her parents hoped she would marry a local boy, but when her horse threw a shoe on the way to the gathering, she was directed to the blacksmith stall, where she met Joran over the neck of her mare. Charris lingered while he attended to her horse and ended up watching him work the rest of the afternoon. Each day of the gathering she found time to stroll the market, lastly arriving at Joran's stall and sharing tales of her life in the Vale, a place Joran had only visited once as a small boy.

Enamored with her charm and outgoing spirit, Joran soon became intoxicated with her. She laughed easily, whipped her dark hair behind her, had graceful hands that playfully stroked his cheek. She flirted unabashedly, but Joran never felt toyed with. After she left, lovesickness overcame him. The more he attempted to put her out of his mind, the more he fell apart. Eventually he couldn't focus on his work. His brothers teased him relentlessly.

While he tried to raise the nerve to send her a letter, agonizing over the possibility that Charris had already forgotten him, she showed up on his cottage doorstep. Joran nearly fell down when he opened his door one evening and saw her face—just as beautiful as he remembered her—smiling at him without a trace of mockery. Evidently, his brothers had been one step ahead of him and had tired of his melancholy. They had sent word to Charris and begged her to come and give them relief from their brother's distracted moodiness. So Charris penned her horse with Joran's old goat and took up lodging in a room next to the mill—housing provided for the weavers—and waited until Joran grew accustomed to the idea of having her in his life.

He had hoped someday to marry and raise a family, but never expected a wife to come from Wolcreek. As was her town's custom, by the end of the month Charris had proposed to Joran, offering to move to Tebron and work in the mill. Joran was a bit startled by her forwardness, but he also breathed relief, for the thought of her riding out of his life again set his emotions in a frenzy. Right then he decided to tether her to his heart—a decision he now bitterly regretted.

Their first year together had radiated with affection, warmth, and mutual encouragement. Then, gradually, Charris's work seemed to consume her. She spent long hours at the mill, and in the evenings at the cottage she pored over her sketches and designs, compelled and bewitched by colors flowing from her brush. Joran tried to share her enthusiasm, offer suggestions. But the familiar feeling from his childhood smothered him; he felt pushed to the sidelines—an observer rather than a participant in life. Never did he suspect she was taking her affections elsewhere; she still rediscovered Joran on nights when her designs relinquished her heart. At those times she fell comfortably into his arms, slept in the crook of his elbow, remembered to make him biscuits and eggs and hotcakes when morning filtered in through the kitchen windows.

Joran hurried up the cart road as snow whipped his face. The village sounds dwindled as Tebron dropped behind and he entered the hush of the forest. He fought with his urge to find the old woman—for she repelled him. But something pulled him along, flattened his resistance. He felt as if in a trance and helpless to run away—which is what he yearned to do. He should just go back to work; customers were becoming impatient with his delays. Tabor was likely to be worrying. Surely Charris would show up somewhere. There had been a misunderstanding, poor communication. Malka probably listened to gossip that had been stretched into a fantastic story. But, even as Joran mused over these things, his feet kept running ahead of him.

Up there, she had pointed. Joran searched for a path through the snowberry bushes, for a goose-trodden trail. Thick mist hung on branches, smothering trees. Finally a path appeared at his feet, and so he pushed his way through the brush, navigating a heavily wooded grove of trees that scraped their crowns against the heavens. Joran stretched his neck, seeking sky and finding only a deep green canopy overhead that scattered rays of light through the fog and muffled his footfalls. Silence grew thick as porridge; calm enveloped him as he stumbled upon a small clearing. There, in the burned-out hollow of a huge tree, her geese huddled, a makeshift fence of thin branches latched across the pen. His arrival set off a boisterous honking, bringing the goose woman out of her tiny planked hovel built on top of a huge stump.

"Back so soon, little cub? We knew you would come." The goose woman took small waddling steps down the stairs carved into the stump, gripping her staff tightly. She came up to Joran and took his hands in hers, laughing and wheezing as she drew breath. Her wrinkled hands felt like leather.

"Please, tell me where Charris is—where is my wife? Do you know?"

Her eyes glazed, and she lost herself in memory. "We have been there, to that place you have put her. We came from the sea long ago, little cub. Towering cliffs, churning waves." She stared into the air, digging for images. "The sea near my home. That nasty Moon, always causing mischief." Anger flickered across her face. She snarled, then spit off to one side. "We never liked her, came here. Hidden in fog, where she can't see us."

Joran squatted to meet her face and collect her gaze. "Please, I don't understand. How can she be at the sea? It is so far away. How . . ."

"You have put her there, don'tcha know? Your anger has trapped her. Your dreams." Her eyes widened, sparking with recognition. She lowered her voice to a raspy whisper. "We see your dreams." She turned away from him and spoke distractedly. "You must loose the three keys and open the lock to get her out. Sand is seeping out." She turned back to Joran. "You will never have peace from those dreams until you free her."

"How do I do this thing?" Joran's heart thumped hard in his chest; nothing she said made sense. "Why should I free her, anyway? She betrayed me. Isn't this her fault?" Did he want her back? He was too upset to dig for a truthful answer that lay under a layer of rock. Yet, he knew he couldn't keep going without sleep, without relief from the nightmares. He knew he couldn't stay in a town where whispers and suspicions would no doubt hound him like mosquitoes in late spring.

The goose woman smiled, her black teeth exposed. "Little cub, you have grown so big. Now a man. We have no answers for you. We just see."

Joran paced, kicking up the soft mulched ground. "So, what do I do now? Where are the keys, the lock? This is madness . . ."

The goose woman pointed a bony finger northward. "Go to the house of the Moon. She is there, with your wife. You saw her. She may help you, if she feels like it. Or maybe not. Tricky and deceitful, she is."

The Moon has a house? "How do I get there?" He looked northward, trying to see past the forest in his mind, but it evoked nothing but waste and bitter cold.

"Oh, it is very far, little cub, far beyond imagining. Your dreams will point the way north, but it is beyond the ends of the known world, and the traveling perilous. You will wear out three pairs of shoes before your journey ends. Yes, you will."

Joran spun around and faced her. "Why? Why so far?"

The tiny woman chucked Joran under the chin and started to walk away, wheezing with each deliberate step. Abruptly, she stopped and turned to him. "We always say: 'The longest way 'round is the shortest way home.' It is the only way, you know." With that, she strained up the carved steps, her staff tapping against wood, and closed the door to her cottage behind her, leaving Joran befuddled.

THREE

AS JORAN floated on the current, blown by a warm south wind, he reached down to touch the water and found himself encased in a bubble. He faced the same starless night, and when he heard the Moon laugh, a chill rattled his bones. Nameless things brushed against his legs, which dangled under the water, causing him great agitation. Queasiness racked his stomach, but he floundered at the whim of the tide, helpless to abate his nausea.

The forceful current hurled him toward the shore and the imposing cliffs. He felt sweat run down his sides, soaking his shirt. Spindrift lit on his face, coating his cheeks with tiny pearls of saltwater. As he tumbled onto the beach like a disgorged fish, he nearly collided with a monstrous sea lion, briny and putrid, that lay sprawled on the sand. Upon standing, he realized the mammal was dead and rotting, with flies amassed on its face and whiskers. Giant holes had been chewed in its side, exposing bleached ivory ribs. Joran gagged.

Somehow, over the droning waves and soughing wind, he heard Charris's voice. She called him! Joran looked up at the dizzying upsweep of cliff and moaned from exhaustion. The thought of making that treacherous climb again filled him with lassitude.

He wrestled with the need to rescue her and the urge to acquiesce to futility.

A sudden chill brushed across his neck, sending shivers down his spine. He watched as the bleeding heart vines frosted over, ice threading its way up the bluff. The ground under his bare feet turned to ice, a transparent shade of blue, freezing his soles and toes. A dread of indescribable proportion coated him like a layer of frost itself. He heard the Moon laugh again, and wheeled around to see the blackness of night grow even blacker.

Night became a void, hungering to be filled with anything it could devour. Joran's vision dimmed as the world disappeared. Sand slipped around him, sucking downward as through an hourglass. Charris's voice called out to him louder. He groped blindly as he lost contact with the roaring sand under his feet and the bluff that, moments earlier, had towered before him. Able to bear no more, Joran screamed and clawed, then fell unconscious.

Joran awoke with a sense of urgency. He realized he had fallen asleep, exhausted, on the divan in the foyer of his cottage. The image of the hourglass was imprinted on his mind as he forced himself to sit up.

Two weeks had dragged along since he heard of Charris's disappearance. He reassured inquirers that Charris was in Wolcreek, even though the scattered reports contradicted him. Joran ignored the air of mystery and intrigue surrounding Charris's absence; the stories grew more fabulous and bizarre with each telling. With each passing day, Joran became more reclusive and hung his head as he rushed past the villagers who watched him, questions in their eyes and forming on their lips.

Finally, tired of their stares, Joran took leave from his work, telling Tabor he was ill and needed rest. But he found no relief at home. Each night he wrestled with the sea and labored up the sandy cliff to reach his wife, only to fail. Anger fueled his waking hours and anger burned in his sleep. It took all his strength to get up each morning, milk his goat, prepare a tasteless breakfast. His larder was now empty save for dried beans, jars of jam from last year's harvest, and a basket of old bread rolls, but Joran had lost all appetite, anyway.

With little resolve, Joran knew he had to leave and start his journey. He chastised himself again for listening to the warped tales of a lunatic in the woods, but how could he stay? This thing had been set in motion, like a runaway carriage heading into a ravine. He would have no choice but to follow where it led. Decency and obligation required this of him. At the very least he could retrace the delivery route, find people to question, explore alternate roads. Maybe Charris, out of spite, decided to travel to see a distant friend, wanting to hurt Joran with worry. Well, she was doing a good job of it, wasn't she? Why couldn't she just go home instead of haunting his dreams? Hadn't he suffered enough?

And what would he say to her when he found her? All he wanted to do was strike out in anger and hurt, throttle her for her heartlessness. He would find her—he must! If only to drive home how much pain she had caused him.

He brushed hair from his eyes and sighed. He consciously unclenched his fists. All he had wanted was to live a simple, peaceful life, raise a family, work with his hands. He had hoped marriage would anchor him to a home, a sense of belonging, but all it had done was cut his moorings and set him adrift in a merciless sea of confusion. Would he ever feel at home again, anywhere?

Before he could talk himself out of it, he stood and set his jaw. Looking around his cottage, he gathered what he needed for a long journey. He tried to think of useful items—what food was left, a knife, handy tools, flint, rope. He packed warm clothes and coins in a pouch. Looking down at his sturdy, wool-lined boots, he pondered the goose woman's words. It would take a few years just to wear these out. Wear out three pair! She was certainly short a few pebbles!

He stopped at the table when he saw Charris's pens and paper. He should write a note to Callen. At some point, his brothers would come looking for him; it would be Callen, more than likely. What could he tell him? That he went to fetch Charris and would be back soon. Anything else would raise concern, and he certainly wasn't going to mention the goose lady's babble. He scribbled hastily, then propped the note against the lantern on the kitchen table. He took one long look around him, fearing it would be his last. Already, the anticipation of a tiring journey burdened his heart.

When Joran entered the barn, the frych poked her head out of the box.

You. Here. Breakfast!

Joran reached into a sack and poured a handful of seed into the dish beside her box. He watched as the bird pecked at the food with gusto. *Yes, I'm back. Aren't you all better by now? How's the head?*

Fine. Great. Ready to fly! The frych flapped her wings excitedly.

Joran lifted the tiny bird into his hand. He stroked her jeweled head. *You're quite a pretty one. But, you need to watch where you're going and stop crashing into barns.*

Yes. Will. Now, give you my name.

Oh, no, little one. That is quite unnecessary. You would have gotten on your feet just fine without my help.

No. Nice box. Very nice bed. Bird food and water. Take my name.

Joran sighed, discomfited. He had collected many names over his lifetime—of birds, bears, foxes, skunks—too many to remember. But, they were all there, catalogued in the back of his mind. Each time he refused, the creature would insist. The law of nature, they would say. They must. Joran had never found need to use their names, but he guarded them all the same. Out of respect.

All right, little one. I will honor your name.

And I will honor your call. My name is Bryp.

Joran bowed toward the frych. *Bryp, I take your name. And I thank you. You are now free to go. And please be more careful.*

Bryp hopped onto the table top, then flitted away through the crack in the barn door. Joran picked up the milk bucket and led the goat to the post, where he tied her up.

She turned her head toward Joran and glared with yellow slit eyes. *So, you are planning to leave. Who is going to milk me? You can't just abandon me here.*

Joran tugged on the teats, filling the bucket with warm milk that steamed in the air. *I arranged for the Agrens to take you for a while. Their daughter, Lyrna, will be by tonight to pick you up. Please don't be difficult.*

The goat snorted. *Are you going to get Charris? Will you come get me soon? Do they have any other goats at their farm? Do I have to ride in a wagon again? I just hate that jostling around . . . hurts my udder . . .*

Don't you ever stop asking questions? I don't know if they have goats. I think they may have a sheep or two.

Sheep! Pah! I'd rather sleep with the chickens.

You may be, at that. I think you'd better behave if you want to get milked. Try not to baa so much first thing in the morning.

All right. The goat loosed a great sigh and chewed her cud. Joran finished milking her and poured some of the milk in a cup and drank. *If you took me with you, you could have milk every day.*

I can't take you. Too long a trip and your hooves would crack. Joran sensed her escalating anxiety and stroked her head. *Don't worry, I won't forget you. You'll be back in your pen before you know it.* Joran reached into a can and pulled out a handful of sunflower seeds. He fed them to the goat, who inhaled them eagerly. She rubbed her head against his leg and Joran scratched behind her ears. *Okay, time to go.* He untied her and released her into the grassy pen.

At least it wasn't snowing today, Joran noticed. He made sure the pen gate was latched and then secured the barn door. He thought about the note on the table and imagined his brother's concerned face upon reading it. By then, Joran was certain, the whole town would be abuzz with gossip. But he would be far away from their stares and judgment. Far away, somewhere. Looking for a tricky Moon, a wayward wife, and a sea he only knew from his dreams.

FOUR

TRUDGING WITH the sun over his right shoulder, Joran followed a deer track up into the high hills. Where Tebron backed up against a ring of ragged peaks, the cobbles of the cart road ended; there were no open roads where he was going. He carried a walking stick Callen had carved, made of black oak from Logan Valley, where massive trees spread their boughs over winding creeks. The wood felt smooth under Joran's hand, and he was glad to have something to remind him of his brother. The knob was scrolled with river and fish designs, and as he climbed rocks he traced the outlines mindlessly with his fingers.

The gentle hills gave way to ragged rock, rugged buttes, and eventually creamy white granite boulders speckled with silver chips. Joran had climbed in these mountains many times, for the view they afforded of his village was panoramic, often reminding him how small he was compared with a huge world he knew little of.

He had occasionally met travelers off on adventures, seeking fortunes, but few came to Tebron—a dead-end town out in the middle of nowhere, leading nowhere. More often what arrived in Tebron were stories, chock full of excitement, danger, rich discoveries. But Joran was sure the tales had been padded by the imaginations and longings of the storytellers. He had known a few who, eager to seek adventure and bored with Tebron's isolation, left home for the wide world. Most returned disillusioned—with nothing to show but empty pockets and in need of a hot bath with plenty of soap.

Joran pondered how the people of the northern kingdom were, by nature, not very curious about other lands. They seemed content to work, raise families, and visit with their neighbors, rarely engaging in anything resembling politics. Tariffs and taxes were paid dutifully; most complaints gravitated toward the upkeep of the road leading in and out of Tebron Village. Elder Tabor never complained; the flow of broken cart axles from the unattended potholes generated a steady business.

Twice a year, a government official came to Tebron from Sherbourne, an ancient city strategically placed on a high moor, where the king's palace stood surrounded by the ruins of the old battlement wall. Joran had never been there, but heard the king was a temperamental and miserly man. Apparently, the king met annually with his councillors and assessed the goods produced to adjust Tebron's tax base. In exchange for their taxes, Tebron was given vague assurances of protection and a voice in the kingdom—whatever that amounted to. Tebron's oldest citizens were still trying to figure out what that meant.

Joran caught his breath after a short, steep scramble and looked down at the fallow fields far below him. Many in Tebron were farmers, as the semimild climate and fertile forest soil encouraged plants to flourish. Goods came in from other villages, but Tebron lacked little it couldn't produce. Still, there was a market for exotic spices from the south—cardamom, curry, cloves—and baubles and lace from cities in the east. The only real traveling his neighbors did was during the fall harvest, when they erected huge tents in Logan Valley and exchanged goods with farmers from all compass points. Produce, honey, and potted plants switched hands from the back of their wagons for the better part of a week. That was only a two days' journey. And now, Joran was setting out on some reckless journey, not spurred by a sense of adventure but haunted by a sense of doom and apprehension. An unwitting traveler.

Dark clouds crawled across the sky accompanied by a mild breeze that wended up the cliffs, growing colder with each hour. Joran breathed hard, making sure of his grip as he pulled himself over another jumble of rock. He stopped and drank deeply from his water skin and wiped his brow. The air smelled of impending rain; the sun peeked out now and then, like a badger from its hollow, but gave no warmth.

As Joran navigated the maze of rock, he chided himself for not telling anyone he had left. He knew Tabor would worry himself sick. Hopefully, he would find Charris quickly and get home before he became the latest exaggerated legend laughed at over ale at the tavern.

As the hours passed, Joran occasionally stopped and surveyed the land below him. Sitting on a ledge, he noticed Tebron grew smaller with each rest, an ever-shrinking circle that encompassed his life. Now his village looked like a small corral of structures, diminutive next to the imposing forest. There he was born, raised, and most likely would die. Everyone he knew and loved, and even those he disliked, lived between those towering trees and the ring of mountains. What he had heard of the eastern cities did not arouse longing in him. Confining walls, crowded streets, wending his way through a crush of people and carts—Joran couldn't fathom a town that took three days just to cross. Yet the lure and comfort of anonymity held a certain appeal for him now. Would he feel compelled to leave Tebron? If he returned without Charris, would the shame and humiliation be too much to bear? He sighed deeply, kicking small rocks over the ledge to tumble and scatter into the brush below.

Joran's thoughts were interrupted by a chilling whimper. He reached out with his mind to find the cry, but heard no voice. He stopped and pulled off his hat to listen. A bee buzzed nearby. Two magpies heckled back and forth from the crags. A flock of ravens scattered in the air like a handful of black rice tossed in the wind. He traced the noise around a large rock face to a deer spur leading down to a dry creek bed and leaped to his feet.

He was unprepared for what he stumbled upon. The immense silver wolf had a paw clamped in a rusted trap. He lay on the side of the trail, curled up in pain, eyes watered over. Even more imposing up close, the wolf's muscles rippled under thick fur, and his sharp teeth protruded over his lower lip. He was larger and longer than Joran himself. Without flinching, the wolf turned his eyes toward Joran as if assessing him. Joran, torn between fear and compassion, stood motionless himself, unsure what to do. A long moment passed, the air reeking with tension, the only sound the panting of the wolf. Finally, Joran heard a voice.

Whatever you are going to do, be about it quickly.

The voice was deep, strong, lacking fear. Joran sensed courage and resignation. Did he expect Joran to abandon him or try to free him? Or did he think he wanted his stunning pelt? No doubt some would be tempted to wander the mountains day and night to procure such a treasure. Joran wondered about the trap set so high in the Sawtooths. Who could have rigged it? Joran had never seen signs of inhabitants up there, although it was rumored there were invisible ones—wizards and magi—who dug homes into rocks and caves that were wreathed in magic, and thus were undetectable. Maybe the trap belonged to one of them. Maybe they were hunting bear or fox. Joran smirked. Maybe the wolf had eaten some of their invisible chickens.

Joran watched the wolf chew at his paw. He could tell the animal was in terrible pain but restrained himself from showing vulnerability. If Joran tried to help him, would the wolf turn on him and kill him? Now, that would be a great start (and end) to his journey. One thing he knew—he couldn't leave this beast to suffer and slowly die from starvation, cold, and infection. If releasing him cost Joran his life, so be it. What was his life worth now, anyway?

Joran called to the wolf. *Please, sir, let me try to open the trap.*

The wolf did not reply, but stared at the ground and panted in discomfort. Slowly, Joran set down his pack and walking stick, then fished around his belongings for a small pry bar. The wolf's keen yellow eyes narrowed as Joran approached, and a snarl edged up one side of his face. Joran stopped, sweat dripping into his eyes. He was close enough to smell the wolf, a deep feral odor, rich with earth and leaf. The left paw, pinned in the jaws of the trap, dripped blood onto the dirt. The pad underneath bulged open.

Joran took a deep breath and knelt next to the trap. Avoiding the wolf's eyes, he inserted the metal bar into the jaws of the trap, levered it against his foot, and pushed hard. He tried various permutations and positions, but nothing budged the teeth apart. After a long while Joran wiped his brow and ventured a look back at the wolf, who watched him thoughtfully.

Use your knife. Cut the foot.

Joran let out a whistle of air. *I really don't want to do that.*

There is no other way. Unless you are content to leave me here to die. In that case, it would be more merciful to kill me.

Joran marveled at the calmness in the wolf's voice. Rather than sounding angry or threatening, the wolf's steady voice was laced with pity. How could the wolf be thinking of Joran's own anguish at such a time?

Joran stayed kneeling in the dirt, puzzling over the trap. He of all people should know how to dissect this thing, but it was welded seamlessly—much finer workmanship than he saw in Tebron, and a much stronger metal. Streaks of rust coated the hinges. How long had it been buried, hidden under loose rocks? He wondered if it had been set years ago, at a time when trappers may have roamed these mountains for game.

As he pondered his decision, he startled at the warm nose nudging his foot. The wolf's soft silver muzzle pushed against him, urging him on.

You can do this. I will try not to squirm.

Joran sucked in a breath. Steeling himself and gritting his teeth, he pulled out his knife from the leather sheath at his side and swiftly sliced the paw, separating the two claws from the foot at the ridge, breaking bone as he bore down. He accomplished his task with one steady stroke, glad he had just sharpened his knife. The wolf's eyes clamped shut as Joran gingerly freed the matted and bloody fur from the last grasp of metal.

Quickly, methodically, he rinsed and cleaned the wound with water from his water skin and pulled a cloth from his pack. With great care, he wrapped the paw snuggly to arrest the flow of blood, then secured it with twine. He collapsed back down, holding the paw in the air, his heart still pounding fast.

The wolf finally opened his eyes and continued his panting, punctuated with deep sighs. Joran sat quietly for a long time, wondering how he managed to acquire a giant wolf in his lap. Unable to resist, Joran gently stroked the wolf's head, losing his fingers in the warm thick fur that gleamed in the midday light. He noticed now, this close, that the fur wasn't truly silver, but captured and broke the light into hundreds of rainbow hues—greens, purples, reds, yellows—a mesmerizing swirl of color that changed as the wolf moved. He truly was a magnificent beast.

Joran reached back into his pack and produced a wooden cup that he filled with water. He set it before the wolf, who lapped steadily, gratitude evident in his face. When the wolf had licked the bowl dry, he turned to Joran.

I am indebted to you, young human. What are you called?
Joran.

The wolf thoughtfully chewed his name. *I have many names.* He rested his chin on Joran's leg while he dangled his throbbing paw in the air. *I have one I will give you.*

Joran considered how to sidestep the wolf's offer. Here was a formidable animal; it wouldn't do to call him by any name.

I can guess what you are thinking, Joran. The wolf pressed up, steadying himself on three good legs. Joran released the paw and the wolf tested it with a little weight. Standing alongside Joran, his withers came up to his rescuer's waist. The wolf gave him a dog smile. *You could have killed me. You didn't. You are a strange one too. Fancy that, you know how to speak wolf.*

Joran met his curious eyes. *Wolf, bird, skunk. You all talk to me. I just talk back.*

The wolf chuckled, if Joran could call it that. He was glad to see the wolf steady on his feet. He was also relieved not to be eaten, and felt compelled to leave this place and get over the ridge before nightfall. He picked up his walking stick, slung his pack onto his back, and looked the wolf over.

Keep the wrapping on if you can. You'll want to chew, but it's better if you don't. Licking is okay.

Joran, I owe you my life. The wolf moved in front of Joran and stopped. *You should know, if you speak with animals, that we have a keen law of honor. We cannot survive without it. Take my name. It is Ruyah.*

Joran bowed his head. What else was he to do? He didn't want a wolf indebted to him, but he could not refuse to take his name. He did not want to anger the wolf he had just seemingly befriended.

Thank you, Ruyah. I will take, guard, and honor your name.

And I, Joran, will honor your call. The wolf tested his steps, and as Joran started to walk away, came trotting haltingly to his side.

Joran stopped and looked at Ruyah. *What are you doing? I do not need company.*

Where are you going? What brings a human up into the Sawtooths? A Tebron man.

Joran thought of the many times he had seen the wolf throughout his life, watching him from the heights. Just how much did this wolf know about him, or care? How many human lives had he tracked with his piercing eyes?

Joran continued walking, the wolf keeping pace with his steps. *I am searching for my wife. It appears she is lost.* Joran looked back at the wolf. *Have you seen any woman wandering about?*

No, but why are you looking for her up here?

I am going to the delivery junction north of these mountains.

You could have taken man's road. Why did you come this way?

Joran didn't answer. He thought by avoiding the road, he wouldn't run into curious people who would report sighting him to the villagers in Tebron. This was a longer, harder way, but it afforded him privacy.

The wolf found a rhythm that favored three legs, and Joran noticed his plush tail swaying as he padded quietly alongside him. *Well, fancy that, we seem to be headed in the same direction. At very least I can keep company with you, and flush out a pheasant or two for dinner.*

Joran noticed this wasn't a request but a declaration. It wouldn't do for him now to start arguing with a companion who could easily have *him* for dinner.

Near nightfall, Joran could finally make out the delivery station at the crossroads, a small wooden structure standing vigil in a barren field. Some hours earlier he and the wolf had crested the saddle between Tebron and the region of Roundvale. Crags gave way to rolling hills and porous boulders. Small streams skipped down the hills to merge into a wider lazy river below. Joran had never been on this side of the mountains. Across the small valley he could see more mountains, taller ones blanketed in snow and encircling the vale. Although the river dissected the land, the ground seemed rocky and inhospitable. A stand of sheep and a lone farmhouse punctured the flat horizon far off in the distance, leaving little else to look at. Joran had no clue what lay north of this valley; the few maps he had seen in his life outlined cities to the south and east. As far as he knew, he had reached the end of civilization.

As he neared the empty building at the cart roads, he turned to Ruyah.

This is where we should part. You have no place down here.

You have piqued my curiosity, Joran. Maybe you will learn where your wife went. The wolf rested on his haunches, and his eyes scanned the lonely land.

It wouldn't do to have you scare the delivery carriage away. Then we'd never know, would we?

The wolf nodded. *I see your point. Maybe it is time to rustle up a little supper. I will hunt, and then, once the wagon has left, we will talk. And eat.*

Joran watched the huge animal pad away, back up the hill and into the cover of trees. He went over to the bench that faced the road, lowered his pack to the ground, and sat. Loosening his boot laces with a sigh of relief, Joran scanned the deeply rutted road that wandered off toward the east. Recent rains had turned dirt to mud and flooded the nearby fields. Clumps of scrub brush pushed up from the uncooperative ground devoid of nourishing soil. A jackrabbit skittered into the brush. At the crossroads another narrower road led northwest and disappeared over a hill. Twilight hung heavy over the tops of the mountains, erasing them into dark smudges against the backdrop of a streaked orange sky.

Evening was quiet here, lonely. Few birds rustled in their ground nests; nothing flew in the air. Joran drank from his water skin, grateful for the plentiful creeks he had found throughout the day. The cold mountain water was flavorful, and he had gobbled handfuls of salmonberries—fat, pink globes that still clung to bare branches. He had also gathered bunches of minty pennyroyal to brew for tea later—something he had forgotten to bring. He found an oat roll in his pack and munched thoughtfully.

Hours dragged as Joran waited on the bench. He had neither heard nor seen the wolf and wondered if Ruyah had finally gotten bored and gone back over the mountains. That would suit him just fine. Wolves were wild beasts, not pets. He was glad he had survived the encounter with Ruyah, but the wolf was a distraction. Joran had pressing concerns that needed attending to. Like finding his wife and deciding what to do with her. He wasn't gallivanting over the mountains just for a bit of excitement.

Joran looked at the night sky. Stars peeked out, and a heavy coldness took the place of the wind, penetrating Joran's cloak and chilling his face. A ground fog rose up and trailed like ghosts around his ankles.

Words from the goose woman plagued his thoughts. "Sand through the glass." "Trapped by the Moon." "Lose three keys, open the lock." "You have trapped her, you have, by your dreams." What did she mean—that because he sent her away in anger, he caused her to come to harm? Maybe the sea and the castle were symbols—but of what? How could he find the Moon's home at the end of the world? He had never heard of anyone who had traveled farther than Sherbourne, let alone to the end of the world! Did the world really end, and if it did, what came after it?

Joran's head spun in confusion. As he sifted through these thoughts, he heard the squeaks of wheels and jingling of breeching. Looking up, he watched the wagon, pulled by two draft horses, come to a halt in front of him. A man in a long, worn coat eased down from the buckboard, carrying a lantern. As the man set down the light and brushed himself off, Joran stood. He approached the grizzled man as he swung open the door of the building and cleared his throat. Joran guessed the driver hunched over from too many years spent loading and unloading carriages.

The man eyed him curiously, then spoke in a crackly voice. "What's a young man doing out here so late at night? Need a ride somewhere, lad?" He turned away from Joran and unlatched the back of the wagon and started unloading crates.

"Here, let me help," Joran said, taking one of the wooden boxes from the man's arms. How many different carriages were there—and drivers? Since the deliveries came through Tebron at night, he'd never seen them. Sometimes there was an early morning carriage, but the station was at the other end of town, and usually by the time Joran arrived at work it had long gone, having dropped off its goods and headed back east.

"I'm . . . looking for a woman. She got on the Friday night delivery carriage two weeks ago—headed to Wolcreek." In the dim lamplight, Joran saw immediate recognition in the man's pale eyes. "I heard she never made it there."

The man set down a crate at the threshold of the building and drew close to Joran, lowering his voice. "Young man, I drove that carriage." Joran noticed his hands shook. "I'm telling you the plain truth—no ale passed my lips that night . . ." His voice trailed off as he resisted his memories.

Joran urged him on with his eyes. "Please. Just tell me what happened."

The man sat back onto the bench with a thud. He shook his head slowly from side to side. "The lady was my only passenger. Don't usually get people riding at night, and not this time of year. I had the wagon, this one. So, the only place for passengers is up front, with me." The man dabbed at his forehead with a cloth he pulled from his vest pocket.

"Everything was quiet and all as we left Tebron and rounded north toward this station. Usually 'bout a three-hour ride. She was very quiet—and very upset, mind you—but I didn't ask nothing. Wasn't none of my business." He nodded vigorously. "It was very dark out, very quiet. Then the horses got upset, snorting, stamping. I tried to calm 'em down, keep 'em moving, but they acted like bees was stinging 'em all over. The lady started screaming and I tried to get her to calm, too, but she was as batty as the horses. I swear there was nothing around, no animals, robbers, nothing."

The old man jumped up as if remembering why he was there. He hurried to the back of the wagon, reached in for another crate, and carried it inside the building. Joran followed him in. "And then what?"

He set the load down on the floor with a grunt. "Then she was gone, lad. I looked around everywhere for her." The man caught Joran's eyes. "We were out in the middle of nowhere—no trees, no buildings, nowhere to hide or run to. I'da seen her." He shrugged and fumbled with the buttons on his vest. "She just disappeared. Into thin air. I ran around looking everywhere, shoutin' for her. I even checked the ground for her shoe prints. There weren't any. Never seen the likes of that in my entire life."

Joran's mouth fell open; words fled. The man resumed his hunched walk to the back of the wagon. Joran watched in silence as the man stacked the next few crates inside the station. With a gentle hand, the old man latched the station door, then pulled himself up onto the buckboard with another grunt, looking weary and despondent. He took a last glance at Joran before gathering the reins. "I'm sorry, lad. I done what I could."

Joran stared blankly as the driver clucked the horses and the wagon jerked and jingled forward. Long after the rig ventured down the hill to the west, Joran shook off his stupor. He sat in darkness, aware of the irony of the crossroads, a place that reflected his dilemma. He could turn back, go home, and what would he face? Humiliation. Reproach. A life too uncomfortable to imagine. He had no home left, not in Tebron.

He could go to Wolcreek Vale in the hope of finding that Charris had somehow arrived safely. But he already knew that would prove to be a fool's errand.

Hadn't he heard the man? Charris vanished before his eyes in some whisk of magic, and it would take nothing short of magic— or a miracle—to find her again. The only one who'd seemed to know how to find Charris was a lunatic who spoke riddles. And yet, she did see his dreams. She saw Charris trapped and recognized the sea. A real place, unless the goose woman confused waking with dream. Nevertheless, deep in his heart, he sensed that the urgency and danger were real. As much as he would like to forget Charris, start a new life somewhere far away, it was unthinkable. What if he *had* caused her entrapment, by some strange twist of magic? How could he abandon her to an uncertain fate?

In the darkness, Joran made out a shadow with glowing yellow eyes moving toward him. Ruyah's bulky shape quietly emerged from darkness; his silver fur rendered him invisible under the mantle of night. A huge fat pheasant flopped against the sides of his mouth. Joran could tell by the wolf's gait that he was quite pleased with himself.

Got one more back there. Are you hungry?

Joran, numb all over, stood and strapped on his pack. He tightened his laces and followed the wolf in silence to a path leading behind large boulders and thick brambles. There on the ground lay another fat bird. Ruyah sat beside his quarry.

You probably want to eat these cooked. I had my fill raw.

Joran groped the ground for small twigs and dried moss. The wolf picked up sticks with his teeth and deposited them at Joran's feet. Joran found his flint and made a tiny pile of tinder. After a few strikes, a spark took and the tinder blazed. Steadily, Joran fed bits into the fire, enlarging the circle of light, exposing his surroundings. Firelight flickered on the walls of the boulders, revealing a small enclave, dry and windless. As Joran busied about cleaning the brace of birds, Ruyah settled down beside the crackling fire, head resting on his paws. Joran was aware of the wolf's gaze upon him, penetrating the thickness of night. It set him on edge.

Don't you have places to go, animals to hunt? People to snoop on?

No. The wolf got up, turned a circle and lay down, warming his other flank by the fire. *Are you tired of my company already, young human?*

Joran cooked and ate in silence, hardly enjoying the pheasant. The carriage driver's words agitated him. His wife had literally disappeared, gone, vanished. And here he was, wandering north with a needy wolf. Indecision plagued him, he was cold and depressed, and what did he look forward to? More nightmares. He seethed with thoughts of Charris that smoldered brightly in his heart like the fire that flamed before him. Why had she betrayed him? What had he done that was so wrong, so failing, that she had to hurt him like this? Joran sat and stared vacantly into the glow, letting numbness coat his mind. All this agonizing tired him out. He spoke aloud without thinking.

"I am so confused."

The wolf lifted his head from his paws and studied Joran. *The world does not explain itself, Joran.*

I don't need to understand the world. Just my life. One day every-thing made sense, the next—nothing was as it seemed. He poked at the flames, sending sparks floating up into the night. Not far away, a creek spilled down toward the river. A peaceful place, Joran thought, if only he could feel peace.

What did the driver tell you of your wife?

That she disappeared before his eyes. The horses spooked, she screamed. And then she was gone. Poof! Joran kicked up a spray of sparks with his boot.

Ruyah lay there awhile in thought.

Ruyah, there has to be a simple answer. It was more a question than an opinion.

It is said among wolves, "It is no good asking for a simple answer. After all, real things are not simple."

Joran grunted and reached for his bedroll. He spread it out by the fire and lay down on it. *The real world is made up of mystery, Joran. It is not just shoeing horses and baking bread. There is much more beyond, below, and above that has substance. You must not dis-count the mystery, for it is said among wolves, "The mystic allows one thing to be mysterious and everything else becomes lucid."*

What—are you a seer as well as a beast?

Ruyah laughed. *All creatures are seers. Except "practical" humans. They think they are grounded in reality, that dreams are silly—fancy that.*

A chill shook Joran at Ruyah's mention of dreams. He wrapped himself in his blanket and scooted closer to the blaze.

Ruyah continued. *This is also said among wolves: "The vision is always solid and reliable. The vision is always a fact. It is reality that is often a fraud."*

So, are you saying that my dreams are true?

Not dreams, young human, visions.

How do they differ?

The wolf grew quiet in thought. *Dreams whisper. Visions yell to get your attention.*

Joran grunted and lowered his head, adjusted his pack for a pillow. He looked at the night punched with a thousand bright holes, the fabric of space chewed by tiny moths. *Then, maybe my nightmares are real. They scream at me every night.*

Every night—the same dream?

Oh, some variation of it. Always the sea. Wind tossing me about. Charris trapped in a castle high on a cliff. The Moon laughing, a black bird. Climbing to try to free her. Sand collapsing underfoot. And always, I am angry, so angry. I cannot free her; she is frozen in ice or glass. I wake up exhausted. I feel I am going mad.

Ruyah narrowed his eyes at Joran. *You are not mad, young human. You are full of doubts. Wolves say, "Mad men never have doubts. Your doubts anchor your sanity. Once you are certain you know the way, then you are truly lost."*

Joran harrumphed and stared at the fire. *No, I am truly lost now. I do not know the way. The goose woman said my dreams will point the way. She said to go talk to the Moon—she will tell me what to do. Have you ever heard anything so loony?*

Joran looked over at Ruyah, hoping a philosophy-spouting wolf would agree. Hoping Ruyah had more sense, and more practical advice for him than searching for the end of the world. He was a wolf—couldn't he sniff out his wife? If Joran didn't know better, he would say Ruyah was enjoying Joran's misery. *What would a wolf know about anguish? Do wolves have nightmares? Do they fear anything at all?*

Greater than the fear of going mad was Joran's fear of wandering the rest of his life in search of a dream that led him nowhere. He did not want to be a mystic! He wanted that world of shoeing horses and baked bread. That was *his* world. Not chasing dreams. If that life was a fraud, then it was *his* fraud. Real things *were* simple. This wolf, with his homilies, had taken life and turned it on its head.

I have heard of the house of the Moon. Your goose woman knows of whom she speaks. It is said among wolves, "The Moon is the mother of lunatics and has given to them all her name." That woman is a wayward daughter of the Moon, a runaway. Hiding in her fog. But just because she is loony, that doesn't make her crazy.

Joran huffed and threw off his blanket. He walked over to Ruyah. *Let me see your paw.* The wolf rolled onto his back, exposing a furry pink underside. Joran was still unused to the huge body with that giant ribcage. He took the bandaged paw in hand. The dirty shreds of cloth barely hung on, and as Joran unrolled the dressing, it stuck to fur matted with blood. Ruyah gritted his teeth as Joran rinsed the wound with cold water and picked out dirt and debris.

This is healing well. Joran bound the paw with a new cloth and set it down with care. Ruyah rolled back over.

It's starting to itch. Ruyah sniffed the wound, venturing an unsatisfying lick. *But I can walk on it now.* The wolf scrutinized Joran. *You have done me a great kindness, Joran. Not many humans would have done so.*

I'm sure it will feel much better by morning. I wish I had been able to break that trap. Maybe I should have tried to smash it with a rock.

It is all right, Joran. You did your best, and I am grateful for your help. Besides, a rock may have smashed more than the trap. This way I still have two good claws left, besides my dewclaw. Fit enough for a long journey to the Moon.

Joran glared at the wolf. So much for sensible, practical advice. *And who asked you along?*

Ruyah lifted his eyebrows like a child caught with his hand in the biscuit jar.

Joran shook his head and stacked more branches onto the fire, which popped and crackled vigorously. He climbed back into his makeshift bed and tossed about until he found the spot with the fewest lumps. He rubbed his hand along his chin where the stubble of a new beard grew. He may as well let it grow out, with a long, cold journey ahead.

Soon, he could hear Ruyah's breathing slow and deepen. He looked over at the wolf and saw the strong furry legs kicking in slight jerks to the pattern of dreams. Wolves *do* dream, he realized.

He envied the wolf. Surely *his* dreams were all about chasing rabbits and sniffing out quail. Surely completely lacking in mystery.

─FIVE

JORAN AWOKE with a jerk. At first he thought the rain splattering his face was the ocean spray in his nightmare, but nightmare faded into the harsh gray around him— his clothes damp, his hair damp, everything he owned damp and musty from countless weeks of trudging and camping in rain. Days had spilled into weeks, and weeks blended together until Joran cold hardly tell day from night. As they traveled farther north, he found less delineation between sky and horizon, dawn and dusk.

He pulled his sodden blanket around him and sat up. A few embers glowed in the fire, hissing as the wind splattered rain onto the coals. Joran remembered they had spotted an overhang of rock in the dim light, but it had taken hours to reach it. He had barely found enough strength to coax a fire under the meager shelter of the cliff, then collapsed in exhaustion.

Since climbing the Roundvale Mountains, they had not encountered any other people, and few animals. The food in his pack had run out long ago, and now he was too far north to find many straggling berries or tubers—even if he could dig out the bushes and roots from the ponderous drifts of snow. His stomach ached from lack of food, and once more he cursed himself for his stupidity. Just what was he doing this far from home? He would surely waste away in these mountains—if he didn't freeze to death first!

Early on, the tedium and seeming futility of trying to reach his destination weighed on him with every step, plaguing him with doubt and tempting him with images of warm fire, hot soup, goose-down blankets. But after weeks, those images lost their substance and power; the saturation of gray washed away their vibrancy and flavor until they were no longer memories but color-less ghosts, too impotent to rouse in Joran any feeling at all. Now, trekking was habit, void of thought, a pattern of walk, eat, sleep—and dream. Joran dreamt while he slept—and daydreamed while awake. He often confused one for the other.

Joran had stopped hoping for sun or even sunlight. Up here, the world around him existed in continual twilight. His eyes gradually adjusted to the murkiness as he climbed higher each day. As he sat up in his soggy blanket, his head spun. The thin air stung his lungs with every inhale, and he suffered from the unmerciful cold. Meager amounts of food combined with strenu-ous climbing had reduced Joran to little more than skin stretched over bones. Joran had no cushioning against the freezing temper-atures, and each night the unyielding ground found more tender places to poke.

A cold nose pressed against his neck. Joran clutched his chest and took a deep breath. *Ruyah! Please stop sneaking up like that!*

Sorry, young human. The wolf gently deposited a huge hare at Joran's feet, so white that Joran could hardly make out its shape against the snow-spattered ground. *You need to eat.*

Joran almost retorted with cynicism. But, one look in Ruyah's eyes melted his irritation. Ruyah had been listening patiently to his complaints for days on end, and never once snapped at him or told him to be quiet. Instead, he prodded Joran with encourage-ment and hope, even told him ridiculous stories to try to make him smile. Guilt edged into Joran's heart. Had he shown the wolf even one bit of gratitude?

Joran looked at the hare at his feet, then raised his eyes to meet Ruyah's.

Ruyah, I'm so sorry. I've been so rude to you. Thank you for this food.

Ruyah lay down next to the smoldering fire and pushed at a wayward branch with his nose, stuffing it into the hot coals. The wood sparked and flared. In the illumination of the fire's struggling light Joran studied the wolf's face, searching for judgment but finding none.

You are cold and frustrated. I understand. And you are forging blindly ahead, having only me to lead you. Ruyah rested his head on his giant paws. *That takes faith—and trust.* He tipped his head and looked deeply in Joran's eyes.

Joran, he mindspoke gently, *I will not abandon or forsake you. We will find the house of the Moon—and Charris.*

Joran reached over and buried his hand in the wolf's thick fur. Warmth traveled up his hand and arm and seemed to heat up every part of him. Even the tears that spilled down his cheeks were hot.

As Joran inched toward the fire, Ruyah scooted closer, wrapping himself around Joran's legs like a second blanket. The bitter wind railed against Joran's face long into what may have been night, moaning in a shared misery with him. Soon, Joran's face was so chilled he could not even feel when he touched his finger to his cheek. As if sensing his need, the wolf unwrapped enough to allow Joran to lie on his side, and once his companion got comfortable, Ruyah sidled up next to him, his bushy tail curled like a hat over Joran's head. A delicious heat radiated from the wolf's fur and even seemed to melt away Joran's icy despondency. Joran's heart lifted a little and, with a sigh, he gathered up as much wolf into his arms as he could and fell fast asleep.

Joran opened an eye and glanced over at Ruyah sleeping contentedly beside him. The fire had long gone out and only gray ash remained inside the small ring of stones. The air was still, no longer cold, as if a sun somewhere in the sky sought to find them. Joran stretched his arms over his head and heard bones crack. He sat up and studied the wolf's peaceful face.

He wondered at this creature that had joined him on his mad journey. Ruyah had insisted; he felt indebted to Joran for rescuing him. But that didn't seem to warrant this loyalty and devotion. Now Joran was starting to feel indebted to the wolf, dependent on him. And he had to admit that he was. He knew that if Ruyah left him in this indecipherable wilderness he would flounder and die. Without the wolf's warm body to keep the winds and snows from buffeting him while he slept, he would be a frozen corpse at morning. Ruyah seemed to know the way, or a way, through all these endless crags and ravines, leading him up, up to—where? Would they come to the end of the world? As Joran stretched more kinks from his back, Ruyah opened an eye.

Morning yet?

Who can tell? Day, night? I sleep in fits and starts. Maybe it is midnight, for all I know.

Joran fished about in the ashes of last night's campfire and dug out a piece of burnt meat. He proffered it to the wolf. *Want some?*

No, you eat it. Ruyah raised his haunches in a deep stretch, his neck still on the snowy ground. He plopped on his belly, then rolled on his back, delighting in the snow as he scratched and wiggled. *Ahh . . .*

How can you still find fun each day? You should be as miserable as I.

Misery is highly overrated. It is said among wolves—

Joran sighed. *Do I have to be subjected to your aphorisms before I've even gotten dressed? Don't wolves ever run out of pithy things to say?*

Ruyah chuckled and ignored Joran, then shook the snow from his fur. As Joran reached for his boots, Ruyah's face grew serious.

You cannot continue much longer in those.

Joran picked up a boot that was little more than patches of sheep's wool and shredded leather. For days now Joran had been stuffing bits of cloth around his feet, using twine to hold the whole mess together. Tromping through snow and the relentless rain had turned his footwear into a soggy mass that left his toes numb.

We need to get you some new boots before you lose your feet.

Oh sure, let's just take a small side trip to the cobbler's and pick up a pair. I'm sure there is one just around the bend. Joran retreated back under the rock ledge as the wind kicked up and pelted rain in his direction. He was as miserable as he thought humanly possible. Of course, if he had that magnificent silver coat and nice rubbery padded feet like that beast over there, maybe he could enjoy a romp in the snow.

As if reading his mind, Ruyah spoke. *Do you know what wolves say about the perfect happiness of humans? "It is an exact and perilous balance, like that of a desperate romance . . ."*

Joran grunted. *What do wolves know about romance?*

It is said among wolves, "Man must have just enough faith in himself to have adventures, and just enough doubt to enjoy them."

Joran sneered at the wolf. *I have plenty of doubt. And if you think I am enjoying this "adventure," you have not been paying close attention.*

Ruyah pushed against Joran's chest with his broad snout. *Yes, well you need to have more faith, then you will see the adventure. It is also said, "An adventure is an inconvenience rightly considered."*

Joran sighed. *Faith in what?* There was nothing worse than having your fill of wolf on an empty stomach. *And why do wolves have so many sayings about humans? You never have any clever adages about wolves. Go catch something. I am taking the day off.*

Ruyah trotted around the rock ledge and returned with fur in his mouth. He deposited two rabbit pelts in Joran's lap. He grasped Joran's pack with his teeth and dragged it over to where Joran hunched under the ledge. *Make yourself useful. Here're the remains of dinner. I will go catch a few more snow hares. That should be enough for a pair of boots. By the time you stitch these together for the soles, I will be back.*

Joran watched the silver wolf melt into the gray distance and vanish like an apparition. He hunkered down to task, threading twine through his farrier's needle, the one he used to stitch breeching—a hundred years ago.

Thinking back to his life in Tebron was like conjuring up another apparition. *Once upon a time, there was a young man who worked as a blacksmith, fell in love with a beautiful woman, ate food that had color and texture, smelled fish on hot coals, felt the warm sun bake his shoulders.* A picture out of a child's storybook. A few days back, Ruyah had told him, *The center of man's existence is a dream.* To Joran, at this moment, the whole of his existence was a dream—not just the center. The man back in Tebron never existed.

Ruyah had been right, though—by the time the wolf returned, Joran had fit, cut, and sewn the beginnings of two boots. Joran, cross-legged by a glowing fire, rubbed the suede with a liniment to waterproof the hide and seams. Ruyah shook a tub's worth of water out of his coat, and after dumping a pile of rabbits onto the snow, gratefully plunked down to soak up warmth instead of water. Steamy wisps started to rise from his fur.

Joran raised his eyes from his work. *You look like a drowned rat. On hot coals.*

Those are coming along nicely.

Yes, I think my feet will be very happy. Thank you, Ruyah.

While Ruyah slept deeply, Joran cleaned the hares, skewered the meat, and scraped the hides. He rigged up a rack of branches next to the fire on which he spread out the skins to dry. As he tended the fire and cooked his dinner, Joran looked out at the landscape—what he could make out in the dimness and rain. They were now almost at the tree line. Up until now they had been fortunate to find dry wood buried under piles of boulders, the result of small avalanches that occasioned the hillsides. When tinder and twigs were plentiful, Joran had stuffed them in his pack, and they proved invaluable. But tinder alone would not keep them warm and fed now. Once the trees disappeared, Joran would freeze to death. Either they would have to turn around or chance continuing on in hope the mountains would yield to a more forgiving terrain. Maybe the wolf was made to thrive in winter's elements, but those elements would be the death of Joran.

At some arbitrary point, Joran determined he'd try sleeping again. Long ago, sleep at the end of a productive day was a welcomed thing. Now he faced closing his eyes with trepidation. He knew he would have no rest. He knew what awaited him on that shore of slumber. From time to time Ruyah raised his head, looked about, but uninspired, dropped back to sleep. Rain droned on, smacking the rocks and lulling Joran into drowsiness as he finished his last stitches and tied a knot. The fire had reduced down to glowing embers that snapped and hissed as water intruded. Joran rubbed the soft leather with more liniment, admiring his work.

Well, nothing to brag about. He had made a lot of shoes for horses, but this was his first attempt at shoeing human feet. Joran slipped on the boots, the soft rabbit fur tickling his ankles. The fit was stiff and snug, but soon his feet heated up and felt wonderful.

Joran picked up the bits and shreds of his former boots—boots he thought would take three years to wear out. How long had he really been traveling? In this place there was no accounting for time. Maybe three years *had* passed, or maybe time came to a standstill in this forsaken land of rain and gray and snow. A place never day or night, never quite dark or light.

Joran threw the old boots into the fire and watched them smolder and smoke on the coals. *You will wear out three pairs of shoes before you finish your journey.* Well, now he was on the second pair—with no stars, no Moon, nothing in the universe to guide him, to answer the riddle of the three keys and show him how to free his wife. All he had was a carefree wolf stuffed with homilies.

SIX

ONCE MORE Joran glared into the frosted sea-glass window, trying anxiously to make out Charris's words. Although encased in ice, she was able to move her lips, but Joran heard nothing but screaming wind and Moon laughter. *Where? Where?* she seemed to be mouthing. Her eyes darted; she strained to see, looking past him into the enveloping darkness that grabbed Joran by the collar of his coat and tried to pull him off the steep ledge that jutted out over an agitated ocean roiling far below.

Joran. Wake up.

As Joran's feet gave way in collapsing sand, his eyes opened. Superimposed over Charris's pleading face were a furry muzzle and two bright yellow eyes. Joran gave a start and knocked his skull against rock. *Ow!*

As his eyes adjusted to the darkness, Ruyah tipped his head and cocked his ears.

Did I startle you, young human?

What do you want? Joran moaned and rubbed his head. Something seemed odd. After a moment, he sat up and looked about him. A huge disk of Moon hung on the horizon, brightly illuminating the expanse of night. The world around him radiated a luminous glow of white, almost as bright as day. The rain had stopped; clouds had fled. Snow, in tufts of meringue, glistened like a million diamonds. Joran found himself camped on a wide rocky butte, every little crevice and mound in crisp detail. Not a living thing could be seen in this barren landscape—no trees, shrubs, insects, birds. The expanse was stark, austere, and yet somehow complete in its beauty. After so many weeks of gray and obscurity, the clarity of his surroundings hurt his eyes. It was as if he had been wandering blind for years and suddenly regained his sight.

Look, Joran. The house of the Moon!

Ruyah trotted across the escarpment and pointed his nose up the fortress of slick rock. Silvery steps of glass were embedded in dark obsidian, a small moon swimming on each. Perfectly placed and identical in shape, the steps zigzagged to the heights and ended at the incongruous warped stoop of a crumpling hovel made of some strange material. The planking looked like wood but shone like matte stone, as if dozens of trees had become petrified at the sight before them. Joran threw clothes on in haste and stuffed the bedroll in his pack.

Ruyah paced restlessly at the base of the stairs. *Fancy that! Here is the Moon's house—a sorry sight if you ask me. Now maybe you will find your answers. But, I cannot stay here much longer.*

Joran rushed over to the wolf's side. *Ruyah, what is wrong? Are you unwell?*

Odd, I have this terrible urge to howl. It grows in me like a rancid meal I must disgorge.

Oh, lovely.

I do not want to make a commotion. What if it upsets the Moon and she sends you away? I cannot risk that.

Ruyah, you can't leave me here alone. What am I supposed to do?

Ruyah clenched his teeth and scrunched his face. *Go. Talk to the Moon.* He turned and stared at the huge Moon lifting herself up from the edge of the world and rising into the night sky. Not a star dared make an appearance alongside so breathtaking an entrance. The wolf rolled his eyes. *Joran, I must leave. Now.*

Joran was overtaken by a wave of fear. *What if the Moon won't speak to me? What if she really is crazy—what will she do to me?*

Ruyah hung his head and started inching away from the steps. *The Moon. Is strong. It is said . . . among wolves, "To what will you look for help if you will not look to that . . . which is stronger than yourself?"* He skulked away from Joran and toward the cliffs he had climbed the day before. *Joran, you will be fine. Do not grow faint. I will not be far, just down the hill a bit . . .*

Joran watched as the wolf loped through the crags and disappeared from sight. Quiet nearly smothered him. Joran took a longer look around him. He found himself standing in a huge rock arena, surrounded on all sides by sentinels of ochre stone, a ragged circle of slabs of similar sizes, rising far above his head, many of the slabs joined together with flat stone caps. Like stacked divining cards, or those spotted wooden blocks that old men played with in the tavern. Moonlight filtered through the massive shapes, splitting into beams that crossed and refracted, bouncing off stone and creating a five-pointed star of brilliant light at Joran's feet. He felt neither cold nor warm as he stood drenched in light.

Joran walked over to the steps and touched one with a hesitant finger. The glass was smooth as ice, and the little moon wavered like a reflection on rippling water. Joran placed a foot on a riser and stopped. The step held his weight, so he continued, step after step, stirring and disturbing moons that resettled as each foot lifted away. His footfalls made no sound, but his soft rabbit boots seemed to sink a little with each contact.

Partway up the staircase, Joran glanced back to the star pattern in the center of the stone slab circle. It shifted to the side as the faceless Moon climbed the starless sky. He searched with his eyes for Ruyah to no avail. He trusted the wolf would be waiting for him when he came back. Joran grimaced. *If* he made it back.

Nearing the top of the staircase, Joran got a better look at the shack at the end of the world. He sensed that at one time, long ago, this had been an impressive palace. He studied the elegant scrollwork wrapping the eaves of the house, now chipped and crumbling. Bas-relief carvings of planets and moons interlaced with waves that foamed and crested. The lintel over the door tipped to one side, and the heavy slat door itself was warped—if rock could warp—and no longer fit into its frame. It hung uselessly from its silver hinges, exposing an entrance that pooled soft light across a smooth glassy floor. The roof seemed to be made of carved stone, half-moons overlapping like baked tile, pearlescent and radiant.

The shack leaned against the backdrop of night, and as Joran cautiously peeked around the side, there was nothing but blackness behind it, a place where no moonlight dared go. Like a heavy black curtain lowered across the stage of existence. No doubt, he *was* at the end of the world, and it was no comforting thought.

As he approached the front door, Joran thought he could hear someone moving about inside, clanging pots and bumping into furniture. He stopped, confused. Even more perplexing were the snatches of tune he heard hummed—a little ditty from his childhood, something about a cat and a fiddle. Who was in there?

Collecting courage, he lifted the crescent-shaped doorknocker and let it fall against the door. Bits of grainy rock broke off and drifted slowly to the ground, capturing tiny moonbeams as they settled softly on the stoop. The pieces shimmered like stardust. A melodious voice called out.

"Entrée, entrée, yes, I'm coming!"

Joran peeked into the entry, at the pool of light coating the floor like ivory paint. A figure in a long gown emerged from shadows and glided to greet him. A hand was offered—bedecked with a silver ring on each finger, and sporting a dozen thin bracelets that jangled noisily.

"Oh, it's you. What took you so long? I am certain the soup has gone cold but—no matter—let's just heat it up, what do you say, darling?" The woman gave Joran no time to react; she led him by his hand across the pool of light into the messiest kitchen he had ever seen. After a quick glance around the spacious room with the intricately vaulted ceiling, he nearly tripped over a mop leaning against an upholstered chair—a rather ratty one at that—and kicked a wooden slop bucket with the toe of his boot, sending it sliding across the floor.

"Oh, my, forgot I left that out. My apologies."

Joran shook his head, trying to make himself wake up. Now he *must* be dreaming. This place had put him under a trance.

"Nonsense." The woman pursed her lips and leaned close to Joran, giving his cheek a little pinch. Joran jerked back and banged into something else. He winced when he heard objects crash to the floor and break into pieces. "Don't worry about that old thing. She collects the most useless junk. And, no, you are not dreaming."

"Who are you?" Joran asked. "Just where am I?"

"Silly. You know exactly where you are. This is the Moon's house."

"And you are—the Moon?" Joran ventured.

Hearing this, the woman laughed hysterically. She slapped her thigh and tried to catch her breath. Between guffaws, she snorted and wheezed in a most unladylike fashion. "You're kidding, right? Weren't you taught your fairy tales at bedtime? Or do humans not do that anymore?" she seemed to be asking herself, rather than Joran.

Joran didn't know what to make of this tall, lithe woman dressed in a sequined gown that trailed around her feet and seemed to drop pearls as she scurried around. Her beaklike nose overpowered a weak chin, and her high cheekbones were rouged in red. Her long white hair, interlaced with ribbons, spread about her like a skirt. Her gown flowed like water about her, never quite touching her skin—unlike anything Joran had ever seen. Although silver in color, it swirled with blues, golds, and greens like a meandering stream, circling and circling her waist, reminding Joran of Charris's buckets of paint when she blended colors together with her large paddle. Tiny glass slippers graced her feet, and rather than walk, she danced and glided about, humming softly and occasionally winking at Joran.

"Sit, my little mince pie," she ordered, pointing to a rickety wooden stool. "That way you won't break anything else." Joran promptly deposited himself at a table brimming with serving platters and bowls of crystal lined with gold filigree. He peered into one tureen and found a collection of sparrow's nests, dusty and cobwebbed.

As the woman busied herself at the stove, stirring an enormous copper kettle, Joran looked around him. Moon globes glowed dimly from the walls, and moonlight streamed in through a round window down the hall. Trinkets and bottles and tins lined cupboard shelves. Unlabeled glass jars of different shapes and colors cluttered the countertops, dirty dishes lay piled in the wash basin, oddities and sculptures crammed every nook. Giant vultures of bronze glared from the walls; strange creatures with tentacles and buggy eyes hung from ornate chandeliers. A stack of moldy books, topped with what looked like a set of antlers, teetered precariously on a stool in the corner.

"I know, I know, she has terrible taste. Where she gets most of this dreck I'll never know."

Joran searched for something to say, but this place overloaded his senses. A strange smell drifted over from the cooking pot—briny and pungent. Joran's stomach gurgled in response.

"Yes, you have some fattening up to do. Your journey has taken its toll on you, poor boy." She lowered a long dipper into the pot and poured a clear liquid into a crystal bowl. As she handed the bowl to Joran, he saw the Moon reflected on the liquid's surface. The woman studied Joran's face.

"It's harmless, trust me. And it will fill you up nicely. Here, I'll fetch some biscuits." She rummaged through a cupboard and found a large, round tin. After blowing off the dust, she pried open the top and handed Joran a handful of crumbs. "Well, they are still biscuits, after all. Let's see, when *did* I bake those? It's been so long, I can't remember." She turned to Joran. "And it's been so long since we've had any visitors out here, I *am* forgetting my manners." She offered her hand to Joran.

"My name is Cielle. I am the Moon's sister."

"Pleased to make your acquaintance," Joran replied politely.

Cielle waved him off. "Enough of the formalities, dear boy. It is just an absolute *joy* to have your company. We do get a bit lonely out here and end up talking to ourselves more than we should." She started in humming another tune. This one Joran also recognized—a rhyme about an owl, a cat, and a runcible spoon.

Joran sipped his soup, which, although only lukewarm, spread a fire through his limbs and dispelled all his aches. He stared at the clear liquid with the floating moon, puzzled, for as he sipped, his mouth exploded with flavors he had never known. He bit down on wonderful chewy things that reminded him of potatoes and river clams and summer squash.

Cielle raised her eyebrows, giving him another wink. "Pretty neat stuff, huh? Ancient family recipe."

"It's delicious." Joran tried not to eat too quickly, savoring each sip. "May I ask, Cielle, where is your sister?"

The woman laughed again, then snorted. "Why, you funny boy. Outside, of course!" She pointed to the moonlight spreading like syrup across the entry floor. "She will be absolutely livid when she gets home and finds I have entertained you all by myself. But, what does she expect? Out there, traipsing about, wreaking havoc with her whims. What trouble that lazy woman gets into, lollygagging as she snoops around. And you think you can say anything to her? Heaven knows I've tried—what good that does." Cielle pulled up a chair, brushing something that looked like a cat off the cushion and onto the floor. The animal scurried away with a squeal. Cielle plopped down beside Joran with a steaming cup in her hands. She sipped at her drink thoughtfully, looking her houseguest over.

"Now, darling, you'll be wanting a bath and some neatening up, no doubt. A few months of sleep and some clean clothes—that should do the trick."

Joran withheld his comment. He had no intention of spending months in this place, but he wasn't going to say anything to upset her. "Tell me about the Moon. Is she able to . . . solve riddles?"

"Dear sweetums, asking her would be folly—the Moon will just load you up with more riddles. How can I describe Lunella? She isn't very bright." Cielle covered her mouth and snorted again. "Well, of course, she is *very* bright, but I meant she is not *bright*, short a few candle marks, if you get my drift. And absentminded as well. Causes a lot of trouble, that way."

Cielle tipped her cup and drained the dregs into her throat. "The Moon is fickle—starts one thing, gets distracted. If I wasn't here to help clean and cook, she would waste away. Oh—and she does! Every month she goes out carousing and forgets to eat. She starts all fat and round and by the time she drags her sorry body into this house, she is just a sliver of herself. After a few nights' sleep and some of my home cooking, she's as good as new. It is an endless cycle. But, as they say, 'The recurrences of the universe rise to the maddening rhythm of an incantation.' That's the way it is meant to be."

Cielle sighed and slumped over the table. "And, between you and me, I am really fed up with her. You think she ever helps out around here? Hah! But I try not to irritate her too much. It is prudent to stay out of her way, you bet. She gets a little steamed and mountains pull from their foundations, tides flood and sweep away cities, destroy whole harbors in one fell swoop. I've seen it, my darling, *I have seen it*." She punctuated the last four words with a pointed finger into his chest.

A heavy lassitude overtook Joran as he finished the last sip of soup and dropped his spoon into the bowl. The little moon still sat at the bottom, round and dreamy. He knew he had important things to ask, riddles to solve, but his tongue grew heavy in his mouth and he forgot what to say even as the words formulated in his thoughts. He felt a soft hand on his shoulder and heard the jangling of bracelets.

"Come, my pumpkin. There will be plenty of time for riddles and answers. But why you humans always want answers, answers . . . Just remember the old saying: 'The riddles of God are *much* more satisfying than the solutions of man.' Let's get you into a soft bed for a well-deserved sleep. Plenty of time for chitchat later." She gave him another knowing wink.

Joran did not know how he found himself under a pile of luxurious blankets, soft as gossamer and both warm and cool at the same time. His wet clothes stripped, boots removed, and satin and silk caressed his skin as he sunk into a bed that swallowed him up in absolute comfort. Cielle was right; there would be plenty of time later to answer all his questions. What was the hurry? And for the first time in what must have been a dozen months, Joran slept deeply—so deeply that, as hard as they tried, his nightmares could not find him.

SEVEN

"WELL, LOOK what the wombat dragged in. Sleepyhead has finally woken up."

Joran, lightheaded, shuffled into the kitchen while Cielle hurried to make a path for him through the morass of clutter. Moments earlier, he had opened his eyes to the dimness of moonlight on his face and was surprised to find himself buried under blankets in such a cumbersome bed. A search for his clothes proved useless, so he had put on the deep blue silk robe laid out on the coverlet and, barefoot, followed the bustling sounds that led him to the kitchen. The room still glowed in the soft light of the moon globes. He imagined it was always night in this place.

"What's a wombat?" he asked, sinking into a chair at the table, while Cielle placed before him another bowl of clear moon soup.

Cielle handed him a silver spoon. "Darling, I have no idea." Cielle looked him up and down. "Ah, that rest has done you some good."

Joran realized that, instead of being skin and bones, he had filled out a bit, almost back to the way he had been when he started this journey. How was that possible?

Cielle nodded her head and snorted. "See, muffin, I told you that was some soup."

Joran lifted a spoonful of clear liquid to his mouth and startled. He bit down on raisins, walnuts, oats, and honey; baked raspberry scones with cream and jam; brick cheese, smoked and aged; slices of peach and apple. Each chew released a new flavor, and by the time Joran finished the bowl, he was unbearably stuffed.

"More?" Cielle asked.

Joran shook his head. "I couldn't possibly swallow another bite. Just how do you make this . . .?"

"Uh uh uh—family secret, sorry." Cielle rested her head on her hands and smiled. "You look absolutely adorable in that robe. That's Lunella's, by the way, but I'm sure she won't mind you wearing it."

"I would prefer my own clothes, if you please. And just how long have I been asleep? Will I be able to see the Moon today?"

Cielle took Joran's hand in her cool grip. "Darling boy, so many questions! I took the liberty of washing those filthy things—I'll fetch them." Cielle went into another room and came back with his clothes neatly stacked in her arms. She set them on the table in front of Joran. She then gathered the dishes and added them to the towering stack in the basin. Joran was amazed they didn't topple over.

"And of course you can see the Moon today." Cielle pointed to the hall window, from which the creamy light spread across the floor. "You can see the Moon every day. Well, almost every day."

"Cielle, please, I do need to talk with her. The goose lady told me she may be able to help me find my wife."

"Yes, yes, we know all about that." Cielle waved him away. "Well, Lunella was here for a brief stop. She thought you looked so adorable, sleeping away under the covers, she didn't have the heart to wake you."

"When was that?"

"Good heavens, sweetling. How should I remember?"

"Well, when will she return again?"

"Oh, not for at least a few weeks."

Joran looked crestfallen. Cielle chucked him under the chin. "Now, now, sourpuss, what are we so sad about? Surely little ol' Cielle can help you with your troubles."

Joran sighed. How long had he been asleep? The goose lady had warned him time was running out; it was urgent he hurry. It had taken him weeks, maybe months, to get this far. No doubt Charris was beyond help, lost for good. Why continue this insane quest? He had failed; he was useless and inept. Somehow he had caused Charris to disappear, and all his foolish wanderings had led him to the end of the world—far away from wherever Charris had needed rescuing. Why had he listened to the goose lady, that old witch, anyway? Maybe she had deliberately misled him, to take him far from Tebron and Wolcreek, to send him off in distraction to wander the world.

Joran buried his head in his hands, his heart hurting. What in heaven's name was he doing with this nutty lady in a strange shack at the end of the world? Joran reached for his pile of clothes. It was time to get dressed and leave. Where he would go, he didn't really know—or care. All he knew was he had to leave this place of continual night and eerie moonlight and find civilization before he lost his mind. If he hadn't lost it already.

"Wait, poochie," Cielle said, "what are you doing?"

"I have lingered here too long. Thank you for your hospitality, the bed, the soup. But I need to be on my way." Joran stood and started toward the bedroom, clothes in his arms.

Cielle pulled him back to the chair. "You aren't losing your mind, dear boy. Not yet. But you will, if you are not careful. I should know! Why don't you tell me your riddles and I will see if I can help."

Joran sat and reluctantly related all that the goose woman told him, about how he had trapped Charris with his dreams, and that he needed to lose three keys to find and open a lock. "What can you tell me about these riddles?" he pleaded.

Cielle thought for a long while and then patted Joran's hand. "Absolutely nothing, my gorgeous boy. Haven't a clue. But, wait. I have something for you. A little trinket, or souvenir, if you like." Cielle dug through the tins in the cupboard again, tossing them to the floor in a great clatter. "Ah, here." She opened a small latched box of tarnished silver.

"What is it?" Joran asked as she placed a smooth shell in the palm of his hand. The shell was large, shaped like a dish with a curled rim. It fit in his hand and felt oddly heavy. Joran turned it over and saw a pattern of rippled lines, swirled and merging in the center of the shell, colors of moon and foam.

"Silly, it is a moonshell. Very rare. She wouldn't like it if she knew I was giving it to you. But, it is very special."

Joran slipped it into his pocket and muttered thanks. Just what he needed. He got up once more to leave.

Cielle grabbed his arm. "You don't seem to understand, darling. She will confront you—when you get to the sea. She has her trapped and will not want to let her go. She doesn't part with her treasures easily. Like I told you, she has a temper." Cielle turned pensive. "It's really a good thing you didn't meet her while you were here. She may not have liked you one bit."

Joran sat back down, tired of trying to make sense of her words. Cielle continued, "This shell may save your life, so guard it carefully. If you do battle with the Moon, unless you use this shell, you will perish—you and your beautiful, *tragic* wife." Cielle reached into her dress pocket and pulled out a dainty handkerchief. She dabbed her misty eyes and then blew her nose in a loud honk.

"What must I do with it?"

Cielle grew serious, lowered her voice. "If it comes to that, dear boy—you must put your whole heart into it. It is the only way to escape."

"Put my whole heart into what?"

"Haven't you been listening, dear boy? The shell, of course."

Joran rolled his eyes. First keys and locks, now hearts and shells. As he walked toward the bedroom to change his clothes, Cielle called after him.

"Where will you go now?

"I have no idea."

Cielle went into the kitchen and brought Joran's pack to him. "I have stuffed your pack with all kinds of goodies. Some extra soup too."

"Thank you, Cielle. I will remember your kindness."

"Oh, and a good juicy bone for your wolf friend."

Joran had almost forgotten Ruyah. Was he still out there somewhere? If Joran had truly been asleep for weeks, what made him think the wolf had waited? Surely he had gotten tired, or hungry, or bored, and went on his way to do whatever wolves do.

Joran dressed, put on his rabbit boots, and swung the pack over his shoulder. He felt refreshed, strong, and well-fed. His clothes smelled vaguely like lilies and cinnamon, and he realized, as he put on his hat, that his hair had been washed and his beard trimmed. He had no recollection of having been bathed.

Cielle came over to him as he stood at the door gazing out at the starless night. The top of the huge Moon barely broke the horizon, shooting beams of light across the snowy expanse. Once more the light bounced around the stone slabs and formed a perfect star in the center. A moment later, Joran saw a shape move into the open arena and stop before the star.

"There's your wolf," Cielle noted with a tilt of her head. Joran looked at Ruyah, sitting still, waiting, then looked at Cielle, hair and ribbons flowing around her sad face, gown shimmering and pearls scattering at her feet. "Now you must go to the palace of the Sun."

"The palace of the Sun. Why? Where is that?"

"Why, in the east, of course. As far east as you can go. That's where he lives. Oh, and it is a dandy of a palace too. Not like this piece of rubbish."

"Why should I go there? How will that help me?"

"Why, snookie, the Sun knows everything, sees everyone. Each day he travels the length and breadth of the world. Nothing is outside his vision. He will surely know where your wife is. No doubt he has seen her." Cielle laughed and snorted again. "The Moon wouldn't tell you anything, anyway. She's the perfect snob. But, the Sun. Now, he is honorable, dependable. Much more compassionate. Go find the Sun and ask him your riddles."

Joran felt as if a yoke of iron had just landed on his shoulders. Here he was at the most northern point of the world, and now he was told to go east, as far east as possible. Just how long would *that* take? If only he had wings and could fly there!

So much for the Moon solving his riddles. All he got for his efforts was a shell, a souvenir. Something to put on a shelf someday and admire. And it wasn't all that pretty to look at.

As he thanked Cielle, she leaned over and kissed his forehead. Joran felt a slight burning and reached to touch where her lips had brushed his skin. He could make out a soft outline of moon. After giving him a wink, she went back into the house, half-closing the broken door, and Joran could hear her humming and singing something about a dream maker, a heartbreaker, and a huckleberry friend—whatever that was.

He shook his head, if only to knock some sense into it. As he placed his foot on the first glass step, scooting the dainty moon to one side, the huge Moon floated up slowly to sit on the edge of the mountain. Below him, he watched Ruyah stretch his neck high to meet her and, without warning, the wolf let loose a piercing howl that filled the night with the sound of yearning.

EIGHT

AS JORAN hiked down the mountain, with the staircase to the Moon's house retreating into darkness behind him, the wolf trotted up beside him and sniffed him over.

You smell funny. Can't put a claw on it. Nutmeg?

Yeah, well, at least one of us has had a bath. I think.

The soles of Joran's rabbit boots were soggy from slogging through miles of mud and puddles. Although it seemed to have taken months of strenuous climbing over cliffs to arrive at the house of the Moon, within hours of skipping down ravines and crawling over boulders, a faint light began to filter in through the dark and gloom, revealing forest and grassy meadows. The Moon had followed them for a while, then set over a peak without incident. A soft fog coated them, clung to their clothes, but Joran was cheered by the change. He'd had his fill of moons.

You have a smudge on your forehead.

Joran leaned down to Ruyah and showed him. The wolf licked the spot with his large tongue. Joran scrunched his face and wiped off the slobber. *Hey, what are you doing?*

I thought it was a bit of jam. It doesn't come off. Ruyah took a closer look. *It's an imprint of a moon. How did you get that?*

Long story. Ruyah sniffed at a bush; Joran stopped to watch. The day warmed, tingling Joran's face. He removed his coat and began walking again on a drier path of trampled knee-high grass.

I must say I was surprised to see you down below, in the stone circle. I thought you would have given up waiting weeks ago.

Weeks ago! What are you talking about? After you started climbing the staircase, I ran down the mountain as fast as I could. And then I felt bad. So, I turned right around and came back. You had made it to the door when I couldn't contain myself any longer. I just had to howl. Ruyah looked over at Joran with puzzlement in his eyes. *I don't know what came over me. I have never howled like that before.*

Joran blinked. Had he imagined it all? That wouldn't surprise him. As far as he knew, he could be back in his barn loft in Tebron, sleeping under straw. One day he might wake up and find none of this journey had occurred. Maybe that was why he never had any nightmares while sleeping in the house of the Moon—perhaps he hadn't been there.

Joran reached into his pocket and found the moonshell. Well, *that* was real. He pulled it out and showed it to Ruyah, who gave up nosing bushes and took a rest in a large mud puddle.

Now it is your turn for a bath. You smell like one of the rumphogs at market.

This feels great, Joran. You should try it. He sniffed the shell. *What is it?*

A moonshell. Cielle gave it to me.

Who is Cielle? I thought you went to see the Moon.

Cielle is the Moon's sister. The Moon was out.

I noticed. Ruyah sniffed Joran's pack. *What else did she give you? Something smells wonderful.*

Joran lowered his pack to the ground. *Oh, I forgot. This is for you.* He handed the wolf the large meaty bone. Ruyah snapped it up eagerly and returned to his mud puddle. Joran smiled. He rummaged through the pack, finding strange things that looked like fruit, nuts, and breads, but in colors and shapes that were foreign to him. He bit into a roll that tasted like summer, and the creek behind his cottage. He could swear he heard dragonflies' wings beating the air as he chewed.

While Ruyah crunched on his bone, Joran told him what Cielle said about the moonshell and the palace of the Sun. That she had no answers to his riddles.

What does she mean that you must put your whole heart into it? What does the shell do? And how do you put a heart in it? Ruyah pulled at a bit of meat, stripping it from the bone. *This is really tasty. How thoughtful of her.*

Ruyah, what have you heard about the palace of the Sun? Do you think it exists?

It must. If the Moon has a house, so must the Sun. It figures.

Then I suppose that's where I am headed. Joran swallowed the last piece of his roll and washed it down with water from his skin. Cielle had replenished it for him, but the water tasted more like a waterfall of cherries in his mouth, sending tingles down his spine. As he sat on a fallen log, he took in the scenery. The sight of trees, with their branches green and snowless, refreshed him. Patches of purple lupine and orange fire lilies added splashes of color to the meadow spreading out before him. He drank in colors as the fog dispersed and sunlight made an entrance.

Colors long lost returned to the world, but as Joran's world became more tangible, so did his anger and hurt. The somnolent cloud that had coated his mind in the Moon's house now parted and exposed what lay raw beneath. Charris's face came to him unbidden. Joran touched that face, traced her cheek, releasing a torrent of memories that struck him forcefully. He didn't notice Ruyah at his side until he felt nudged by his nose.

What is the matter, Joran? Do you want to go home?

Ruyah, I have no home. This journey is hopeless and stupid.

The wolf lay down next to the log, and Joran scratched the top of his head. *You are searching for truth. That is not a stupid goal.*

Why is it so hard?

Ruyah leaned into Joran's fingers, enjoying the scratching. *It is said among wolves, "The road to truth has not been tried and found wanting. It has been found difficult—and left untried." Joran, at least you are trying. That counts for something.*

Not if it leads me nowhere. What if I have been wasting my time, traipsing the world, while Charris is really back in Tebron somewhere? How can I know?

You have to follow your heart, Joran. And your dreams.

I didn't ask for those dreams.

No one asks for dreams, but you have been given them. They are your task.

Joran scowled. *From whom? Who hands out these tasks, anyway? Can't I get a different assignment?*

Ruyah rubbed his head against Joran's belly. *The goose woman said you have power in your dreams, that you have trapped Charris there. Perhaps the way to get peace from your dreams is by getting peace in your dreams.*

Joran stood, restuffed his pack, and swung it onto his back. Ruyah straightened, then rolled in the dry dirt and shook clumps of mud from his fur.

And how do I do that—get peace in my dreams?

I have an idea. We will work on it together. Tonight we will start.

Joran began walking down the hillside, with Ruyah alongside him. In the cheering sunlight he noticed new buds on the trees below him. Bulbs sprouted through patches of grass—flowers of violet and pink—and berry bushes sprouted sprays of white flowers. Somehow, while he had been sleeping at the end of the world, spring arrived down below.

Usually spring lightened his step, but Joran's heart remained heavy and troubled, and each step took effort. He knew, with dread, that tonight he would be ravaged by his nightmares. He felt the sea

calling to him louder than any cry of Charris's. Even as he walked,
he could hear the lapping of waves against the shore. Salt spray filled
his nostrils and the rhythm of his walking became the bobbing of
the sea. As the Sun rose high and mighty in the sky, Joran felt the
insistent tug of current, pulling him under, calling his name.

And somewhere behind him, he heard the Moon chuckle.

By midday, Joran began to see indications of civilization. Hills
flattened into prairie, where tall grasses waved with the westerly
breeze. Wagon ruts matted the vegetation leading to skeletons of
farmhouses and barns, weather-stripped planking barely hanging
on to posts and beams. Joran wondered where on earth he was,
and if there was a village nearby where he could get his bearings
and supplies. The air buzzed with clouds of insects, their wings'
song droning in his ears. The aroma of damp grass baked by the
sun invigorated Joran, lifted his spirits. Even if his journey led
nowhere, at least he had a beautiful day to enjoy. Ruyah amused
him with his bounding and leaping through the fields, pouncing
on mice and digging heatedly for some furry escapee.

You look quite undignified behaving like a rowdy puppy.

A wolf head popped up from the sea of grass. *Who says wolves
have to be dignified? Besides, dignity is more a state of mind than a
behavior. You should know that.*

Joran scanned the fields around him. *And you should be paying more attention to your surroundings. I doubt farmers here, as
anywhere, would welcome a wolf of your size cavorting around their
livestock.*

My nose will alert me if humans are near. The head vanished.
Ruyah's paw had healed and didn't seem to hamper him in the
least. Joran had stripped down to a sleeveless shirt. His hat kept the
sun off his face, but his arms were getting baked. After so much
time in rain and snow, Joran welcomed the heat.

The mountains shrank behind him, and stretched out before him were endless fields, an ocean of green. Joran frowned. He doubted this would lead him to the real ocean he sought. Who knew where the sea was? He had only heard of it from childhood stories or songs sung off-key late nights in the tavern. Tales conflicted—the sea was treacherous and filled with snakelike monsters; the sea was emerald green, flat as a mirror, teeming with sparkling fish and enticing creatures that lured you to its depths. The sea went on forever, and swallowed sailors who tried to reach its edge. Maybe there was no sea; maybe it existed only in dreams—and nightmares.

Joran sat on a rock beside the wagon road. As he drank water and wiped his forehead he looked for signs of Ruyah. Probably off on a hunt. He thought of all the nights Ruyah had kept him alive, bringing him game to eat when there had been nothing else. Curling his thick body around his to keep out the cold. Now, thanks to Cielle, he had a pack full of odd food that filled and strengthened him even after few bites. He wondered why the wolf stayed with him. Ruyah told him he couldn't resist an adventure—and a mystery. He was curious to see how Joran's tale would end. To Ruyah, this was just a bit of fun, but it wasn't fun to Joran. Why couldn't Ruyah see that?

Joran traveled along the road for hours; now the sun was westering behind him, and the air thickened with bugs. Still no sign of Ruyah. Joran decided to keep walking until dusk, then set up camp. He had accumulated a small bundle of sticks along the way, enough to start a fire. Off in the distance sat another dilapidated house. Maybe he could scrounge for wood there. As he turned south toward the homestead, Joran froze.

He thought he heard a squeal, a whine pierce the din of insect wings. He heard it again. Ruyah!

Joran threw down his weighty pack and ran toward the sound, battening down swales of grass and tripping over gopher mounds.

Then he heard a brusque voice. Joran fell flat to the ground, digging his face into dirt. He stilled his breath and listened.

"Ooh, he's a nice one, this is."

Joran heard more squealing and Ruyah's snarl. Another voice, a second man spoke. Joran's heart pounded.

"Get that muzzle tighter. That monster'll rip out your throat give 'im half a chance." Joran heard thrashing, and then a smack of wood.

"That'll quiet 'im some. Get a look at that fur. You seen anything like it?"

Another man, this one with a nasally voice, coughing: "Take off the choke. Bind 'is legs tight now. It'll take the lot of us to toss 'im into the wagon. Hooey—wait till the others sees this one. Must weigh at least eight stone. Will make us rich, can bet."

Joran panicked. What could he do against three men? Surely they had weapons; all he had was a small knife. He could not let them take and kill Ruyah! He slowly lifted his head, hoping to get a look in the dimming light. He heard the first man speak again.

"He won't be out long. We should skin 'im now."

"Aw, Greb, we're all knackered. Kin wait till morning, don't ya think?"

"Yeah, it's gettin' dark an' I'm starvin'," said the third. "I'm not going start any knife work this late."

"Well, then you better make doubly sure that critter is well tied. Fent, go fetch some wood and get to cooking. Demar, check that beast. Hit 'im again if you have to."

Joran inched his way back to a spot where he could lift his head without being seen. The three men were big and heavy, plenty strong. Joran had no doubt if they had been able to tackle and restrain Ruyah, they could make short work of *him* in no time. They were dirty and unshaven and one carried a hefty rope on his shoulder. He was relieved Ruyah was still alive, but what on earth could he do?

While the men busied themselves preparing camp and dinner, Joran could make out Ruyah's limp body on the ground next to a rickety cart. He heard the snuffle of horses and tried to reach them with his thoughts, but to no avail. He was probably too far away.

He fell back down under the cover of grass, sweating and anxious. He had to do something! He didn't dare try to sneak in late at night and free the wolf. If he could talk to the horses, maybe he could enlist their help. Maybe he could convince them to trample the men, or create a distraction. Would they feel loyalty toward these rogues, or be willing to help? There was no way to know unless Joran could get closer. Just the idea made his knees quiver.

Joran waited for hours, his legs cramped under him, but he dared not crawl back to his pack. Once the sun set, the air cleared of bugs and all was quiet except for the men talking and laughing boisterously. Joran could see a fire and smell meat cooking. Ruyah hadn't moved or made a sound and Joran worried for his life. He was tired of waiting, and angry at himself for just sitting there. Quietly, he crawled, ever so careful not to make a sound, and worked his way around so he faced the horses. There were two of them, pulling at the grass and tethered to a high line. Before they saw Joran and could make a noise, he spoke to them.

Please, don't make a sound. I am a friend.

The horses both jerked at their leads and looked for Joran in the grass.

Don't be startled. I am just a man. But I need to stay hidden.

One of the horses spoke. *I see you now. What are you doing? Lose something?*

The other horse laughed. Joran shushed him. *Please, if those men find me, I am a dead man.*

That's for sure.

Joran sighed. This was not looking promising. *They have a wolf—my friend.*

Wolves are no friends of ours. That's for sure.

This one is a noble beast. He would never hurt you.

The horses snorted. *And what do expect from us? To save your precious wolf? How would we manage that?*

Would you help me? Maybe cause a commotion, or break away so the men would chase after you? I just need a chance to get to him and untie him.

If we did that, said one horse, *we would be beaten. No, thanks.*

The other horse nodded. *We dare not. We have felt their whip more times than I can count.*

So, why don't you help me? I will free you from those men.

And they would come after us. No, we will not help you.

You would rather stay under their cruel yoke?

The horses thought for a moment. *Yes. That is our decision.*

Joran sighed. *Will you at least keep quiet while I leave? I have done you no harm.*

Yes. Leave us now. The horses returned to their grazing, ignoring Joran.

As he crawled back a safe distance, he fumed. All the times he had helped animals, rescued them, listened to their complaints. And now here were two horses, clearly mistreated, who would rather stay with brutal men than leave. Who wouldn't even lift a hoof to help him.

As Joran grew still, a thought formed in his mind, but he began to dismiss it. There were some creatures who had been grateful to him over the years—most had. These had even given him their names. The law of nature demanded they do so. Joran did not understand the world of beasts and their honor code, but he respected it. He knew they were sincere when they entrusted him with their names, and promised to make good when called. Joran had never stepped over into their world, fearful of abusing their trust. But this situation was desperate! Could he count on any to help him in saving another beast? Would they be able to hear his cry, and would they resent his intrusion and need?

This was not a time to worry about the ramifications. Ruyah was in danger, and he would be dead soon. He must do what it took to save him, regardless of the consequences. Ruyah had saved his life many times over; he owed it to the wolf to rescue him, even if he died trying. *He* had his own code of honor too. He may have lost his wife by some failure on his part, but he would not lose this friend if he could help it.

Joran reached into his mind, stirred his heart, and sorted though the names he held in a secret place. He felt each one, saw the face that went with the name, and, with his heart and the strength of his will, he called to them—not to all, but those he thought could come swiftly. Over and over he reached out his mind, sent his urgent cry, and throughout the night, like a mantra, he repeated their names until he fell to the hard ground, fast asleep.

A terrific pain throbbing through his skull snapped Joran out of his nightmare. When he tried to reach back to feel for a lump he found his hands bound. So were his feet—in thick rope with double knots. His back ached and his clothes were ripped and dirty. In the early dawn dimness, he saw that he had been dragged all the way over to the men's campsite, clearly after they had knocked him out. Quickly, his eyes searched for Ruyah and found him close by, his muzzle clamped shut with rope. Joran's heart skipped. Was the wolf dead?

Ruyah, Ruyah!

Relief flooded Joran's body as he saw the huge beast slowly move his head toward Joran.

What . . .? Where . . .?

Rest, Ruyah. You have been struck and bound.

Joran, where are you? I smell you but my eyes won't work.

I am close by. But I am also tied up. I am afraid my rescue attempt failed.

There was a long silence. *I am glad you are here, but you should not have tried to save me.*

I could not leave you to the knives of those men. Although, now, I . . .

Joran was interrupted by a sharp kick in his side. He curled up in pain.

"So, the little sneak's awake. We saw you scouting our camp. What were you hoping to find? Coins, pelts? Come now, 'fess up." Joran recognized the man and voice as Greb, the apparent leader of the three.

"I . . . am lost. Just trying to find my way home."

Joran heard laughter; the other men were nearby. "Right, just wandered off a bit from the ol' farm. That's a tall tale."

Don't say anything to them, Joran. Maybe they will let you go.
Not likely.

"You wouldn't a'been hunting after our wolf, would ya?" Greb circled around Joran, kicking dirt in his face. "What do you blokes think we should do with the little thief?"

"We kin take 'im with us. May come in handy when we need to fetch us things," one man said.

"Aw, he's too much trouble. Just leave the lad here," said the other.

Greb spat something out of his mouth. "I don't like this. Maybe there's others. Demar, break camp and put out that fire. Let's git going."

"What about breakfast?"

"We'll eat as we go." Joran noticed his pack over by the fire circle, its contents spilled out on the dirt. "Take the boy's stuff— might be something worth eatin' in there." He looked at Joran. "Where'd you get all the strange food?"

Joran kept quiet and felt another sharp kick in his side.

"So that's how it's to be, eh? You're a strange fish. What's that drawing you have on your face?"

The men set to loading the cart, and after dousing the fire they went over to the wolf, keeping a safe distance. Demar spoke. "Well, that wolf's awake. See his eye."

Greb looked around nervously. "We should slit him now, drain 'im out. I'm not going to try to load 'im in the wagon alive."

The other man, Fent, pulled a long sharp skinning knife out of a sheath at his side. "Well, I kin do it. But someone needs to club him again before I get any closer."

Joran looked over at Ruyah, who had closed his eyes in resignation. He searched frantically for something to say.

"Please. Don't kill him. Let me pay you for him."

The men all laughed and wagged their heads. "So the boy wants the wolf. An' with what will ya pay us? We've been through your pack—and your pockets. How 'bout that funny ol' bowl—the one that looks like bone? Now that's worth something, ain't it? Or what about your set of tools, or those goofy boots you're wearing." The men laughed harder, buckled over.

While Joran struggled in vain to think of something to dissuade the men, out of the corner of his eye he noticed a dark cloud gathering. Lying near Ruyah, beside the wagon, he strained to lift his head as the air shuddered with a low rumble. Gradually, the men stopped laughing and continued arranging the wagon, harnessing the horses. Fent pulled out a leather strap and began sharpening the knife against it, eyeing Ruyah with a grin. All the while, the cloud grew larger, coming closer. The air vibrated with energy and buzzing, and the ground started to rumble. Ruyah looked over at Joran with questioning eyes, blood trickling down his muzzle. The noise grew to a deafening volume, but for some reason the three men were oblivious to the sound and the approaching cloud.

Ruyah tried to bury his head in his paws. *Joran, what is it? Something's coming!*

Just then Joran heard a high-pitched shriek, a frightful, not frightened, one.

We are here, Joran! We come! Joran recognized the voice but could not identify its owner. In moments the sky turned black, engulfing them in a huge whirlwind of noise and fury. Joran could barely see anything; he felt wind whip at his face as flying things sped through the air around him, yet never touching. The air tried to choke him with dirt, leaves, and grit. He clamped his eyes shut and then felt hundreds of tugs and taps at his wrists and feet. The ropes restraining him fell in pieces to the ground and his hands and feet sprang loose. And then the screams started.

The horses stamped their legs and cried out, but even louder than the roar of the invasion and the panicked horses were the voices of the men. Joran's blood curdled as they howled in pain. He could make out the men running wild, thrashing the air, grabbing at their eyes and throats. As one man stumbled in agony right beside him, Joran saw a column of bees dive down his mouth, and hordes of birds peck ferociously at his skin, ripping clothes into shreds. Small creatures leaped at him from behind, biting his legs and ankles. Sounds of suffocation followed as one by one the men faltered on the ground around him and Ruyah. The wolf, free from his fetters, had slid to Joran's side and huddled with him in shock.

Joran, whom did you call?

Joran suddenly remembered. His silent plea for help before he went unconscious. Before he could speak, the drone and wind began to die down. Joran watched as a million bees dissipated into the sky in all directions and morning light filtered piecemeal upon the scene. Birds of all shapes and colors lit upon the ground, the wagon, but the three men were nowhere to be seen. Foxes and badgers slowly scampered away. Joran stared at a half dozen blackbirds pecking at the scattered and trampled breakfast scraps lying in the dirt.

Slowly, a shroud of calm settled over them as day broke over the horizon to the east. The prairie lit up with crisp morning light and the snowcapped mountains in the distance shimmered. As quickly as the attacking hordes came and ravaged, they left. As Joran wobbled into a sitting position, a small bird flew down to him from the wagon.

Joran. We came. Stopped those bad men. Helped your wolf.

Now Joran put a face to the voice. *Bryp! You are here. How did you find us from so far away?*

You called. We came. The little bird shook and ruffled her feathers. *Speedy we are. Brought friends.* The bird nodded at the other birds. *Never far away. Birds fly great distances. Always ready in a pinch.*

Joran tried to stand; his head ached mercilessly. Ruyah rose up on shaky legs. A large bumblebee wove through the air and lit on Ruyah's head. Joran recognized the queen bee, whose hive he had saved in the forest years ago.

You came, too!

We honor your call, Joran. Her tiny voice was joyful.

Joran began to cry, feeling the release of pent-up fear. Sobs racked his chest. Ruyah pressed against him, and Joran hugged him with all his strength. *I don't know what to say, how to thank you . . .*

The bee lifted off the wolf and hovered before Joran. *No need. It is the law of nature.*

Bryp hopped excitedly on the ground. *And fun! We love adventure. Bored at home. Till you called. Now. Something important to do. Save Joran! Save wolf!*

Joran smiled, still wiping tears. He still couldn't believe his eyes. He stroked Ruyah, felt the wolf's head for lumps. Blood matted the back of his neck, and his eyes were clogged with dirt and more blood. Joran took the edge of his shirt and gently cleaned the wolf's eyes.

I am all right, Joran. What about you?

Well, I could use another bath. You too.

The queen bee hovered and said good-bye. Joran thanked her and gave her back her name, and then watched as she flew off after her contingent. Gradually, the birds also left, but Bryp stayed behind.

Snotty horses. Finked on you. They make noise—men catch you.

I figured as much.

We didn't hurt them. Much. Poked them a bit. Teach lesson.

Joran looked around him at the camp. In terror, the horses had snapped their harness lines and run for their lives, with the panicky men following, no doubt. The front board of the wagon, where the breeching attached, had pulled apart, and the wagon lay broken in pieces. As Joran picked up the items from his pack that lay littered around the campfire, Ruyah licked at his fur, with Bryp perched on his back.

Bad men gone. Lots of bites and stings. Deserved that.

Joran found Callen's walking stick—broken in two. His fingers traced the scrolled knob that had been so carefully carved, and his heart ached for his brother. He tossed it to the ground; it was of no use to him now. Sifting through the mess, he found the moonshell, unbroken under one of his shirts. He was glad to find it, although he wondered how on earth he would use it to save Charris. He lifted a finger to his forehead and felt the etching on his skin. Bryp flew over and landed on his arm.

Nice moon. Pretty.

Joran couldn't help but laugh. *You are a funny thing, Bryp. I am glad you came. Now I owe you my life, for you have saved both me and Ruyah.*

Even Steven.

Still, take back your name, Bryp. You have more than repaid me. You can leave now. Joran leaned over and gave the bird a kiss on top of her head. He was sure she turned an even deeper shade of crimson. Joran wondered just how far away Tebron was from here, as the bird flies. *Did you notice any towns as you flew here?*

Too busy flying. Dark. Do not think so. Bryp jumped up and down on Joran's arm. *I will scout. Find you a town.*

Don't you want to go home? All your friends have left.

Ruyah ambled over to Joran, his legs stiff. *There is a small creek close by, Joran. Will you join me in a bath?*

Before Joran could answer, Bryp chirped. *Bath! Love baths. Let's go.*

Joran surveyed the campsite: the shreds of clothing and pieces of wagon splayed on the ground, pots and food and tools littered around him.

I don't think there's anything here we could use. Everything is broken or torn. Joran looked at the frych, who nodded confidently. He was content to leave the squalor and horror behind him. A good dip in fresh spring water would cleanse more than his body. Bryp hopped impatiently.

Don't you want to go home? Back to your friends in Tebron?

Bryp flew ahead, spun in circles. *New friends now. Mystery. Adventure. Home—pah!*

Joran lifted his pack to his back and dusted himself off. Just what he needed—another companion bent on adventure. What was it about animals that they were so happy and carefree? Didn't the evil in the world put any dent in their spirits? They certainly weren't heartless. Maybe, Joran thought, as he followed his companions to a clear, quiet creek, they were created to teach humans something about joy. He watched wolf and bird dive recklessly into the sparkling water, splashing and prancing in delight. As if the horror moments earlier had never occurred.

Images of the men screaming replayed in his mind. Images of Charris trapped in ice, calling out to him, floated into his awareness like a fish coming up for air. The weight of the world and the enormity of his quest smothered him. He had already come so far—and had barely begun.

Joran noticed his hands shaking. Was Ruyah right, that it had value, this search for truth? He stripped off his torn shirt and pants, yanked off his boots, and allowed the glory of the morning sun to seep into his bare skin. As he plunged into the cold shock of water, he willed the weariness, the fear, the pain in his head to drift away. He knew they would return—many times over—but for now he would allow himself to feel a small portion of joy in the midst of all the turmoil.

NINE

RUYAH HAD wanted to push on, but Joran could tell that the wolf was hurting. After they had bathed, Joran assessed the wounds inflicted on the beast, and they were not pretty. The back of Ruyah's head had been bashed many times and probably needed stitching. But he refused to be babied and urged Joran on in the warming sun.

So they followed the winding creek, startling frogs and flushing out quail as they trampled water reeds. Joran's eyes followed the flow of water as it gracefully danced around tumbled stones, clear and pure, revealing darting fish under the surface sheen. A kingfisher swooped down and skimmed the water, gracefully slicing a seam along the creek's face and snatching up its targeted prey. Joran stopped and took a deep, refreshing breath. The serenity of the prairie acted like a steady eraser, slowly rubbing away the horror and pain of the previous hours. Even Ruyah's step gradually lightened and his hanging head lifted in curiosity from time to time, giving Joran hope that healing would come.

At midday, Joran insisted on setting up camp, back behind a small copse of scraggly oaks—private, with an easy view of the prairie. They had neither seen nor heard other humans and Joran did not want to. For all he knew, this land was filled with nefarious men bent on trouble. He would not let down his guard any more. Bryp eagerly volunteered to fly around and watch for danger. Joran saw her flitting in the sky, weaving in circles while he did a poor job of stitching his shirt. It seemed there were more rips than fabric. He gave up and pulled another shirt out of his pack to put on. He'd save the pieces of the old shirt to patch his pants later.

Joran stopped and watched Ruyah sleeping in the grass. The day grew hot, and by afternoon flies gathered and became a nuisance. Joran came beside the wolf and brushed the insects off his wounds. Ruyah lifted his head.

What? Is everything all right?

Don't trouble yourself. Go back to sleep. You need a good rest.

Where is Bryp? Ruyah scanned the prairie.

Off scouting, she says. Her new passion. She will let us know if anyone comes near. Joran stroked the silver fur. *I forgot what color you were. All those mud baths made a mess of you. Now you are gleaming.*

Ruyah snorted. *All dressed up and nowhere to go.* Ruyah sat up a bit. *I have had enough rest. I should get up and hunt.*

Not today. I am getting tired of rescuing you. You seem to have a propensity for falling into traps. Ruyah made a sad face, but Joran ruffled his fur playfully. *You can share some of my food.*

The wolf frowned. *Moon food?*

You'll live. Joran reached for his pack and found a blue-tinted roll. *Here, try this.*

Ruyah sniffed at the roll and took a small bite. His eyes opened wide. *Tastes just like field mouse.* He took a larger bite and chewed heartily. *Mmm, just like a tasty mouse, with crunchy bones too!*

Let me see that. Joran pinched off a piece of roll and cautiously put it in his mouth. Blueberries and creamy butter, sunflower seeds. *You're crazy, Ruyah. Field mice!*

Ruyah ignored him and devoured the roll, licking crumbs off blades of grass. His eyes begged for more. Joran reached back into the pack and proffered another roll, which the wolf accepted greedily. As he ate, Joran glanced up at the webbing of tree branches overhead. Sunlight filtered through them and splattered the ground with mosaics of light. Aside from the hum of insects, the day was quiet and undisturbed. Joran turned to Ruyah, who had finished his roll and stared thoughtfully out over the fields.

Ruyah, I am curious about the law of nature. Will you explain it to me?

Ruyah looked over at Joran and cocked his head. *I thought you didn't want to hear wolf philosophy. Humans are practical, not interested in mystery and all that.*

I changed my mind.

The wolf scooted closer to Joran, resting his head on his paws. *The law of nature is sometimes called "the perfect law of freedom." It is also a mystery, and all creation is subject to it. Freedom is bound by the law, but the bindings free you.*

I'm not following you.

Imagine you are bound and tied.

Joran gave a wry smile. *I was. You were.*

Yes. So, the bindings restricted you. You could do some things, like breathe or wiggle your fingers. But others things were prevented, like running away. So you were bound, but also free. The freedom we creatures have, though, is a perfect *freedom.* Ruyah thought for a moment.

Let me give you a man's example. Let us say you are in a boat. The boat has boundaries, it restricts your freedom. Within the boat, you are free to move around, do many things, row, fish, eat, sing. The boundaries keep you safe, keep you heading down the river. But let's say you violate the boundary. You overstep and fall in the water. Now where are you? Adrift and floundering in the current, out of control and in danger.

Joran reached for his pair of torn pants and began applying a new patch. *So, the laws of nature are just rules. Rules you follow by instinct.*

Mostly. Some are by choice. But, unlike humans, animals never break the law of nature. They know that the law that binds them also sets them free. It is said among wolves that men, long ago, became bewitched by an evil power that enticed them with a promise of greater freedom beyond their bonds.

The wolf nudged Joran's leg with his nose. *Joran, remember I said that man's perfect happiness is an exact and perilous balance? That is the way it is for all creatures. A balance between law and freedom. But men ignored that truth.*

Joran scratched his head. *They upset the balance and tipped over the boat?*

Right. Another saying we have is this: "It is always simple to fall; there are an infinity of angles at which one falls, only one at which one stands." Humans must rejoin the rest of creation in embracing the law of nature; they must make a deliberate effort to "stand," and it requires a struggle against the current of complacency.

Joran sighed and put down his sewing. *So, if I just follow the laws of nature, I will be happy?*

It is much more complicated than that. For humans.

Joran grunted. *I figured as much.*

It is said when man broke the law of freedom, he came under a dark curse. He could walk about the streets, see and appreciate the world around him, only he could not remember who he was. The ancient legend states, "Every man has forgotten who he is. He may understand the stars, but his self is more distant than any star. Man has forgotten his true name; a part of that name is missing. And what is worse, he forgets that he has forgotten."

Like walking in a dream. I know just what that feels like.

Yes. So men wander about, forgetting. Left with a strange sense that they once had freedom and lost it. Another great wolf once said, "Man's birth is but a sleep and a forgetting." They forget they are in an exciting and puzzling adventure. They have lost the joy that is the ground of the whole universe.

Joran laid his head back and rested on the wolf's shoulder. *It sounds so hopeless.*

Ruyah grew quiet. Joran stroked his paw and tried to make sense of the wolf's words.

Remember I also told you there was much going on, hidden from the world of men. There are other powers in the world, at battle with evil, trying to restore balance to the world of men, trying to find a way to remove the curse. Someday—we wolves believe—men will return to the law of nature. And find the joy in doing so.

I hope you are right, Ruyah. Being human is a lonely road. But you have made it tolerable for me, at least.

Joran heard a cry from the branches above.

All clear. No bad men. Time to eat.

Bryp winged down and landed in the grass, then began pecking for bugs.

Joran patted her head. *Thank you, Bryp. You give us peace of mind. Having fun.*

Ruyah chuckled. *Tell Joran what you think of the law of nature. Fun.*

Joran laughed. *To you, everything is fun.*

No point to journey. All roads lead nowhere. Life is but a dream.

Where'd you pick up those sayings?

Here and there. Songs. Birds know many songs. With that, the little frych began to warble, and across the fields Joran heard birdsong in reply.

Hey! Bryp stopped singing. *I wonder. Who is that?* In an instant she flew off. Ruyah again nudged Joran with his nose.

Remember we talked about helping you with your dreams.

Joran nodded. *These nightmares are eating me up. The goose woman said I have trapped Charris with my anger. I have been trying to understand what she meant, but it doesn't make sense.*

Ruyah got up to stretch, causing Joran's head to slide off his back. Joran scrunched his face. *Are you in much pain?*

Some. My whole body is stiff.

The wolf hunched his back and then flopped over and rolled in the grass. *This feels good. You should try it.* After shaking out his fur and sitting down, Ruyah turned to Joran. *You know, Joran, you are different from most humans.*

Because I can talk with animals?

Not just that. You have other gifts. Powers others do not share.

What do you mean?

There is a special connection between you and your dreams. Somehow you empower them; they are not random images that come to you, but, rather, it seems you create them from the core of your being. All emotions are powerful; they can be wielded for good or evil. But most humans can only express them while awake. I believe your power extends to your dreaming.

But I don't control my dreams. How can I control my emotions while I am asleep?

Ruyah grew thoughtful. *There is a way. It takes work. But, it is worth a try.*

Joran picked up his stitching again and for a while worked in silence. When he finished, he went over to the creek and washed his dirty clothes, scrubbing them and squeezing out the water. He draped socks, shirt, and pants over the scraggly bushes lining the banks. The heat of the day and the weariness caused by recent events combined to put Joran in a stupor. His head thumped with a dull throb. He spread out his bedroll under the swaying arms of the trees and lay down, letting the warmth filter in and soak his aching limbs. As he closed his eyes, he could hear Bryp's light-hearted song tickle the air around him. Ruyah settled down beside him with a sleepy yawn, and Joran, enfolding the wolf in his arms, fell fast asleep.

• PART TWO •
THE ANGRY SUN

TEN

THE DAYS stretched longer the farther east they traveled. Fields, roasted by the searing sun, dried up and withered. Water grew scarce as the terrain flattened out before them. Soon, instead of trees, gnarled shrubs, ancient with peeling bark, dotted the landscape. Eventually, the mountains fell behind them, shrinking more and more each day, until they finally flattened and vanished.

Joran dug for pockets of water where vegetation struggled to survive, but those submerged oases were becoming fewer with each passing day. Ruyah found plenty of game to hunt, and Bryp tagged along, chirping cheerfully all the while. Joran was hot in his boots and woolen clothes. He ripped off shirtsleeves and shortened his pants to gain some relief. And although his hat protected his head, he suffered miserably from chapped lips and burnt skin. For a while, he had been able to shave; he didn't need a hot face full of hair. But as water grew scarce, he gave up trying to scrape the razor across dry skin.

Soon, shelter from the sweltering heat grew just as scarce. Night gradually dwindled away, leaving the Sun dangling on the western horizon, never truly setting. Joran took to traveling after dusk, when the heat shimmers died down and light breezes gave them merciful relief. In the twilight sky, no stars could be seen, and the Moon had fled long ago. Dirt became sand, and soon every step exhausted them, as dune after dune spread out before them like endless seas, and their steps sunk without purchase, the sand burning their ankles.

Joran sucked on his water skin, emptying the last hot drop down his throat. Ruyah panted behind him, tongue lolling out the side of his mouth. Bryp perched on the wolf's back, too tired and hot to sing.

There's a mound of rock up ahead. Maybe some bushes. Joran watched the morning sun lift off the horizon in the east, a glaring fireball that gazed at them like a baleful eye. *Maybe we can find some water there. And get some sleep.*

His companions were quiet; it took too much effort to even mindspeak. Joran wondered about the boundless desert before him—dunes that rolled on forever. Somewhere, there would be an end to the sand and they would arrive at the palace of the Sun. Or so he dared hope.

Nowhere along their path had they found a town or any other people. Bryp scouted for many miles each day but came back without promising news. Joran had never seen or heard of country like this—with huge rubbery plants that sported prickly needles. Strange animals crossed their paths: huge, furry, horselike creatures with lumps on their backs; rabbits with gigantic ears, and back haunches the size of large melons. The oddest were the gray crawlers in armor that trudged on their short scaly feet, snuffling with long noses into the sand, looking for bugs to eat.

Joran spotted a sandstone overhang that afforded enough space for him and Ruyah to sleep in shade. He scurried underneath, removed his boots—to the relief of his scorching feet—and took off his pack. Joran's shirt was drenched in sweat, and Ruyah's fur nearly burned Joran when he touched it. Joran grunted as he pressed back against the sandstone wall. Ages ago he had worried he would freeze to death on a barren mountain. Now he feared he would die of heat and thirst in another barren wilderness.

He studied the soles of his boots. The twine holding the pieces of skin together was wearing thin, and Joran had run out of twine. Gaping holes in the seams were letting in hot sand, making walking unbearable. It wouldn't be long before these boots disintegrated. He needed to manufacture another pair. But without twine, how could he stitch skins together? The idea seemed futile.

Joran was tired, so tired of this journey. He had been gone so long he could hardly remember what Tebron looked and smelled like. He tried to envision the towering trees, the misty rain, the cobbled streets, but the images wouldn't come. He had eaten, smelled, and rubbed against sand for so long his senses had eroded.

Each night, before he went to sleep, he had tried to find a way to tap into the power of his dreams. Ruyah told him he needed to enter his dreams somehow, grab his anger and his hurt, redirect their current. But try as he might, he failed to see a way in. His nightmares took hold of him; he was just a hapless victim of the forces that carried him along. He did not understand what he was supposed to do.

Joran took out Ruyah's bowl and the moonshell, which he used for a scoop in the sand. He dug quietly for a while under some prickly bushes, reaching damp ground after a foot or two.

At least that shell is useful for something, Ruyah mindspoke.

Hand me the water skin, Ruyah. The wolf lethargically nosed around in the pack and withdrew the skin with his teeth, then plopped it at Joran's feet. Joran used the shell to fish out water into Ruyah's wooden bowl. As the wolf lapped gratefully, Bryp hopped off his back and dipped her beak in. Her head followed, and upon retracting it, she shook her feathers and stretched her neck.

Ooh. Feels good. So sick of this hot.

Joran dug deeper, and more water seeped into the hole he had formed. He filled the water skin and drank deeply, drinking and refilling over and over. Thank the heavens he had found water. It lifted his spirits some.

Waves of heat rose in ribbons from the sand outside, bending the desert into a wavy pattern. The Sun inched up in the sky, and shadows shifted on the desert floor. Ruyah drank his fill, then settled down in the shade next to Joran.

You have never told me why you are so angry at Charris. Why you sent her away.

Joran grunted. *You wouldn't understand.*

You should know me better than that, Joran.

I don't want to talk about it.

The wolf laid his huge head in Joran's lap. *Maybe your telling would help me find a way into your nightmares.*

Joran grew pensive and thought back to a day, oh, so long ago. Had any of this really happened? He could barely recall Charris's face; only the image of her trapped in ice was lucid, since it haunted him every time he slept.

There's a farm down the road from my cottage. I pass it every day going to town. From time to time, I see someone there. But, it is set back from the road, and I have never met the man who lives there. There's an old waterwheel, a rundown barn, and a small cottage in the back by a stream.

Ruyah nodded. *I know that place.*

Well, I had seen a man working in the barn from time to time, hauling hay, repairing tools. We waved to each other a few times when I passed by. But, one day I was returning from work early. I had some supplies in the shed at home that I needed to finish a cart axle I was working on. When I passed that farm I saw the man in the breezeway between the barn and the cottage. He was talking to someone, leaning close. I didn't pay much attention. Until I looked harder. He had his arms around a woman, was kissing her. Joran stopped; his throat constricted and his face flushed hot. *It was Charris. She must have thought I wouldn't know. It was her day off from the mill. And there she was—in this man's arms, kissing him, her hair flowing out behind her.*

How could you be certain it was she?

Of course it was. I know my wife. She had on her favorite shawl, one she made. There is no other like it—a deep burgundy and blue, with wisteria vines interlaced. Her back was turned to me, but it was Charris! While I was away at work, there she was, throwing herself at this man.

Joran grew quiet, clenched his teeth. *I couldn't take my eyes off them. I sneaked up closer, to watch from behind a tree—to torture myself, I suppose. They were kissing, laughing, embracing each other. Then he walked her into the barn, out of my sight. I was devastated! I thought about running in and confronting them, but I was in shock. I stood there for what seemed like hours, waiting, waiting. I thought when she came back out . . .*

Ruyah interrupted. *What did you do then?*

I . . . I was so angry, I just wanted to kill her, kill him. Burn down his barn. If I stayed there, I knew someone would end up hurt. So I ran. I ran down the road, into the woods. For hours. Until I could not run anymore. I collapsed on the ground and cried until I had no more tears left. Joran exhaled deeply and hung his head. *She destroyed our lives. Everything we had. I thought we were so happy. I was such a fool!*

Ruyah and Bryp waited quietly for Joran to continue. After a few moments Joran gathered his thoughts. *I finally dragged myself home after dark. It was cold; I was hungry and worn out. When I came inside, Charris acted relieved to see me. She said she had been worried sick, wondering what happened to me. She acted as if nothing had changed between us, tried to hold me. But I wouldn't have any of it. I pushed her away and sulked. So many thoughts rushed at me, things I had rehearsed saying to her while in the woods. But once I was there, sitting in the kitchen across from her, all I could do was fume. She pretended she didn't know what I was upset about, but I told her I had seen her. Then she acted innocent and started crying. It was a good act, but I wasn't fooled. I demanded she tell me the truth, but she said nothing. Finally, I made her pack and I took her to the station and sent her off that night on the delivery wagon.* Joran sighed, aware of his stomach tangled in a knot. *You know the rest.*

Ruyah stood and paced under the rock overhang. Bryp sat in the water bowl, occasionally dunking her wings and head. An oppressive silence beat down on Joran, stronger than the Sun's rays. The wolf came back to Joran and stood before him.

Now I understand your anger and the power it wields over you.

Joran buried his head in his hands. *How can I love her any more after what she did? How can I let go of this anger?*

You must find a way. Before it destroys you.

Joran matched eyes with the wolf. *It* will *destroy me. If the desert doesn't take me first.*

Joran felt the wolf's nose on his cheek and opened his eyes. Ruyah was hovering over him. *Joran, are you asleep yet?*

Almost. Not now.

Joran sat up to get his bearings. They had walked many more days in harsh sun. There were no longer any bushes, any rocks providing shelter, and even Bryp, in her short excursions, could find nothing that promised an end to this desert—or a source of water. Joran languished from hunger and thirst, and he knew his companions fared as badly. Too late to turn back, too weak to continue on, Joran had collapsed at the bottom of a windswept dune and made a makeshift tent out of shirts. He was beyond caring about anything. Rather than tormenting him, his nightmares gave him relief with their deceptive images of water, wind, and cool nights. Joran longed for one last dream to sweep him out to sea and into oblivion.

Joran, you must try again to get into your dreams.

I have tried for months. What will that accomplish?

We will die here. You, me, Bryp. We need water. You must try to save us.

I want to. But how?

Bryp lay on Joran's pack, listless. Ruyah panted in the heat. *I am going with you. Into your dream.*

You can do this?

When I concentrate, I can eavesdrop on your dreams when you sleep, as if I am in the next room. Tell me, have you ever had a strong dream like these? A dream so real that when you awoke you were changed?

Joran searched his memory. The heat beat down on him through his tent cover, dulling his thinking. *I remember . . . one time. Maylon's daughter, Bela, was small, just a crawler. She got very ill, high fever. I was at the house with Maylon and Malka. I rocked her in my arms late at night, cooling her with a cloth, giving Malka a break. Somehow I fell asleep in the chair. I had a vivid dream I've never forgotten.*

Tell me about it.

I was in a strange room; there were no walls or windows. Bela sat on the floor, burning in flames. I was horrified, unable to move. All I could do was watch as the flames licked at her clothes and hair and started to devour her. She was unconscious, I think. She didn't scream.

Joran wiped his forehead. All this talk about fire made him even hotter. His tongue, dry and chalky, stuck to the roof of his mouth. *But I started to cry. And as I cried my tears began to fill the room—cold, quenching tears that rose in a flood. The tears gradually put out the fire, but then Bela became engulfed in their flood. She started to flounder and drown. I stopped grieving at that moment and the flood stopped. I felt this overwhelming surge of love, and reached out to her—and my arms finally moved. I rushed to her and held her. At that instant, I awoke suddenly. I was in the rocker, with Bela in my arms, and she was completely soaked—every inch of her. And her fever was gone. From that moment on, she was fine.* Joran paused for a moment. *At the time I thought she was wet from her fever sweats, but now that I think of it, she really was dripping wet.*

Joran looked curiously at the wolf. *Are you thinking that I saved her? That somehow I had gone into my dreams and found a way to ease her fever? That's impossible!*

Ruyah shook his head in disagreement. *Don't underestimate the power of dreams, Joran. The substance of the universe is the stuff of dreams. Everything begins as a dream in the great mind of the One who dreams and sustains all creation with His dreaming. We are manifestations of those dreams, and we also have been given the power of dreaming.*

Ruyah paused, his eyes heavy from the heat. *But few have power* in *their dreams, to mold and direct them with their intent. You have been given this gift. You gave Bela back her life with your intent, and now you must enter* these *dreams with intent. You nearly drowned her with your grief, but once you found your love, you directed its current. Do you understand?*

Joran was awed. It made sense, in some obtuse way. *What now?*

You have been trying to barge your way in. This time, try climbing in through the back window, where you won't be noticed. I will show you the way. Your emotions are running amok! Your anger is unmoored. All emotions are like wild wolf pups—bent on doing mischief. They need discipline and harnessing to respond to your intent. You must fasten your anger to something so it can't run loose. Anger is like fire, like the burning sun. Until you can quench the anger, you will never be able to quench your thirst.

The goose woman's words intruded into his mind. *Anger burns cold, but it will leave only ashes.* She was right.

Joran looked into the wolf's yellow eyes. He saw so much more there than just animal. Somehow he saw something of himself in their depths, and a deep sadness and longing welled up in him, choking his throat.

I am ready.

I will be behind you. You can do this, Joran. You must.

Joran rode the crest of the wave toward shore. Upon rolling onto the beach, he stood and looked around. Night surrounded him, and the Moon rose ominously over the ocean. The black bird dove at him, and Joran ducked quickly to avoid its outstretched talons. Looking up, he saw the sand castle and felt anger well up in him, sharp and fierce. As he reached for the trailing vines, he heard someone behind him. He froze in fear. Who was there?

He turned and saw no one. Each time he turned, he found himself facing the cliff. He heard his name and spun around. The waves called to him. Curious, he moved closer to listen. In the curl of the wave he could make out a shape. The shadow of the wolf shimmered, caught under the water.

Joran waded out to him, water crashing around his legs. He heard his name again, and followed that shadow, wading out deeper and deeper into the water.

Suddenly, the water was gone, as were the cliffs and beach. Joran now stood on the sand, and saw nothing but sand in every direction. Night dissolved into day and day to heat. He no longer saw the wolf shadow or anything for miles around.

On the horizon, something small caught his eye. As he walked toward it, the heat grew proportionately. A fireball spattered, with flames darting skyward in all directions. The air burned with flame and spark and explosion. The heat nearly suffocated him, and now the flames surrounded and engulfed him. Anger surged in him like lightning, filling every pore and fiber of his body. He felt as if he were pure liquid anger.

It raged inside and outside of him, and the angrier he felt, the higher roared the flames. He rolled with the anger across the landscape, and everything in his path combusted instantaneously. He did not feel pain but a power, a strength that raced through him. He knew the anger intimately; yet, he also knew if he let it rage, he would soon be incinerated.

Ruyah's words came into his mind. *Use your intent. Fasten it to something.*

Joran concentrated. He imagined the anger as a giant ball and focused his mind on containing it. It snarled and snapped at him like a cornered beast. In an instant, Joran separated himself from the fiery beast and grabbed it with his hands. The beast struggled, sending sparks and currents of lightning into the air, but Joran held on. "I will tame you!" he cried.

For hours he wrestled with it, his arms and face burning, his strength dissipating. But Joran was determined to subdue it. Gradually, the giant fireball lost heat and radiance. It shrank in size and might to where Joran could manage it, and with all his remaining strength, he confined it to a small space in a corner of his dream.

Joran collapsed in exhaustion on the sand across from it, watching it hiss and spark sporadically like a defeated animal. Once he had subdued it, Joran was able to walk beyond it and found, to his relief, a bubbling spring coming up from the ground, filling a pool at his feet. He looked back; the anger was not completely gone, but contained. Joran watched it burn quietly. He felt a raw emptiness in his gut. Then, as he leaned over to drink, he awoke.

When he opened his eyes, Ruyah was lapping heartily from a clear pool of water, surrounded by tall trunks of trees topped with swaying feathery branches. Bryp dove and flitted about, submerging herself in the water and bursting out exuberantly. She flew over to Joran and ruffled her wet feathers, sprinkling him lightly.

Water! Bath! Joran look!

Ruyah turned to Joran and gave him a toothy wolf smile.

Well, don't just sit there. Come on in. He pulled on Joran's shirt with his teeth and brought him to the water's edge.

Is it real or am I still dreaming? Bryp started whistling a tune that Joran recognized. Something about rowing a boat down a stream.

Instead of answering him, the wolf pushed Joran from behind, knocking him into the water. Joran splashed back and tackled the wolf, and they rolled and tumbled in the coolness and wet of the pool. Joran laughed as he dunked Ruyah under the water, and Bryp darted around them, diving and splashing with her tiny wings.

Joran took big gulps of delicious water, and a flood of relief filled his heart. He had carried so much anger for so long that without it he felt light and free, a feeling even more refreshing than the cool water on his skin. Ruyah licked his face eagerly as Joran laughed again.

See what happens when you put your emotions in their place?

Ruyah—you were there. I saw you. I think.

The wolf rested in the shallows with a contented sigh. *You did well. In time you will find your own way in and around. Now that you know you can.*

Joran fell back on the damp shore; a soft breeze brushed his face. Ruyah joined him, paws flailing the air, and wiggled and scratched his back. Joran stroked the wolf's head as the intractable sense of longing returned with a force. *Am I awake, Ruyah? Or, when I die, will I truly awaken from sleep?*

Still on his back, Ruyah closed his eyes and was soon snoring peacefully, Bryp asleep atop his chest. Joran raised his eyes to look out over the water, and across—on the other side—something shimmered under the hot sun.

Something large and beautiful that, when the heat waves settled, became a dazzling gold palace rising up from the desert sand.

E LEVEN

J ORAN AND Ruyah approached the towering door with
awe. Made of tempered gold like the rest of the enormous
palace, the door stretched high above their heads. The brilliance of the Sun reflected off the palace, nearly blinding them. Joran
had never seen anything so bright in his life. His bare feet tingled as
he walked a winding pathway of gold pavers that led to the door.
Two sparkling fountains spewing golden water in golden bowls
flanked the entryway. Joran heard strains of music coming from one
of the upper windows, three stories above them. Before he could
lift his hand to the sunburst knocker, the door opened, slowly, cautiously. Joran and Ruyah exchanged glances and stepped back.

A head peeked through the opening. A small woman, pale and
blonde, her hair swept up on her head and pinned on top with two
thin sticks, peered over the top of her spectacles and strained her
neck toward them.

"Oh, Joran, Sir Wolf, and Miss Bird, you've made it. Welcome." She pulled back on the door and ushered them into a massive entry hall. Her arms overflowed with heavy bound books, and
after her guests entered she kicked the front door closed with her
foot.

Bryp, perched on Joran's shoulder, chirped excitedly. Similar
to the Moon's house, a flood of light spilled across the floor from
a round window, but this light was stark white and much more

brilliant than the faint moonglow. Joran looked at the pale woman, who was a bit shorter than he, and found it hard to determine her age. She seemed almost childlike, but her eyes carried a wisdom seen in one who has lived a long life. She wore odd white trousers, like a man's, that flared out at the cuffs, then gathered at her ankles with gold bands. Sandals, bejeweled with small colored stones like the ones on her spectacles, adorned her small feet. She wore a gold blouse, buttoned to the neck, pressed and starched. Her spectacles, with their thick lenses, made the woman's eyes loom large like a bug's. She readjusted the load of books and offered Joran a clean, manicured hand with nails painted in gold polish.

"I am Sola, the Sun's mother. Please, come in and let me feed you. You must be famished, poor dears."

As they traversed the cool, cavernous hall into the dining room, Joran couldn't help but notice the difference in housekeeping from the Moon's dwelling. Row upon row of huge tomes flanked the walls from floor to ceiling, everything neatly stacked according to color and size. Spotless floors sparkled, and the air smelled like a fresh spring day. What little furniture there was looked new, without a speck of dust. And everything in the palace was made of gold.

The curtains that hung from the dining room windows were woven gold thread; the long wooden table was lacquered with gold lamé, richly illustrated with desert scenery, dunes, and tall fronded trees. The fat stuffed chair cushions were also gold fabric, and as Joran sat in one, he sank into a soothing softness. Sunlight filtered in throughout the entire palace, giving it a cheerful tone, yet the rooms were pleasingly cool. Joran's feet were cracked and sore from the short trek from the pool to the palace; he was grateful to give them a rest. He had tried to pull on his boots, but they completely fell apart.

Joran surveyed the remarkable palace in awe. Just a day before he had resigned himself to dying in the desert, lost, starved, and dehydrated. Now he was lounging in the most beautiful place in the world, and set before him on the massive table were platters of sliced fruit, flat breads, spreads of unusual colors, and pitchers filled with punch and stuffed with chipped blocks of ice. Ethereal music wafted around him, sounds from instruments he had never heard before. The rich sadness of the timbre made his heart ache, and a wave of longing and melancholy settled over him. He removed his pack and placed it on the floor. Sola handed him a warm, wet cloth with which to clean his hands.

"Schumann's *Faust*. Isn't it absolutely glorious? The Germanic composers of the nineteenth century were geniuses. But, please, my guests, help yourselves."

Sola deposited her books on the sideboard and brought another platter laden with sliced smoked meats and cheeses to the table. She set a small bowl of sesame and sunflower seeds on the table for Bryp and handed a large golden bowl to Joran.

"Here, fill this up for your wolf." She turned to Ruyah. "We have plenty more in the kitchen, so don't be shy." Ruyah gave her what Joran thought was an appreciative smile.

Joran filled Ruyah's bowl with meat, and another with water, and set them on the floor by the table. He noticed Ruyah ate politely, trying not to make a mess on the floor, although bits and pieces made their way over the edges. Bryp perched on the bowl's edge and pecked happily at the seeds. Quite a few of her seeds, as well, ended up on the floor, although she did her best to find them.

When Sola returned again from the kitchen, this time with a tray of exquisite chocolate and cream pastries, Joran spoke.

"Thank you so much for your hospitality. But, how is it you know my name?"

Sola sat across from Joran and put a pastry on a plate. She took a bite and rolled her eyes. "Delicious! Joran, I have been following your journey here. The Moon told me you were coming. She said she had a lovely visit with you."

Joran was puzzled. "I never met the Moon, just her sister, Cielle."

Sola laughed and waved her pastry in the air. "The Moon has no sister. She lives alone in that awful house." Sola took a dainty bite and dabbed a napkin at the side of her mouth. "She is a bit confused." She leaned over and whispered, "Every family has a skeleton in the closet, don't they?"

Joran's jaw dropped, to Sola's amusement. "A skeleton?"

Sola laughed again and reached over and touched his forehead. "I see she has left her mark on you."

Joran scowled with worry. "What does that mean?"

Sola smiled warmly. "Do not worry, Joran. She may claim you, but she cannot hold you. You are much too clever for that."

Sola seemed to enjoy watching them eat, and as Joran finished one plate, she pressed him to eat more. He finally had to turn her down. Ruyah also ate his fill and, contented, lay down on the cool floor tiles and rested. Bryp worked her way quickly to the bottom of her bowl, then hopped to Ruyah's water bowl for a long drink.

"You have had a long, difficult journey getting here. Not many can find the palace of the Sun; not many dare. You are a determined young man, Joran." She looked over at Ruyah. "And you are blessed with some very special friends."

"Yes. They have both saved my life on many occasions." Joran sat in silence; Sola studied him. "I imagine you know why we have come."

"Why, yes. To see the Sun. Unfortunately, he is out." She gestured to the sky. "As you have seen."

"Does he ever come home? I mean, this is his palace, right?"

Sola chuckled, amused. "He comes home every night—if he didn't it would always be daytime, wouldn't it? But he is formidable. I do not think you will want to speak with him."

Joran sighed. "But, please, I must. There are so many things I need to understand. The Moon said he sees everything. That he would know where my wife is and how I might free her."

Sola grew contemplative. She got up and took Joran's hand. "Come, let us sit somewhere more comfortable and we will talk." She led Joran into a room of overstuffed couches topped with plump pillows and slipped off her shoes. As they sank into the cushions, Ruyah padded in after them and lay down at Joran's feet. A waterfall slid down one wall into a small rock-lined pool filled with golden fish. The room had no roof; instead, a lattice of beams crossed overhead, draped with chains of lavender flowers that drenched the air with a sweet perfume. Bryp flew over to the pool and gazed at the glittering fish, mesmerized. This room, like the others, had shelves of books covering every inch of wall space.

Joran stared at the books. "What are all these books about?"

"Why, Joran, they contain the entire knowledge of the world— the world of men and animals, the world of Sun, Moon, and stars. I have a lot of time on my hands and I love to read. You can never have too much knowledge." She removed her spectacles and rubbed her eyes. "Although, I think I need a new pair of these. My eyes seem to be getting worse these days."

"Do these books tell how to solve riddles?"

Sola thought for a moment. "Some do. But why don't you tell me your riddles and I will see if I know some answers. And if not, I am sure we can find a book or two somewhere in this house that will help you." Sola pulled one of the sticks from her hair and began chewing the end thoughtfully as Joran spoke.

Joran related the account of how he had lost Charris. He told her about his nightmares and the warnings of the goose woman, and of their journey to the Moon and finally to the Sun's palace. She gasped when Joran recounted the incident with the three men, and how Bryp and his friends had saved him and Ruyah.

"My, Joran, you have been through so much." Sola walked over to the sideboard and poured two tall glasses of an amber liquid. She handed one to Joran, who took a sip of the most exquisite nectar he had ever tasted. Liquid sunshine coated his throat.

Sola nodded in approval and took a long pull from her glass. "This is from a vintage year—apricot and palm date wine—from sun-ripened fruit. I grow the trees in my conservatory out back." Sola gestured with her hand. "But, Joran, please, continue."

"The goose woman says I have trapped Charris—my wife—in my dreams. My wolf friend has shown me how to enter my dreams and tame my anger. So, since I have trapped her with my anger, isn't there a way I can get into my dream and free her there?"

Sola put her hand on Joran's arm. "Joran, dear, you are going too fast. You cannot enter that dream until you deal with the three keys."

"Yes! She said I have to lose three keys to open the lock. But, if I lose them, how can I use them to open a lock? What does that mean?"

Sola laughed, and her face lit up. "*Loose* three keys, not *lose*. You did not hear her correctly. You have three keys to set loose, and you have loosed one already. Otherwise you would never have made your way here, to this palace." Sola smiled at Joran's confusion.

"Let me tell you about my son, the Sun," she said, pausing dramatically and removing her spectacles. "Each day the Sun rises to look out over mankind. He takes what is called a 'random walk.' But each day he sees all the evil the men do and he grows angry and hot. Their cruelty and insensitivity makes him seethe. By the middle of the day, he is burning up with fury. Each day he burns up a little more of himself, yet the fuel for his anger is never used up. Anger is a self-perpetuating thing, you see, and the evil is the fuel. As long as he rises to look over mankind, as long as men do evil, he will keep burning. It all has to do with hypostatic equilibrium."

Joran frowned. "Hypostatic what?"

"Hypostatic equilibrium. The balance between gravity and fusion. You don't need to be a rocket scientist to understand this."

"What is a rocket scientist?" Joran asked, growing more befuddled.

Sola waved away his question. "Let's just say the Sun exists in a state of delicate balance. The photons contained inside the Sun's photosphere explode—that is his anger unchecked. But gravity—his self-control—holds the photons in, keeps them from tearing out into space. Too much anger and he would explode; too much gravity and he would implode. A delicate balance."

Joran was reminded about what Ruyah said about man's perfect balance of happiness. It seemed everything in the world balanced precariously—even the Sun.

"The ironic thing is," she continued, "the Sun will not speak to the sons of men because of his anger, yet his anger is what keeps them alive, for if he ever stopped burning, that would be the end of man. So another balance is required. Men must keep doing evil to keep the Sun burning. You could conclude, then, that maybe wickedness has a place in this world, and in another sense, is its very foundation." Sola looked at Joran with compassion.

"Which brings us to you, Joran. There is a place for righteous anger, just as the Sun's anger serves all living things. But, you have discovered that your anger, unchecked, is destructive. Your anger, when out of balance, was destroying your world. Too much fusion and not enough gravity, you could say. But now! You have learned how to release this anger from your heart, to loosen its grasp. You have loosed the first key, Joran, and it has opened the door to my son's palace."

Joran leaned back into the bulky cushion. The soothing splash of the waterfall set his heart to rest. He was relieved that Sola understood the mystery of the keys.

"But what are the other two keys?" he asked. "I have traveled to the end of the world, to the house of the Moon, who did not help me at all. And now I have worn out a second pair of shoes journeying east to the other end of the world, to this palace. Where else is there to go? How much farther until I find Charris? Until I can go home?"

Sola smiled kindly. She reached under her couch and brought out a soft glistening blanket of gold. Covering Joran with the blanket, which felt lighter than air, she said, "Now, just get some sleep. There is an old saying: 'There are two ways of getting home—and one of them is to stay there.' It is no good complaining now that you chose the alternative. Of course you know this other saying, for it has been told to you before: 'The longest way 'round is the shortest way home.' The journey will take as long as it takes."

Joran heard the goose woman recite those words in his head. He tried to sit up but Sola gently pressed him back down. "But time is running out," he insisted. "I am afraid I am already too late to save Charris."

Sola patted Joran on the head, then traced the moon on his forehead with her finger. "Time is an affair of the will. And so is love. Both can be stretched to the limits—and beyond."

Sola tucked the blanket under Joran's neck and a luxurious warmth spread over him. "Do not be troubled. Get some sleep, and when you wake we shall speak again." Sola reached up and pulled a book from the shelf above Joran's head and tucked her legs underneath her. She opened the massive book and began to read, repositioning her spectacles on her nose and chewing absentmindedly on her wooden stick.

Joran watched her turn pages, one after another, until his eyes grew heavy and closed. Music tickled his ears and his limbs lost feeling. With a full stomach, a head spinning with words, and a heavy heart, he slipped quietly, quickly into sleep.

TWELVE

DAYS FLOWED into one another in the palace of the Sun. Every time Joran mentioned the need to leave, Sola would open another book and read to him. She enticed him with stories of distant lands, the behaviors of strange animals that lived in worlds of ice and fire, tales of bizarre anomalies in the sky she referred to as quasars and binary stars. Subjects she called physics, chemistry, geology filled his mind, opening his eyes to the depth and breadth of a world he never imagined could exist.

Much of what she told him went over his head; much he found hard to believe. How could there be animals that breathed underwater, larger than the palace itself! How could there really be holes in space where all time stopped on something called an event horizon? In his village, you learned your letters, how to manage numbers—and practical experience and apprenticeship taught you everything else. Few in Tebron knew about the wide reaches of the world, and there were no huge books as these with beautiful illustrations depicting the fabulous and terrifying things that covered the earth, air, and seas.

One book particularly interested Joran. Sola had found it for him on her biology shelf—a book with drawings of the sea and the many creatures that lived in it. Joran recognized the sea lions from his dreams, and he read about riptides and currents, undertows and tide pools. Now he knew for certain the place he dreamed was real.

Sola unfurled huge parchment maps of the ocean's shelf—with indecipherable lines showing the depths and trenches, and the outline of coasts far away. But she had no map that showed the path to travel from the palace of the Sun to the sea of his dreams.

"I am afraid there are no maps that lead to or away from here. Arriving at the palace of the Sun is an affair of the will and the heart. It cannot be found by studying maps," Sola stressed.

"Well, then, how am I to make my way to the sea? Where is it from here?"

Sola rolled up the parchments and laid them on the golden table. She reached for one of the jam cookies on the plate in front of her and nibbled thoughtfully. "Joran, I really have no idea. I have never been to the sea. Or anywhere outside my own gardens. This home is all I know. But there must be a way."

Something Sola called a symphony drifted on the air from an upstairs room. Each day she played him different musical pieces, some dramatic, many sad. In Tebron, he had never heard more than three or four minstrels play together at the tavern. This sounded like a hundred strange instruments worked up into an emotional frenzy. Joran found it distracting and irritating.

Sola noticed his mood. "Stravinsky's *Firebird*. Maybe too contemporary for your tastes. I'll put on something less assaulting." As Sola climbed the staircase to rooms he had never seen, he wondered how she could "put on" music. Was it like putting on clothes?

Joran became despondent. Ruyah had been quiet for most of their visit, enjoying the cool floor for his afternoon naps. When Joran asked him about leaving, he just shrugged complacently. Bryp spent her days hypnotized by the golden fish in the pool and rarely left the water's edge except to eat seeds from her golden bowl. Joran sensed something was wrong, that his friends were under some enchantment, for Ruyah had never behaved like this. Surely Ruyah knew how important it was that they leave and find

Charris. And with each passing day, Joran found it harder and harder to muster up the urge to continue his journey. He was lapsing into lethargy.

How easy to fall into a daily routine of bathing in a warm golden tub with water that smelled of lavender and roses, eating delectable foods that were different each day, and thumbing through fascinating books! Sola had given him a new set of clothes—a shirt and pants made of soft, breathable fabric that hung comfortable and cool against his skin. He never saw another person in the palace, although he imagined someone must be preparing and cooking all the food they ate, for Joran never saw Sola leave his side. She was always curled up on a couch or sitting at her desk, her hair pinned to her head, poring over her books and chewing her stick. Her clothes never changed, and she never seemed soiled or wrinkled. No one cleaned or dusted, but the palace was immaculate day after day. He came to the conclusion that Sola somehow kept them from leaving, that she was lonely and wanted company.

And another odd thing—Joran never did see the Sun return each night as Sola said he did. For it was never night, and yet at the end of each day Joran fell fast asleep on the couch—under that marvelous airy blanket—and would awake each morning to find Sola studying nearby, and sunlight streaming onto the floor. He still had his nightmares each night, and although they were filled with fear and panic, his anger was absent. Many times he tried to climb into his dream and free Charris, but without Ruyah's help he could not find his way in again.

Finally, Joran had had enough. He knew if he stayed much longer he might never leave. He hoped he would be able to navigate the treacherous desert once more and find a way back to the prairies before running out of food and water. The thought of venturing out into that wasteland filled him with apprehension and fear.

Miles of desert stood between him and Charris. Yet, he reminded himself, he had made it here; he should be able to make it back. But—then where? Wherever it was, he would not save Charris by lingering in the palace any longer.

Thinking of his wife made him petulant and heartsick. For the hundredth time he berated himself for his failure as a husband. He must have done something to push her away, to make her look for love and comfort elsewhere. He thought he had been attentive to her, but maybe it hadn't been enough. He'd tried to give her space to work, to express her creativity, something he knew she needed. What had gone wrong?

Joran got up from the table where he had been reviewing the maps with Sola. He picked up his pack and began to rearrange its contents. Sola returned to the room, and a loud male voice sang out in a strange language.

"Boito's *Giunto Sul Passo Estremo*. You should appreciate his Faust—turning his last dream before dying into a beautiful aria. Much better."

Joran pulled out his water skin from his pack and handed it to her. "Could I please fill this before I leave?"

Sola put her hand on Joran's shoulder. She took a long look at him. "So. Have you tired of me so quickly?" She smiled, but disappointment clouded her face.

"Sola, you have been wonderful, and you have taught me so much. I have learned more from you than all I have learned in my lifetime. But you know I have a task before me. You yourself said I still have two more keys to loose, and I need to find them. Your generosity will never be forgotten."

Sola took his pack and water skin. "Yes, you are right. You should leave. Let me replenish your provisions and give you some ointment for your face and lips. The Sun will not spare you this time, either." Joran watched Sola go through the doors leading to the kitchen. He woke the wolf and bird, who were asleep by the waterfall.

What is it?

Ruyah, time to rise. We are leaving.

Ruyah stood and stretched, and Bryp fluttered her wings and settled on Ruyah's shoulder. *Time. Where?*

We have lingered too long. I need to go rescue Charris. Do you want to come, or stay here? You would have a nice life here in the palace of the Sun.

Ruyah shook the sleep from his head. *No, we are coming. You are right; we have dallied too long. My head is thick.*

Sola returned with his pack brimming with food. She handed Joran the water skin. "Do not worry about finding water—this will not run out." She handed him a strange pair of sandals. "Try these on. You will never make it barefoot across the desert."

Joran held the sandals up to the light. They were made out of the oddest leather. Sturdy, but stretchy, and black and smooth to the touch. They smelled of heat and desert and dust. Joran strapped them on and found them quite comfortable. When he walked, the thick spongy soles squeaked against the floor. "Thank you, Sola. You have been so kind."

"Aren't they a kick? They are made from the compressed fossils of ancient beasts long extinct. Oh, I have one other thing for you." She walked over to the waterfall pool and reached her hand in, picking up something from the bottom. She brought it over to Joran. In her palm lay a dull round stone, the size of a coin and milky in color. Ruyah came over and looked at it curiously. "I know you said the Moon didn't help you, but she gave you an invaluable gift, one you need to guard and cherish."

"The moonshell?"

Sola nodded. "This is the sunstone. I have given one to each guest who has found the palace. But, it is probably a wasted gesture." She looked intently at the stone and it began to glow faintly. "This stone contains all the Sun's light with none of his anger."

Joran wondered how a small, dull stone could be as she described. "What do you do with it?"

"For most, it is just a souvenir. Something to remember me by." She leaned closer to Joran, the stone between them. "But, know this—the sunstone is the most powerful thing in the universe. Can you imagine what you could do with all the light contained in the Sun?"

Joran noticed that she gave Ruyah a curious, penetrating look. "However, this stone can only be wielded by a pure heart void of all anger. A heart with no darkness. No human has ever been able to unlock its power, and, believe me, many have tried. Now, you must leave quickly, for if my son finds out I have given you the sunstone, he will be enraged. He doesn't want his power to fall into the hands of men."

"Why, then, do you keep giving away these sunstones?"

Sola sighed. "It is said that someday, one with a pure heart will unlock the power of the sunstone. In that day, darkness will flee." Sola rummaged through her mind. "Somewhere, in an ancient book, it is written: 'There is one who is light, and in him there is no darkness. The light shines in the darkness, but the darkness does not overpower it. The true light is to come into the world, and the light will bring a healing to the world of men.'" She paused and chewed hard on her stick. "I wish I could recall which book that was! Anyway, it is my hope, and my deepest wish to see those words fulfilled. For then my son could come home for all time—and stop being so angry." Her expression revealed how much she missed him, and how lonely she truly was.

She placed the dull white stone in Joran's hand. "Maybe you are the one, Joran."

Joran shook his head. "My heart is full of much darkness, Sola. I am just an ordinary man."

It is said among wolves, "All men are ordinary men; the extraordinary men are those who know it."

Joran ruffled the wolf's head. *I am glad to hear you spout aphorisms again, Ruyah, however useless.*

Ruyah snorted.

Joran turned to Sola and shook her hand. "Nevertheless, I am grateful for your gift and will treasure it."

Joran walked to the large golden door, Ruyah and Bryp following behind him. Sola stopped him before his hand turned the latch.

"You must find the cave of the South Wind, Joran."

Joran made a sour face. "The South Wind? I don't even want to know how far that is."

"Not far. For distance is also an affair of the will. This much I can tell you from the books I have read: Upon crossing the oasis where you first saw the palace, journey south. The South Wind is the wisest of all nature's powers, and she circles the earth not just east to west, like my son, but north and south as well. She has traveled everywhere, and remember—she is there, in your dreams, blowing you across the water and pressing you toward Charris. She is able to stir up the sea and is the only one who can fight the forces of the Moon. I have read she is kind . . . but brutally honest." Sola took Joran's chin gently in her hand and turned his face to meet hers.

"She will not coax and coddle you with soft words, Joran, for she embodies raw truth. The South Wind penetrates between soul and spirit, between thoughts and intentions of the heart. She searches into all things and wanders where she wishes, but you do not know where she comes from and where she is going. If you do not want to face the truth of your heart, then do not go there. But,

Joran, I suspect she is the only one who can truly help you." Sola paused. "For it is time you learned the truth."

Joran's heart pounded fast. "What truth? What are you saying?"

Sola lowered her head and pulled open the heavy gold door, welcoming a wave of scorching heat into the entry. Before them were the endless dunes, heat shimmering up from the sand. Through the distortion of the heat waves Joran could make out the small oasis with its stately fronded trees. The air smelled acrid and dusty. Sola pulled Joran's hat from his pack and adjusted it on his head, then patted him affectionately.

"Don't forget to use that ointment; you'll see it does wonders. Put it on Ruyah's muzzle as well. I made it from the cocoa plants in my conservatory."

Joran put the sunstone in his pocket. Now he had a shell and a stone. A shell that seemed practical for digging sand, and a stone that had a power he could never unlock. What good were they? He had worn out two pairs of shoes and was on his third pair. He had loosed one of the keys, but there were still two to go. And now, he faced the imposing task of trekking back across the burning desert in search of the cave of the South Wind.

Sola's words made him anxious and afraid. What truth? he wondered. And did he really want to find out?

As the golden door closed gently behind him, he stood hesitantly in the scorching heat, listening to the soft bubble of the fountains beside him. Ruyah and Bryp watched him in silence and waited. Finally, stepping onto the sand in his squeaky new sandals, Joran walked toward the oasis, the strain of soft music wafting out of the third story window behind him.

• PART THREE •
THE REVEALING
WIND

THIRTEEN

THE DESERT stretched on for many days with its grueling heat and blinding sunlight, but gradually the terrain changed. At first the Sun refused to take his eye off them, but then he dipped lower and lower below the horizon, allowing evening to rush in and drape the sky. Maybe it was his imagination, but Joran sensed the Sun's reluctance to let them go, and he wondered if it had something to do with the sunstone in his pack.

The more they headed south, the more daylight and heat gave way to a familiar diurnal rhythm, with cool nights emerging after the Sun set across the expanse of wasteland. In the late hours, stars formed strange constellations above. Sleep came more easily for Joran in the dark shroud of night, and from time to time Ruyah found a way to climb into Joran's nightmares, but he could not find the key to unlocking Charris's prison. Sola had said he must first loose two more keys, but what could they be? The Moon reappeared, both inside and outside his dreams, setting Joran on edge, but Ruyah told him to ignore her.

Joran couldn't recall when the slight breeze first appeared, but it pressed them southward, never leaving, never abating. Sand gave way to dirt; vegetation thickened and grew lush. Water, in creeks and rivulets, pooled around their feet as they walked, and the air grew balmy. Warm mud squished between Joran's toes.

Although it was not as hot as the desert, Joran awoke drenched in sweat and stayed that way until he fell hard asleep at night. Lush trees with thick hanging vines replaced the scraggly desert shrubs, and the cries and screeches of strange animals and birds filled the canopy above them. He strained to make out the creatures flitting overhead, but saw only shadows darting among the branches and heard something that sounded like raucous laughter. Silvery snakes as thick as his thigh slithered up tree trunks, making Joran nervous. He imagined they could swallow a rumphog whole if they had a chance!

Bryp was intrigued by a land spilling over with birds. She spent her days warbling, flying from tree to tree, and engaging the other birds in chatter. Their long colorful plumes awed Joran, feathers of every brilliant color, and their strong hooked beaks, shiny black or red. Some birds had crests on their heads or fans that opened and closed at will. They perched themselves like jeweled adornments on all the branches around him. Sometimes the woods were so noisy from birdsong that Joran could hardly think.

Bryp rarely visited Joran; she was busy socializing. But from time to time she landed on Ruyah's head to give a breathless report of all her adventures. Joran was fatigued and miserable, but at least Bryp seemed happy, and that cheered him considerably.

His sandals sank in mud, and he had to pick off crawly things that stuck to his ankles. Soon the vegetation was so prolific and confining that Joran had to use his knife to hack through the branches and vines to seek a path. The air always smelled fetid and dank, like moldy clothes. Ruyah found strange things to hunt, but Joran wanted no part of his meals. After weeks, he still hadn't eaten through half of the delicacies in his pack, and the trees around them hung heavy with ripe, sweet fruit that Joran found delicious and filling. He would leave the meat to Ruyah.

In the warm evenings they had no need of making a fire, although Joran wanted one to keep wild animals at bay. Ruyah assured him there was no beast in the jungle stupid enough to take on a wolf of his stature. All the same, the creepy howls he heard after dark made him nervous, especially when Ruyah snored deeply at his side. Joran slept fitfully, waking at every shriek and caw, aware of dozens of glowing eyes floating in the darkness just beyond his purview.

Ruyah pushed his way through a maze of plants with broad leaves the width of a wagon wheel. Joran followed behind, grumbling quietly. The wolf stopped and turned to Joran.

Do you want to rest again, young human?

I am not tired, just sick of this jungle. It has been days since we've found a clearing large enough to spread out a bedroll. Joran drank from his water skin. It amazed him that what Sola had predicted was true—he never seemed to get to the bottom of the skin, no matter how much he drank. And despite the heat around them, the water was always refreshingly cool.

Joran found a vine-entangled log and straddled it. Ruyah came to his side and sat on his haunches. He scratched absently at his ear with his hind leg.

There is so much life in this place. It is overflowing with animals and birds.

And bugs! Joran slapped his bare thigh, then his arm. *It's too bad that ointment doesn't repel these pests.* Joran slapped again. Within moments of his sitting, swarms of insects hounded his face and legs. *I'm going to be eaten alive before I make it to the cave of the South Wind.*

Too bad you never befriended any mosquitoes. That would have come in handy.

Lucky you have fur.

You wouldn't think so in this heat. Even soaking in the creek doesn't cool me off. I wish I could take off my coat as easily as you remove your clothes.

Joran poured some of the cool water from his skin into the palm of his hand. *Here, drink some of this. I'm sure it is more refreshing than that warm creek water.*

Ruyah came over and lapped the water. He sighed. *You have been sullen lately—and quiet.*

I'm sorry I don't have your sense of adventure, Ruyah. It's just that I am so fed up with wandering the world. I feel so lost. I've been away from Tebron for so long I think I have forgotten everyone I've ever known. Even Charris. Here I am searching to find her and I barely remember her. She's become a faint memory from another lifetime. I just don't see why I should keep going. I am not getting anywhere.

Ruyah sat back down and rested his head on Joran's leg. Joran continued. *I keep thinking about what you said—how the center of man's existence is a dream. I am hounded by dreams at night, and I am living a dream by day. You told me men are under some curse, wandering about, forgetting who they are. Well, that certainly sums me up, doesn't it?*

Joran fell quiet for a long time. *I don't want to wait for some magical day when the curse will be lifted and I will remember my name. I need help now. And nothing seems to help. Every night I still have that nightmare. Even when you are there, in my dream, I am powerless to free Charris. She remains trapped in the ice, crying out to me to save her. How can I save her when I can't find her? When I can't even find the cave of the South Wind? We have been slogging through this jungle forever, and I wouldn't doubt that we have been going in circles. Ruyah, I can't go on any longer.*

Joran hoped Ruyah would have something encouraging to say, but the wolf just sighed and sunk his head into his plush neck. The constant breeze ruffled his fur, and Joran smoothed it out.

Sola said the cave wasn't far. What did she mean that distance is an affair of the will?

Perhaps it means you need to focus hard on your destination and then you will arrive.

I've tried that. I concentrate hard, imagine the cave, see it before me. But I also feel hampered by a sense of dread.

What is worrying you, Joran?

It's what Sola said—about finding out the truth. She said it was time I learned the truth. Just the way she said it scared me.

She did? I didn't hear that.

Well, that's what she said. That the South Wind would pierce my heart and reveal things. I am not sure I want to hear what she has to say.

What are you afraid of, Joran? Do you have something to hide, something you are ashamed of?

Joran squeezed his eyes shut. *I can name many things I am ashamed of, and don't want to look at. Maybe you animals never feel shame, but it is something humans know too well. We don't like to have those things pointed out, either.*

I think you are too hard on yourself, Joran. But, nevertheless, can you rally enough courage to face her? Maybe unless you are ready to find her, she cannot find you. Perhaps if you steel your will to discover whatever it is you need to learn, we will arrive.

Joran swatted at more bugs. *Do you remember my dream last night? I kept trying to climb the vines to get up the cliff to the castle. But something weighed me down. I felt in my pants pockets and they were bulging with rocks. They were so heavy I couldn't lift my feet from the sand. So I reached in and started tossing them onto the beach, and the faster I dumped them out, the faster my pockets filled up again. Then, the current grabbed hold of my legs and pulled me into the sea. Wave after wave crashed over me and I fell down, unable to drag myself from the water. The rocks anchored me to the sand. If you hadn't dragged me out by your teeth I would have drowned.*

It was only a dream, Joran.

No less real than being lost in this jungle. More real, even.

Joran fell silent as the wind blew around him. The bugs eased off a little.

She is here, I think, Ruyah said, looking up into the canopy of rustling branches.

The wind is always here. But it seems to be growing stronger. Joran studied the hot, panting wolf, who had sticks and leaves protruding from his silver coat.

You need a good brushing, Ruyah. Joran took a comb from his pack and started in on Ruyah's head, picking through the fur and pulling out debris. *I will try to do what you said—steel my will to confront the South Wind. I know in my heart I have been dreading our encounter. That's probably why we have been wandering lost. I have been avoiding our destination. Walking around it, so to speak.*

If truth will help you find Charris, then what do you have to lose?

I'm not sure. And that's what I am afraid of. Once he had Ruyah's fur cleaned, he combed it until it shone. *Now you look presentable. Let's go.*

Ruyah smiled. As soon as he and Joran got on their feet, the wind kicked up, blowing strongly to their right. *Follow the wind, Joran. She seems to be showing us the way to go.*

The wind pressed them southward late into the evening, keeping the insects at bay. Joran was grateful for the reprieve; red welts covered nearly every inch of exposed skin. Ruyah was right; as soon as Joran made a decision to face the truth, whatever it would reveal, the wind urged him along, nearly pushing him from behind. The sweltering heat eased as the sky turned a dusty pink beyond the branches arching overhead.

Joran hacked his way through more vines and sloshed through mud. His arms ached from days of swinging his knife and sawing through fibrous plants. Pushing aside a large clump of growth revealed a beautiful deep pool lined with moss and ferns, with a wide, soft waterfall emptying down from a rock face. Joran spotted tiny fish lounging below the surface, and Ruyah was in swimming before Joran had even taken off his shirt.

Ahh, the water is cool, Joran. Join me.

Joran stripped and dove into the emerald water. When he surfaced, Bryp splashed beside him.

Nice to see you again, my little bird friend.

Been busy. New friends. Like cool water.

Bryp dove under the water and popped back out by Ruyah, who paddled slowly in circles around the pool's perimeter.

Learning to swim. Part duck. Bryp stopped and tried to float, but immediately began to sink. *Oops!*

Bryp, you don't have the right kind of feathers for that. Joran reached over to the edge of the pool and grabbed his grimy clothes. He dunked them in the water and scrubbed them diligently.

Keep trying. Maybe learn. Bryp flew to the wolf's head and perched herself there, preening her emerald feathers.

Bird calls echoed around them, and from time to time Bryp answered them in her singsong voice. *So much to learn. Many beautiful birds here.*

Yes, they are breathtaking, Bryp.

Stay here maybe. Much food. No rain. Watch out for red and yellow snakes. And sticky frogs.

Joran smiled. *If you are happy here, then you should stay. Unless you have family worrying about you back in Tebron.*

No family. Left the nest. All gone.

Joran sighed. At least Bryp had found a place to call home. He watched her flutter off overhead to join a circling flock of squabbling red-winged birds.

Ruyah spoke. *I thought of another old adage: "Wolves have dens and the birds of the air have nests, but man has nowhere to lay his head."*

You are reading my thoughts, Ruyah. You always seem to know exactly how I feel. How is that?

Ruyah paddled over to Joran and swam circles around him. *Humans are much like glass. Naked and exposed.*

Joran looked down at his bare body as he swam. *Yes, that's what I am, all right. I've never been good at masking my feelings. My brothers often played tricks on me because I was so gullible. I never could figure out when they were serious, or just joking with me.*

Ruyah continued circling. *I have observed many humans over many seasons. You are unusually sensitive—empathetic and gentle. Unlike many, your heart is soft and pliable. It may mean you are more easily hurt, but you also more easily love. Among wolves, that is a worthy trade-off.*

Joran grunted. *My mother used to tell me that when I was small. That I was too sensitive. But she meant it as a criticism. I was to toughen up, be strong and hard like the trees in Tebron's forest. That way I would not bend with every wind, but stand firm.*

Joran swam to the edge of the pool and pulled himself up. The persistent wind sent shivers down his spine, so he rubbed himself off with one of the shirts Sola had given him and dressed quickly. He squeezed water from his laundry and laid those clothes out to dry.

Ruyah climbed out of the pool and shook from head to tail. *It is getting hard to stand firm in this wind as well. At least my fur will quick-dry.*

It'll be dark soon. Maybe this clearing would be a good place to sleep. Fresh water and no more biting bugs.

Ruyah agreed. By the time they settled in for the night, a chorus of frogs entertained them. The wind moaned relentlessly and

Joran had to batten down his pack and clothes so they wouldn't tumble into the pool. After eating his fill of fruit and something dried and chewy that reminded him of perfume, he wrapped his blanket around him and dozed off to the wild music of the jungle.

After so many encounters, the instant Joran felt the tingle on the back of his neck he was seized with a fear that clenched his heart in a vise. The black horror that snuck up behind him was all too familiar. Joran lay prostrate on the crumbling ledge above the sea, shivering erratically. What began as a howling wind gathered violently into the dark mass of undulating blackness, hurting his ears with an acute chatter, a clamor that ripped the night into shreds. The stars had long since dispersed; now even the Moon was blotted out, but Joran could still hear her laughter underlying the invasion.

He strained his neck toward the sand castle but Charris's face was lost in obscurity. He knew she was there, safe behind sea glass, and he ached to go to her. But he also knew in his heart she didn't want him. He felt that pain as a knife through his gut. As he lay on the sand, grit filling his eyes and the black cloud swallowing him, he felt Ruyah's bulk pressing against him. The wolf's whine turned to a howl that joined the wind's mournful voice.

Joran covered his ears. Frost sprang from the ground and began crawling over his fingers. The ledge gave way. Joran wrapped his arms tightly around Ruyah's thick neck. Terror sank claws into Joran, pinning him to the falling chunk of sandstone cliff. As he fell to the sea, he screamed—a scream quickly sucked up into the void of black. He could see nothing, feel nothing but the frantic wind whipping around him. When he awoke, the jungle vanished.

Joran found himself enwrapped in darkness. A damp, warm breeze tousled his hair. Gradually, his eyes adjusted and he could make out jagged walls and a ceiling above him. The pool was gone along with his pack and bedroll. He startled when he felt a touch on his hand, but it was Ruyah's wet nose. The wolf stood beside him, looking around. His yellow eyes shone dully.

What do you see, Ruyah?

We are in a cave. There appears to be a tunnel over there.

Joran rubbed his eyes. *What was that thing—the black cloud in my dream? You were there with me. It terrifies me.*

I do not know if this is the time or place to discuss it.

It is always there, somewhere in the background. But lately, it has grown more and more forceful. Joran shook his head, chasing away the memories. *What should we do, Ruyah? Wait here or follow that passageway?* Joran noticed a faint glow of light off to his left.

This must be the cave of the South Wind. Since the wind is blowing toward that opening, we may as well see where it leads. There do not seem to be any other tunnels.

Joran trailed Ruyah as he cautiously padded ahead. They followed the tunnel for a long time as it wended through rock, finally emerging into a cavernous chamber filled with dangling vines and birds in multitude. Torches of fire stationed around the huge cavern revealed a tropical paradise, with small waterfalls filling pools chock full of red and orange fish—fat, lazy fish that surfaced and pecked at the water. Huge ferns and bushes bursting with blossoms bordered a grassy knoll, where tall, lithe birds with trailing feathers waltzed in graceful stride. The sounds of the water and bird chatter wove together into a stirring song, music so rich and invigorating that Joran felt as refreshed as he had been at the palace of the Sun.

Joran stood at the entrance of the cavern, astonished. Fragrant, sweet flowers overpowered Joran's senses. How everything grew and thrived in a dark cave mystified him. Ruyah sniffed, eyeing the surroundings with curiosity. He sat and waited, remaining alert. The wind circled playfully around Joran's feet, then settled down.

Fancy that, Joran!

Someone emerged from behind a small waterfall, passing through the water like a wisp of cloud and then reappearing at the top of the grassy knoll. A tall, graceful woman beckoned him over, and as Joran approached he was awed by her beauty. Her skin was so rich and dark, he felt he could melt into it. Her shiny black hair fell in a braid down her back. She wore a skirt of resplendent colors, with bird designs woven into the fabric in red, green, yellow, and black. Her blouse shimmered in silver. Silver loops hung from her ears and circled her wrists and ankles. Every finger and toe bore a silver ring.

As she walked to meet him, Joran noticed her bare feet did not touch the ground, but rather she floated effortlessly and with graceful elegance. Birds of all colors and sizes were drawn to her, pulled into her orbit. They lit on her shoulders and rested attentively.

The South Wind's presence took Joran's breath away. Both he and Ruyah stared unabashedly. From moment to moment she seemed to waver transparent; Joran could see through her to the waterfall behind. He rubbed his eyes and looked again. The outline of her body blurred and softened. Perhaps she was a ghost, but how could a ghost be so beautiful?

The South Wind took Joran's hands in hers; her skin was soft and tender, and her hands felt light as air. A breeze encircled him, wrapping him up. Ruyah surprised Joran by his deep bow, lowering his eyes and waiting for acknowledgment. Her gaze lit on the wolf; she then turned to scrutinize him. Joran quickly lowered his eyes as well. After a moment, she released him and spoke.

"Welcome, Joran, welcome . . . Ruyah." She turned to the wolf. "Shall I use that name to address you, or another?" Joran watched his companion nod respectfully. "Well, then." Her voice was deep and melodious, but at the same time like a whisper.

Joran squirmed; the Wind's stare unsettled him. A gentle finger probed his mind and heart. Even though he had so many questions to ask, he could not gather his words. Each time he thought to speak, the words in his mind seemed silly, vacuous, unimportant.

The woman spoke evenly. "You have nothing to fear from me, Joran. Men are often afraid of what they do not understand, but know this—man can understand everything by the help of what he does not understand."

She looked up and held out her hand. "Come here, Bryp." Joran hadn't seen Bryp join them in the cavern, but the little bird flew over from a nearby waterfall. The frych lit on the South Wind's arm and cocked her head curiously. The birds on the South Wind's shoulders shifted and resettled.

"You are welcome to stay here, in my land. Your big heart and inquisitive mind please me."

Bryp hopped up and down. *Hear that? Stay here!*

The woman turned to Joran, and as she moved, wisps of her body floated away, then rejoined to make her whole again. "You may call me Noomahh. My other names are too difficult to pronounce."

Joran's voice came out on shaky breath. "Thank you, Noomahh. Sola, the Sun's mother, sent us. She said you might be able to help me find my wife and free her."

"Yes." She walked slowly around Joran; a breeze followed where she stepped. "Your heart is burdened, Joran. Weighed down. You have buried your heart in a deep hole and cannot dig your way out."

She stopped in front of him. "Tell me, Joran, what do you seek?" Joran looked into eyes that reached deep within him and touched some hidden, uncomfortable place. "Happiness? Comfort? Peace?"

As Joran sifted these words in his heart, he realized he did not know the answer. Months ago he might have said happiness. Or that he just wanted to find his wife and go home. A week ago he would have chosen comfort, relief. Now it was not that simple. There was something buried deep, just as Noomahh noted, that burned a hole in his spirit, made him long for something he could not put a name to. Now that his anger held him no longer, he did feel naked and exposed. A strange empty feeling sat like a lump in his stomach.

Ruyah looked up at him, concerned. *Joran. Tell her what you seek.*

Joran met Noomahh's eyes and lost himself in their ebony depths. "I suppose I really do want peace. Peace in my heart. I don't care whether I am happy or not."

The South Wind nodded her head. "That is a wise choice, Joran. In man's life, as in everything else, happiness is the one thing you cannot get by looking for it. If you look for truth, you may find happiness in the end. But if you look for comfort, you will not get either comfort or truth—only wishful thinking and, in the end, despair."

The South Wind slowly circled him. Joran felt uneasy and restless. Her words went down his throat like a potent draught. The cavern grew ominously quiet. All the birds stopped singing, and even the waterfall sounded muted. All Joran could hear was the soft brush of wind and the loud thump of his heart.

"Do you understand, Joran? Men close their minds to the truth in their search for happiness, and because of that, happiness eludes them. Are you willing to accept the truth in your quest for peace?"

Joran nodded and a thick lump formed in his throat. "But . . . I am afraid."

Noomahh took Joran's hands and kissed them. Her lips were butterflies on his skin. "Few men will admit their fear. Few men are so honest. But, know this—to find true peace you will have to enter despair."

The South Wind turned to Ruyah and stroked his head. "Your loyalty and patience have served him well. You have a tricky path ahead of you, Ruyah. You risk much to gain all." She looked into the wolf's eyes for a long time. "I will help however I can." Joran listened, puzzled. If Ruyah answered her, he could not tell.

Ruyah bowed to her, lowering his head to his leg. Joran had never seen the wolf behave so oddly. What could she be talking about?

"Joran," Noomahh said, turning back to meet his eyes. "Someone once said, 'Do you know the terror of he who falls asleep? To the very toes he is terrified, because the ground gives way under him and the dream begins.'"

Before he had a chance to reply, the cave disappeared in a whoosh.

FOURTEEN

FOR A MOMENT Joran felt dizzy and disoriented. He reached out his arms to feel his way in the darkness, taking careful steps. The warm dampness of the cave condensed and a vapor spread around him, shrouding him in mist.

Joran was stunned. Materializing before him were the trees of Tebron, tall and stately with their fibrous bark and flanked by giant ferns. The ground beneath his feet became the spongy mat of conifer leaves. Daylight filtered in through the branches, revealing a fall day, crisp and refreshing. Looking down, Joran saw he was dressed in different clothes: his work shirt and pants, and his sturdy lined boots. He smelled the fragrant burning of alder wood wafting through the forest, and the familiarity of it set his heart aching. A steady wind blew him toward a trail, urging him along. He looked around but Ruyah was nowhere in sight.

As Joran walked along the forest trail, mushrooms sprang up at his feet; a creek appeared on his right, shallow and clear. He raised his eyes and stopped. Not many yards away was the goose woman's shack, perched up on the old stump and buried in fog. Geese milled around, pecking the ground and honking. Joran touched his face, his clothes. This was not a dream. Somehow, the South Wind had transported him home. Or had she?

Joran hid behind a tree and watched as the door to the shack opened and the woman stepped out, carrying a birch basket full of eggs. Dressed in her long smock with the scarf around her head, she carefully found her footing and navigated the stairs to the bottom, using her burl staff to support her weight. Joran could tell the basket was heavy, as she worked hard to hold it up. He saw her reach in and rearrange her eggs. She was probably heading to market.

Why was he here, watching this? He then heard a strange sound come from the basket. Joran wasn't sure, but it sounded like a baby crying. To his left, branches rubbed and cracked. He spun around and peered into the thicket, catching dark movement and hearing footfalls fade. Something or someone was there, watching him.

Before he had a chance to get a better look, he heard a huge crash far away in the woods. He recognized the boom and shudder of a tree falling, and it spurred him running toward the sound. An unnamed fear gripped him. He ran wildly through the forest, sideswiping huckleberry and salal, dislodging their clusters of berries until he arrived at the fallen tree. He couldn't have been more bewildered at the sight he stumbled upon.

His two brothers, Felas and Callen, were at either end of the fallen giant. But they were much younger, not men yet. Their faces were smooth and their black hair long and unruly. Heavy gloves protected their hands and conifer needles stuck to their woolen shirts. They were terribly distressed; Felas yelled something to Callen, but Joran could not make out the words. Felas had thrown off his coat, and his long saw lay on the ground beside him. Joran noticed Callen was crying.

"Callen, lift! You must try harder!" Callen strained at the end of the tree but could not budge it. "We need to get some leverage."

Felas leaped to his feet, grabbed his axe, and began hacking away at a thick branch. Joran walked closer, making his way around the downed tree. Callen sobbed in great heaves as he leaned down to the ground. Joran edged his way in, to see what Callen was doing. Felas, finally freeing the large branch, jimmied it under one end of the tree. He rolled a massive cut round of wood over to the branch. He worked furiously, trying to get the branch levered on top of the round. Joran heard a moan that rattled his heart.

He came to Callen's side, and although he knew what he was about to see, he was still shocked. Oreb, his father, lay pinned on his back, the fallen tree across his body at the waist. Joran was filled with a morbid fascination; it had been so long since he'd seen his father. Looking once more on his face was both joyful and agonizing—to drink in his dark eyes, the shape of his chin and nose, his thick, black beard that wrapped around his neck. Pain seared his father's eyes, and Oreb panted in short, shallow breaths.

Joran had always wondered what had happened the day his father died, but his brothers had come home distraught and never spoke of it; they were broken and heartsick. His mother had fallen to the kitchen floor and screamed. Joran remembered hiding in his room, under his bedcovers, while Maylon tried to comfort him.

Life after that day had turned somber and joyless for many months. Joran had sought out distraction and purpose by beginning an apprenticeship with Elder Tabor at the blacksmith stall. That day changed all their lives, began the unraveling of their family.

As Joran stared at his father, he was overcome with sadness. He missed him terribly. Even though Oreb had been a stern, distant man, he had raised Joran with love and acceptance. He wished he had been closer to him; he was never the type of father who would take you in his lap and tell you bedtime stories. But he worked hard for his children, and he made sure his sons knew how to behave and treat others with respect.

Joran watched as Callen floundered helplessly, unable to do anything to save his father. Felas kept at his task with frantic attention but was unsuccessful. He stopped when he heard Oreb calling him in a strained voice.

"Felas . . . Callen . . ."

Felas came hurrying over and knelt at his father's side. He and Callen waited, watching Oreb as his mouth formed words. "Tell Mother . . . love her. Maylon too."

Oreb took short gasps, unable to gather enough air. His face grimaced in pain. Callen squeezed his hand, tears running down his cheeks.

"Joran." Oreb forced out the words; Joran leaned in closer, startled at hearing his name mentioned.

"Yes, Father," Felas urged. "What about Joran?"

Oreb turned his head, his eyes glassy, and searched for Felas's face. "Must not." Callen kept sobbing and stroking his father's hand. "Must not tell him. Promise . . . keep secret . . ."

Joran stumbled backward. Felas and Callen exchanged glances, but Joran could not tell what passed between them. Felas turned to his father. "We promise, Father."

"Tell Joran . . . love him too . . . proud of you both . . ." Oreb's eyes glazed over. Felas leaned his head on his father's chest. Callen's look turned to horror as he realized their father was dead. Felas put his arm around Callen and together they sat weeping for a long time.

Joran, overcome with emotion, ran into the woods. His father's words echoed through his head, and his mind reeled in confusion. What did they promise? What were they hiding from him? The South Wind may be showing him the truth, but what truth? He gained no peace from witnessing this scene, only more questions, more confusion.

Why did he have to see his father die? It only reopened long-buried wounds and made him miss his father and brothers terribly. A wave of homesickness battered him. He ran until he thought his heart would burst. Finally, he came upon a small creek and stopped. He heard someone singing and playing music on a stringed instrument.

Catching his breath, he stood immobile, mesmerized by the sweet, sad voice. Wind kicked up again and spurred him on. He waded across the creek to a pasture, in search of the voice, and stopped beside a rundown barn, the planks weathered and broken. Next to the barn was a waterwheel, turning slowly in the creek.

Joran froze. He knew exactly where he was, and it was the last place in the world he wanted to be.

He found a stump in an overgrown field of grass and sat down wearily upon it. As much as he wanted to flee, he knew he had been brought there for a reason. A painful, sick curiosity gripped him. A woman sat on the steps of the cottage, dressed in formal clothes, like someone at court. She held a lute on her lap and strummed the strings slowly. A velvet cap covered her head and her blond hair peeked out from underneath. Her voice rang clear and sweet, and she looked up at the sky as if recalling words to a song she had forgotten long ago.

As she sang, Joran felt a melancholy ache within him. The day shone bright and around him the world glistened in its beauty. Even though his father lay dead in the forest, a sublime peacefulness permeated the air. He could see, overlapping her image, the village of Tebron with its cobbled streets and vendors in the marketplace. There was the bakery; the scent of fresh bread filled his nostrils. And down the street Elder Tabor wrestled with a broken buckboard. Joran smiled as he thought affectionately of the jovial man. He saw his mother's home at the end of the lane, and there she was—at the window, staring out at the fruit trees. And farther down the road was the mill.

His breath caught in his throat as he saw Charris get up from her loom, stretch, and gather her things. He watched, spellbound, as his beautiful wife, her long hair flowing behind her, left the mill and walked through the village.

His eyes returned to the woman singing on the cottage steps. Her voice sang out sadly; Joran was sure she looked directly at him.

Oh, come thee back,
My own true love.
The rocks may melt,
The seas will burn
If I should not return.

Joran's eye was caught by movement over at the barn. There was the man! A strong wind kicked up and pushed Joran over to the remains of a broken pull cart nearly consumed by wild cucumber vines. He ducked out of sight and watched as the man, tall and strong, reached out his hand. A woman appeared from the breezeway; her back was toward Joran, but Joran knew who it was. Oh, he knew.

Charris! The man enfolded her with his arms and kissed her passionately. The burgundy and blue shawl with entwining wisteria vines draped over her shoulders, and her long, black hair blew in the wind behind her. Joran watched as she fell longingly into the man's arms and returned the kiss. Familiar anger and hurt rose in Joran's heart and he longed to run. But he remained glued to his spot, behind the cart.

As he watched them, the wind blew harder, pushing Joran forward, closer. He fell to his knees, hating what he saw, yet unable to avert his eyes. Now he was only a dozen yards away, watching the man and Charris grow more heated in their passion, driving Joran insane with jealousy. The strains of the song wove with the wind and played around Joran's ears, mocking him.

The man laughed aloud, playfully reaching for the buttons on Charris's blouse. Joran squirmed with agitation. He would stop this. That is what he should have done the first time he saw them! Joran stood, wind swirling about him, and began striding over to the barn. Maybe this was what the South Wind meant about his confronting the truth. He had been a coward, and now he would remedy that.

Suddenly, a violent gust whistled around the barn, stirred up water in the creek, and spun the waterwheel with fury. Wind whipped leaves and dirt on the breezeway floor, and then, with a subtle finger, lifted the shawl off Charris's back and sent it floating directly toward Joran.

With a boisterous laugh, the woman spun around to catch her shawl, which danced and played on the wind. The man grabbed at her playfully and she slapped his hand away in fun. As the shawl settled to the ground in the abating wind, Joran stared in horror. The woman who faced him only a few feet away was not Charris!

Joran's jaw dropped. He froze in place as he watched the woman reach down and pick up the shawl, shake out the leaves, and run back to the man, laughing. This did not make sense. Everything about the woman—her hair, her stature, her shawl— was Charris's. But it wasn't she!

Joran fell to the ground as if stabbed with a thousand knives. Nothing in his life prepared him for the pain and despair that coursed through his body. He grabbed his gut and moaned. Back in the breezeway, the man and woman continued their amorous play, and in the distance, at the cottage, the minstrel strummed her lute. The words of her mournful song floated over to him, coating him with numbness.

> *Oh, don't you see*
> *That lonesome dove*
> *Sitting in an ivy tree?*
> *She's weeping for her own true love*
> *As I shall weep for mine.*

Superimposed over the minstrel's playing, Charris's form appeared. As she walked up the cobbled lane from the mill, Joran noticed she was not wearing the wisteria shawl. She carried a package in her arms, tied with twine. A shock of understanding hit him as she turned into the walkway of his mother's home and knocked on the door. As Malka opened it and embraced Charris, ushering her in, the image faded, leaving only the face of the bard as she played her last few lingering notes on the strings.

The singer slowly dropped her strumming hand into her lap and sat quietly, staring at Joran. She put her instrument away in its cloth case, stood, and walked purposefully toward the cart road that led to town. Joran watched her absently, his heart despondent, as she disappeared down the road.

Once more the wind rose and spun, circling Joran and weaving him in a cocoon of misery. The world around him melted; the forest dissolved. The barn and the waterwheel blurred in a swirl of color. A warm, musty current of air released him in a slump in the middle of the dark cavern.

As Joran lay there, alone and in the dark, there was nothing he wanted more than to curl up and die. He had learned the truth, oh, yes. And Noomahh was right.

He had entered despair, and it was insufferable.

FIFTEEN

JORAN LOST track of time; all he knew was that every moment, every breath he took, condemned him. Over and over the images replayed in his mind—the woman reaching for her shawl—Charris's shawl!—and then seeing a stranger's face before him. How had he been so mistaken? And look what his mistaken anger had done to his wife, his marriage. If Ruyah was right, if he himself had trapped Charris through his dreams, then her suffering was due to his error—and stupidity!

A dim light filled the empty cavern, revealing hard gray rock walls and a dirt floor. Joran felt a breeze, gentle and inquiring, spin around him. He lifted his head. Ruyah sat near him, and the South Wind gathered herself by his side. Strands of wind solidified, formed colors and fabric. Noomahh's dark skin radiated warmth, and her ebony eyes spilled compassion.

He could tell with one look that Ruyah knew. Maybe he had known the truth all along. How many months had Joran spent in hurt and fury, thinking about Charris's unfaithfulness, feeding a festering bitterness that had nearly consumed him? And all unfounded. Charris's face, trapped in ice, crying and frightened, tore at Joran's heart. It was *his* fault she was trapped, *his* fault their marriage was in ruins. All this time he had blamed her, distrusted her, and now—everything pointed to *his* failure. Failure to trust his wife. Failure to give her respect.

He cringed as he recalled the evening he sent her away. There she was, pleading with him, crying, confused and hurt. Did he even give her a chance to speak, to defend herself? No, not for an instant did he think to let her speak. All because of his anger and jealousy. Charris—who loved him, who loyally stood by him. And he betrayed her. How could she ever forgive him? How could he even ask her forgiveness? He wouldn't be surprised if she never wanted to see him again. She had every right to leave him, hate him for what he had done. *And I don't deserve any better.*

Joran, she will understand. You made a mistake.

An unforgivable one. I am despicable.

Ruyah came alongside Joran and nestled against him, his warm, silver coat brushing Joran's legs.

Don't try to comfort me, Ruyah. No more wolf philosophy.

"Joran." The South Wind spoke in a soothing but firm tone. "Your anger and hurt created the prison Charris is in. Only you can unlock her. You have loosed your anger, but now you are imprisoned as well by your despair. The bonds of despair are much stronger than the bonds of anger. Once despair sets its claws in you, it takes you deep and abandons you in some unknown wasteland of misery. Anger you can see and feel. You can grab it with two hands and master it, for you can either feed and fan it or quench it altogether. Despair is elusive. You will not find it in your dreams, for it always hides in the deepest recesses of the soul. It is the shadow behind all that is light and pure. You will have to work hard to find your way out of your prison, to loosen the grip of despair."

"There is no way. It cannot be done."

"Not by your own strength, no."

I will be with you, to help you.

Ruyah, why don't you go home? I want to be left alone.

Wind circled slowly, wrapping Joran in softness. "Joran, take some rest and nourishment. Let the peacefulness of this place refresh your heart."

Joran stood on shaky legs. He wiped his eyes and nose on his shirt. "I will not find peace here—or anywhere."

Joran looked at the Wind, her face, her body flickering in and out as she stared at him. "Please, just leave me alone for a while."

He walked over to the wall of the cave and slumped down, his back against rock, burying his head in his hands. The wind blew gently through his hair. Ruyah stayed where he was, plopping down on the ground and resting his head on his paws with a sigh. Clearly, the wolf had no intention of leaving.

After a while, the Wind gathered herself together and drifted down the tunnel to her waterfall. Joran dozed fitfully; he had no idea how long he sat there in the dark. The dimness of the cave never changed and the temperature remained warm and balmy. From time to time he looked up and saw Ruyah, who hadn't moved. What was he to do now? He couldn't stay, couldn't go home. How could he face Charris, if he could ever find her? Hot tears poured down his cheeks as he thought of Charris. Guilt ate at him. If only he had let her speak. If only he hadn't jumped to conclusions, been so suspicious and quick to accuse. If only . . .

You can't go back and make it come out differently, Joran. You must go forward in trust.

Trust what?

Trust in Charris. In her love. Trust that she will understand and forgive.

I don't deserve forgiveness.

Men never *deserve forgiveness. It is not something you earn. It is a free gift. Given from a gracious heart.* Ruyah walked over to Joran and sat before him. *You must allow Charris the choice herself.*

I can't.

The choice is not yours to make. Ruyah nudged Joran with his nose. *No matter what has happened, no matter what you have done, you must still free her. Only you can do that.*

Ruyah, I do not know how. I do not know where to go. I have traveled to the ends of the world and am still no nearer than when I started.

Suddenly, Joran found himself standing in the middle of the grassy knoll, in Noomahh's garden, with birds strolling around his feet and torches burning in a circle around the airy cavern. The cloying scent of blossoms once more assaulted Joran's nose, and a choir of birdsong rang in his ears, this time an irritating annoyance. The South Wind, in her elegance and grace, stood in front of Joran, her bronze skin glowing in the torchlight.

"You know where you must go, Joran. To the sea. It is calling you, as it has all along."

Joran fell to the grass and buried his head in his hands. "But I do not know where the sea is. In all my journeys it has eluded me. I have been north to the Moon, east to the Sun, and south, here, to see you, and never found the sea."

"Well, then, is it not obvious? The great ocean lies west, at land's end. Where both the Sun and the Moon are pulled over the rim of the world. There is a strong force at work there, and you will see a vastness of water beyond your imagining, water with no end and immeasurable depths."

Joran looked up at Noomahh. "Let me guess—it is very far, and a treacherous journey," he said bitterly. "I have heard all this before."

"Joran, life itself is a treacherous journey. But, as your wolf friend once told you, it is also an adventure. 'Man must have just enough faith in himself to have adventures, and just enough doubt to enjoy them.'"

Joran snorted. "What is it with all of you—rattling off platitudes as if that makes living more bearable?" He knew his voice sounded rude, but he was tired of all this meaningless talk.

Noomahh and Ruyah exchanged glances. Joran seethed at the smirk on Ruyah's face. "Go ahead, laugh at me. I know I'm a pathetic man."

Noomahh rested her hand on Joran's arm, tickling him with her breeze. "No one is laughing at you. We smile because we have faith in you. We see things you cannot see. We know things you cannot yet know. In the end, truth-seeker, you will find the peace you long for. And happiness as well."

Her words gave Joran small comfort. How could she know the anguish he felt? It was easy for her to bestow vacuous words of comfort while she lived in a paradise, unmarred by the world outside. What did she—or Ruyah, for that matter—really know about pain, human angst? Nothing. They had no idea at all. So how could they think their words of comfort actually comforted?

"Joran, will you go and rescue Charris? Will you journey to the great sea?" Noomahh wavered before Joran. A hush enveloped him.

Joran hung his head in hopelessness. His life was now more a nightmare than the horrors he faced each time he slept. It crumbled like the sand castle perched above the ravenous sea. He could hear the sound of the sand sucking away around his feet, dragging him under. That was the sound of his life—slipping from his grasp.

"Joran, if you intend to go, you must go to her now. There are more forces hindering you than just your own despair."

The South Wind withdrew from Joran and stood at the crest of the knoll. "I had hoped to send you off with a different gift," she said with mournful eyes. Joran watched, detached, as Noomahh spoke in a strange language, and gathering the air around her, began spinning it with her hands as one holds a drop spindle loaded with wool.

Ruyah stood next to Joran and stared attentively. The Wind's voice grew voluminously as the currents of air began to whip and pull around them. Joran hunkered down; his hair flew into his face. Birds scattered to the safety of crevices in the cavern's walls. The torch fires flickered violently.

Soon, the noise was deafening; Joran covered his ears as his clothes were nearly ripped from his body. Ruyah huddled against Joran and buried his nose. Through the windstorm Joran caught a glance of a gray funnel spinning erratically before Noomahh. It tore at the ground near her feet, hurling clumps of uprooted grass, and scraped the rock roof above him. Dislodged pebbles and dirt spattered him, stung his skin. He fought the urge to run.

Gradually, the maelstrom subsided, and when Joran was able to see through the dust, he saw a silver coil spinning in the air before Noomahh. With her hands she spun wind and purpose, honing and refining until what she manipulated was radiant and malleable. The South Wind herself was torn apart in wisps of cloud, and as the coil of silver tightened and coalesced, she did also.

By the time she reached out and encircled the spinning coil, bringing it to rest in her hands, she was once more the tall dark woman with ebony eyes, hair braided down her back. Fatigue etched her face; her shoulders slumped. After a few moments, she raised her head, her chin strong and her eyes focused. The cavern settled back into tranquility, and the birds returned to light on her shoulders. Water poured delicately down the rocks and bubbled in the pools. Blossoms, ripped from their branches, blanketed the grass like a rainbow coverlet. Bryp flew over to Joran and perched on his arm.

Scary. What was that?

Joran stroked the bird gently. *I have no idea.*

Big wind. Too noisy.

I am sure, Bryp, there was no harm meant.

"I apologize. This required a bit of intense concentration." The South Wind floated gracefully from the knoll over to where Joran and Ruyah stood. For a long time Noomahh and Ruyah gazed at each other in a quiet stillness. Joran looked from one to the other, wondering what was passing between them. No doubt Noomahh could mindspeak with the wolf, but why was Joran unable to hear what they said? Finally, Ruyah turned to Joran, his face deep in thought.

Ruyah?

The South Wind has a gift for you. Ruyah's mindvoice sounded tired, and his face displayed a sadness Joran could not fathom. The wolf tipped his head toward Noomahh and the circle of silver she held.

Joran looked at the South Wind as she extended her hands. The circlet was the length of a man's arm, thick as a finger, and woven of a dozen fine threads that shone brighter than any silver he had ever seen. Sparks hissed and crackled, blue as lightning. But, even as he studied it, the coil dulled and tarnished until settling to pale gray, the color of fog and steam. The South Wind offered it to Joran.

"Take it. It is safe to handle now."

Joran took the circlet, light as air, nearly transparent. But when he pulled on it, it unclasped and became a line of wire or rope. And it was surprisingly strong, for Joran tugged on it with all his might and it was unyielding.

He looked at Noomahh. "What is this for?"

"You have been given the moonshell and the sunstone. Each is a powerful gift. But the silver circlet is by far the greatest and most dangerous of all. When you get to the sea, you will have to contend with the Moon and her tides. She will not willingly give up her captive. She took advantage of your unmoored anger and trapped your wife. This you now understand. Wind will help you, guide and strengthen you. But you will need much more than wind to escape the Moon's clutches."

Joran looked at the wire, touched the ends together, and they reconnected into a circle again. Ruyah sat by his side, unusually quiet.

The South Wind blew through Joran's hair like a caress. "Whatever you bind with this cord, Joran, you will lose. Listen carefully."

Joran looked to meet her eyes. "Whatever you bind with this cord you will lose," she repeated. "But take heart—for whatever you lose you will ultimately bind to yourself, and forever it will be bound. You may only use it once, so take care to use it only when dire circumstances demand."

Noomahh studied him. "At this moment you do not understand. Do not try to. Just remember what you have been told, and at the right time you will recall all that has been said."

Noomahh turned to the wolf. "Ruyah, lead him to the sea. Do not let him drown before he gets there."

The wolf bowed deeply one last time and cast his eyes on Joran. *Are you ready, young human?*

Joran made no answer. He picked up his pack and put the silver circlet inside with the shell and the stone. He noticed his pack, once more, had been filled with fruit and nuts. His water skin bulged; Joran slung it over his shoulder with the pack. Bryp hopped onto Joran's shoulder and tipped her head.

Maybe visit you. Sometime.

Joran could not imagine ever seeing Bryp in Tebron again. Why would she ever want to leave this place? He tried to sound pleased. *I would like that.*

Maybe get bored. More adventure.

Joran sighed. More adventure was right. And it was the last thing he wanted.

Find Charris. You will. You will see.

Joran petted the crimson head. *I will miss you, Bryp.* Joran watched as the tiny frych flew to the waterfall and dipped her head in the pool.

Joran turned to Noomahh. He knew he should thank her, but for what? She had sent him down the path of truth, so shouldn't he be grateful? Without her help, he would have never known the error he had made in accusing Charris and sending her away. He supposed a gift of truth was more valuable than all the jewels in the world. But she also gave him the silver circlet, woven of wild wind, and like the shell and the stone, he had no idea what good it would do him, or how to use it. Despair filled him so deeply he felt he was drowning, unable to come up for air.

As he walked toward the tunnel he had first come through, the South Wind circled around him, blowing him gently with warm strokes.

"Joran, have hope. Grasp it with both hands. The poetess spoke, 'Hope is the thing with feathers that perches in the soul, and sings the tune without words and never stops at all.' Hope is the anchor of the soul, to keep you focused and steadfast. Find hope, hang on to it, and set your heart to it as if grasping a northern star." Noomahh's face began to fade and blur.

Joran walked as if asleep, with Ruyah at his side. A soft breeze followed them out of the tunnel and into the jungle, where sunlight greeted them, rays of bright light dissected by the mesh of branches. The calls and cries of the animals and birds rang out, filling the air with a joyful zest for life that Joran could not share in.

SIXTEEN

SIX DAYS later, leaving the jungle vines and raucous birds behind, Joran grew too weary to keep trudging one step after another. Muted fog enveloped him, coating his surroundings in a gray shroud, erasing scenery so all he could see were his feet plodding before him. For hours he mindlessly put one foot in front of the other, his black sandals embedded in mud. He could not tell if the air was warm or cool; he had stopped feeling his own body.

Was he hungry? Sleepy? It did not matter. His head thumped as if there were a hammer pounding in his skull. An unruly beard covered his chin and neck, and his clothes smelled fetid. Without sunlight, he had no idea if he was heading west or east. But he set his attention on Ruyah's tail, which floated on the fog like a disembodied swatch of fur. Ruyah had taken the lead and was confident he would lead them to the sea.

Joran wondered with little curiosity what Ruyah was doing, why he was on this journey. What business did he have that the South Wind counseled him? Why did he interest himself in Joran's dreams and his task to rescue his wife? Ruyah was a strange creature, no doubt.

Joran frowned as he thought back to the day he found the wolf in the trap—a trap that just happened to be near the path Joran followed. Somehow it didn't make sense that such a formidable and intelligent animal could have landed in the claws of that trap.

And there really was no logical reason for a trap to be set so high up in the mountains, away from paths most wildlife trod, away from human habitation. Ruyah had been with him since the first day of his journey and still hadn't gone home. And now Joran just wanted to be left alone with his misery—but the wolf would not even grant him that.

Joran slumped down on a boulder. For days they had walked though a flat, open land with little disruption of the landscape. They followed no trail; all Joran could see hour after hour were dirt, rocks, rotted leaves, and a few small bushes that hugged the ground, flowerless and prickly. If there were any trees or creeks nearby, Joran could not tell. An occasional bird call punctured the thick mist, but all else was silent.

A few minutes passed before the wolf realized Joran had stopped. He moved so quietly that Joran did not hear him until his cool nose pressed against his head.

Drink some more water, Joran. You look flushed.

My head is hot. I'm sweating buckets.

Ruyah leaned his muzzle against Joran's neck. *You are burning up with fever. You should rest now.* The wolf hovered while Joran let the pack slip to the ground. After taking a long draw from the water skin, Joran stripped off his coat and formed it into a pillow. He curled up on the dirt and moaned.

What is this place? It is so desolate.

I do not know. But I do not like the way it feels. Animals choose not to live here.

Ruyah peered into the gloom. *Perhaps we should find some shelter. You will need to sleep and shake off this fever.*

This is as good a place to die as any.

No one is going to die. You will not get better if you talk that way.

I don't want to get better.

Charris needs you. You must save her.

Joran snorted. *Why don't you save her? You know how to get into my dreams. I have already loosed my anger—and she is still trapped. So what if I make it to the sea? Nothing I can do will save her. And she will hate me, anyway.* He pulled his hat down over his face and shivered. Ruyah nosed into the pack and, with his teeth, pulled out the blanket. He covered Joran, who lay listless and silent.

Just sleep, Joran. I will keep watch, see if I can find something for your fever.

Joran wanted to cry but the tears would not come. He lay on the dirt in a nameless, forsaken land. All he had in his possession were a backpack, a cloak, and a wolf. The rest of the world was lost to him.

Charris, Charris, he cried silently. *Oh, what have I done to you?* He recalled a time when he had been happy with her—for such a short while. Was that all the joy he would ever know—those ephemeral moments of intimacy and companionship? Day, night, even his own name seemed to be swallowed up by the blanket of gray despair that smothered him. The South Wind was right when she told him this despair would be even more difficult to loose than his anger. It was an impossible task. She had told him to find hope, to hold on to it—but hope did not exist. Not in this place or any other. In his heart he knew this was the end. All would end here—he would die in gloom, and his bones would lie unburied, with no one to mourn or care.

Joran's mouth was dry, his throat parched. His head was a forge that burned behind his eyes. As the wolf's tail vanished in the gray, Joran heard the sea. He rocked and tumbled over waves and his stomach roiled. He forced himself to sit up, then retched and wiped his face. Sand was dirt, dirt became sand. Either he was slipping into his dream, or his dream was spilling into his waking life. Joran did not care which it was. Sometimes he thought he heard the Moon chuckling; other times, he saw the wolf pacing restlessly around him. He saw Charris's long hair blowing in the wind. He watched Callen and Felas sawing at both sides of a massive tree trunk. His father and mother fussed over him, tugged at his clothes, smoothed out his hair. Joran wondered why his family was there, in the wilderness with him. Or had he somehow gotten home? He was too weary to care. His hand sifted sand, and sand was all he could feel or see. Each time a wave crashed, the ground rumbled. At one point Joran was able to open his eyes with great effort, and there was Ruyah, standing beside him, plants gripped in his mouth.

Are you real? Where is Callen?

I am here, Joran. All I could find were these fever weeds. Since I cannot brew tea, I suppose you should try to chew these. Ruyah dropped the plants by Joran's face, but Joran did not respond.

Please, Joran. And you need to drink more.

Joran tried to sit up but his stomach rebelled. His head rattled with rocks. He fell back down onto his coat-pillow.

Ruyah nosed the water skin closer to Joran. *Drink. You must.*

Joran forced himself upright and fumbled for the water. More of it dribbled down his face than went into his mouth. He took one of the slender stalks and tried to chew it. It was like chewing twine, tasteless and fibrous.

We have been here for many days and you do not seem to be getting better. If these herbs do not bring down your fever, I am at a loss what to do. Ruyah sighed. *Maybe you can call Bryp to come. She could ask the South Wind for something that will heal you.*

Bryp. Can't focus. Hurts too much.

And I cannot risk going back to the cave and leaving you here unattended for many days on end. Ruyah reluctantly lay down next to Joran and watched him thoughtfully.

Joran could not keep his eyes open, or even understand anything else the wolf was trying to tell him. He spit out the wad of leaves from his mouth and hugged his arms around his knees. Suddenly, his chill deepened and sent his body into a convulsion of shakes. His teeth rattled loudly as the ground around him began to frost over. Unsure if he was dreaming or awake, he felt the cold blast against his neck and watched as the dirt turned to sand again and a coat of ice corralled him and spread outward into the gloom. Just like in his dream.

A hum began to resonate in the air, growing louder and sharpening into a shrillness that made Joran wince. He looked out of one barely opened eye and saw Ruyah leap to his feet, ears alert and head cocked. *So*, Joran thought, *the wolf hears it too.*

Instead of feeling terrified—as in his dreams when the black void engulfed him, swirling around him with a coldness that clutched and squeezed his heart—he felt relief. Why fight this thing over and over and over? Whatever it was, it had pursued him relentlessly in his nightmares, and each time Joran had fought back in terror and desperation. But there was no reason to fight now. It could have him, if that's what it wanted. Joran was too weak, too disinterested to fight. What was it, anyway? Maybe just a conjuring of his own imagination, his own deep fears.

Joran felt his limbs go numb; feeling fled from his fingers and toes. He closed his eyes in resignation.

The chill started at his extremities and inched up his ankles and wrists. Joran looked down and saw hoary frost creep up his skin. He watched in vague curiosity. The gray around him filled with black, spreading like ink on a wet page. And as he watched, detached, he heard Ruyah let out a blood-curdling scream that Joran could have sworn sounded almost human. And then—blackness.

SEVENTEEN

JORAN JOLTED awake. Strong arms grabbed him under his armpits and hoisted him. Two more lifted his legs. He had trouble focusing; pain throbbed behind his eyelids and all he could see was a dull glare of light around him. Sounds were smothered before they reached his ears. His whole body felt on fire, and fever shook him mercilessly as chill air brushed his face. The arms swung him around and Joran's stomach lurched. Whoever had picked him up now tossed him onto a cot and began carrying him, jostling him in haste. Joran moaned and gave up trying to discern his surroundings. Where was Ruyah? Who were these people and where were they taking him?

Gradually, Joran identified cries and yells encircling him, all faint and indecipherable. An hour, maybe two, passed as Joran bounced along at the whim of his carriers. From time to time Joran strained to see, but could not penetrate the thick haze. Even his clothes appeared muted, as if the color of the world had washed away. He had on his shirt and pants and sandals, yet he couldn't feel them touching his skin.

He thought he could make out shapes, even bodies, on the ground as he passed, and these his carriers stepped over and around without interest. The ones carrying him were silent until they came to a stop. Joran inched his head up with much effort and saw before him a massive stone wall—yellow hewn stones stacked far above his head. Now he heard voices, clear and close by, but they spoke in a language Joran did not understand. A heavy wooden gate to his right creaked open, and Joran made out two more figures in long hooded robes, the hoods hanging down over their faces so Joran could not see the visages beneath. They moved efficiently and quickly, ushering his carriers in, and once they were all on the other side of the gate, they secured the entrance with a huge crossbeam. Joran let his head fall to the side and noticed that the hands of the figure at his side wore long fitted gloves that disappeared under his gray robe. The one positioned at his feet was dressed the same.

They resumed their march through some sort of corridor—narrow, with high stone walls on either side. The air hung heavy but scentless. More voices barked around him, anxiety and fierceness in their tones. Finally, after winding through one corridor after another, his captors deposited him in a small, cold chamber. He wondered at the strange haze that masked all before him.

After they lowered the cot to the ground, they silently left the room, bolting the door behind them. Was he hallucinating from his fever? Could this be just another dream? Was anything real?

Through his stupor, Joran tried to piece together how he had arrived at this strange place? Turning painfully onto his side, his head screaming with pain, he squinted to see through the glare. Yet it was not so much a glare as a blurring of everything around him. Nothing was in sharp enough focus to identify; the walls, the floor, the cot were alluded to, implied, but not fully there. Even his own hands, which he held up before his face, seemed fuzzy and undefined. Then he touched his face and startled—his fingers sank into a liquid cheek! Now he knew he must be hallucinating!

Joran faded in and out of sleep; chills shook him awake. He could find no blanket, no pitcher of water as he scanned the stone chamber. Every inch of his body ached. Clearly, his captors did not have his comfort in mind. As hours dragged by and nothing changed, Joran grew fearful. His resignation to die became replaced with dread. He was alone in this bizarre place, no one by his side. He missed Ruyah so much his chest heaved with sobs that shot waves of pain through his skull. And he was so very cold.

From time to time he heard faint voices, more cries of pain, more yelling of orders. Once, a huge explosion shook the walls so hard Joran nearly fell off his cot. He surmised he had been mistakenly captured, but there had been no warning, nothing that had alerted even Ruyah's keen ears to danger. Where had all these people come from? Had he and Ruyah stumbled into the middle of a battle? Joran now remembered the chill and blackness that had engulfed him—and Ruyah's wail. *Ruyah!* He listened through the sharp buzzing in his head but heard no response.

He drifted off to sleep again only to be awakened by the snap of the bolt on the door. Joran squinted and made out a shape moving toward him, a robed figure carrying an earthenware container. He struggled to sit up. His visitor set the jar down on a nearby table and approached Joran, pulling back the hood to reveal a young, pale face. Joran guessed she was a girl, but her features were unformed, blurred. Her hair, almost absent of color, framed her face and fell back behind her shoulders.

As she looked at him, he felt probed, and it discomfited him. Even though her features held no expression and her black eyes were vacant, Joran grew distraught. Nothing about her seemed real or solid, and as much as her outer appearance looked human, his gut told him she was otherwise. He fought a frantic need to escape but knew he was too weak and ill to even stand.

The woman reached over and picked up the canister, removed the lid. She handed the jar to Joran in a slow, precise movement. *Drink,* she mindspoke to him.

Joran jumped. Her voice—or his—was deep and terrifying. A voice that did not fit the face. The effect of that intrusion in his mind made him recoil. The eyes betrayed no emotion, but the voice conjured up things fearful and dangerous to Joran. How could he keep his thoughts concealed? If she could intrude into his mind, could she overhear his musings? He had to shut her out—but how?

The robed figure stood over Joran's cot, the jar in her outstretched hand. She made no other movements nor spoke again, and if she read Joran's thoughts, she gave no indication. As thirsty as Joran was, he was afraid to drink. "Who . . . who are you? And where am I? What is this place?"

Do not fear, Joran. We are your friends. There is no need to trouble yourself with questions.

A shiver coursed through Joran's body. She knew his name! His terror grew. Her tone conveyed nothing resembling comfort and friendship. His captor's voice sounded forced with friendliness and reassurance, but behind the words were knives and poison. Why he believed that, he did not know. But he knew it in his heart as surely as he knew he was alive. It was as if he saw past the face and the robe to something more fundamental, for when he stared hard, the figure dissolved, revealing something dark and creepy and altogether horrible. Why had they captured him—what did they want? He sensed he was in great danger, but what could he do about it?

Finally, the woman retreated and returned the jar to the table. She pulled her hood back over her head, masking her face in shadow. At the door, she turned back to Joran. *Drink. Or you will surely die.*

Through the haze, Joran watched the door close quietly, then heard the bolt slam shut. He realized he had been holding his breath. Letting out a deep sigh, Joran sank back on the cot; his head seemed to melt through the fabric. He touched the cot, the table, the stone floor. Nothing felt solid. Even his nightmares were more substantial than this place.

As he picked up the jar, his fingers became lost in the ambiguity of the surface, making it difficult to grip. The more he tried to hold the jar, the more his fingers fell through. He nearly dropped the container to the ground before he was able to lighten his grasp just enough to secure it. Sweat trickled down his face and neck. The robed figure was right about one thing—if he did not drink soon, he would die. Yet he faced the jar with trepidation. If nothing was solid in this strange place, how could he drink? Were they trying to poison him? If so, why had they gone to such lengths to bring him alive to this godforsaken place?

Tears filled Joran's eyes. Loneliness smothered him. He had now lost everything—not just Charris. His pack with food and water—and the gifts from the Moon, Sola, and the South Wind—were gone. All his efforts to find his wife and save her—futile. And the most upsetting was losing Ruyah. He had to admit that after so many months of journeying with the wolf he had grown attached. Ruyah had become more of a friend to him than any human ever had and seemed to understand him more truly than any other. No one else had shown such loyalty and patience with him. He longed to bury himself in fur.

The memory of Ruyah's wail tore at his heart. What if Ruyah had been captured too? Or killed! The temptation to shrivel up and die was great, but the worry over Ruyah was greater. He would have to gather strength somehow and find a way out. How, he had no idea; the task seemed insurmountable. But he must.

He rallied what little energy and concentration he could. *Ruyah! Ruyah!* He called over and over in his mind, placing the name and face before him like a lantern hung from a hook. He pushed away the screaming pain, the chill racking his bones, the commotion outside the walls of his cell. He filled his heart to the brim with all the love and need he could imagine and lay unmoving, for hours. He received back only silence.

After some time, Joran opened his eyes. He realized he had slept—or blacked out. No nightmares had plagued him, but his mouth was painfully dry. The glare still permeated the room, neither day nor night—so unlike either sunlight or moonshine. There was no quality of light to it at all, just a superficial glow that had no source. The color of nothing, of absence rather than substance.

Joran shakily sat up and reached for the jar. He removed the lid and looked in. He dipped his finger in the liquid and brought it to his mouth; it was tasteless and clear, like water, but different. What choice did he have? He must regain his health and strength if he hoped to escape and find Ruyah—a task he couldn't even imagine undertaking.

Joran brought the jar to his lips and emptied it. The liquid soothed his dry throat and quenched his thirst. As he lay back down, a warmth spread throughout his body. The chill that had plagued him dissipated and he stopped shivering. Lethargy replaced fear; peacefulness replaced loneliness. A wonderful feeling filled his heart and relief coursed through his veins. He placed the jar back on the side table and sighed. A weight lifted off his heart and he sank into a hard sleep.

The next time the robed figure entered his room he did not even look up. Others came in and refilled his jar, and although no food was ever offered, Joran realized he had no hunger or any other bodily needs. Even his thirst had been satisfied by that one drink, but his captors held the jar toward him again, and he drank without thought. Again the clear liquid spilled down his throat and again he lay back in a stupor of complacency.

Joran lost track of time. Long stretches of solitude were interrupted by the robed figures silently entering, refilling his jar, then leaving. Over time, the glare in the room lessened and things appeared more solid. Soon, his hands stopped sinking into objects. He could focus more clearly and his fever lessened. He actually began to feel so comfortable that the thought of having to rise or leave stirred up an unpleasant anxiety that he quickly buried. Words from some distant past echoed through his head: *Every man has forgotten who he is; they have all forgotten their names. And, what is worse, they forget that they have forgotten.* The words were like moths winging around his head; they meant nothing to him.

Eventually Joran stopped thinking of Ruyah, Charris, and his life back in Tebron. He stopped thinking of anything at all. In time, even the intrusion of his captors annoyed him, for they interrupted the peaceful repose he luxuriated in. And even though he stopped sleeping, he never felt tired. He lay hour after hour bathed in quiet, the outside world gone. He had finally found peace and comfort, and it was more than enough.

EIGHTEEN

NOT A STONE'S throw from the towering fortress a figure hunched over, willing invisibility, or at least camouflage. His hands worked quickly, undressing the body on the ground, and from time to time he glanced up with darting eyes. The glare masked his surroundings; he could make out little more than the trampled grass around his feet, although the air echoed with cries and shouting that seemed dangerously close. Smoke and dust made breathing difficult.

He donned the gray robe, peeled off the long gloves of the slain, and worked them over his own fingers and wrists. The boots were unyielding, clinging to the dead man's feet, but after a few muttered words and focused concentration, the boots slipped off the cold feet and were soon on his warm ones. So clothed, he straightened and with bowed head walked purposefully to the barricaded gate, which was guarded by more than a dozen robed men.

The minds of the guards were dull and easily manipulated; they were lackeys, low on the chain of servitude. He didn't expect any real resistance until inside. Without even a word of protest, they opened the gate for the unknown figure, who, like the others, hid his face beneath his hood. Once inside, he navigated the corridors from memory. Even though it had been a very long time, he sensed more than recalled his way correctly through the labyrinth of walkways and tunnels.

Walking was an expected difficulty. His legs ached in remembrance. Balance was an issue, and his back hurt when straightened. So he made slow progress, passing those who never noticed him, hugging the confining walls, and blending into the gloom. He was no fool—there was great danger here, and this danger was not apparent. He knew exactly what would happen if he slipped but once. His attention remained heightened and clear, and he spent all his intent on manifesting a shield around his body and heart, betraying no feeling and letting none in.

He found the room he was looking for—it was little more than a cubicle, a storage room off the upper catwalk. He ducked in and found it littered with weapons and shields. Careful not to touch anything, he ducked into a crevice in the back of the room and slid to the floor. He was breathing hard, and his heart pounded. After spending a moment calming himself and rubbing the chill from his hands, he closed his eyes and conjured up a mental map of the fortress. One by one, he visited each room, each chamber, with his mind, careful to move quietly and masked in emptiness. He was a cipher, a nothing that seeped through walls and doors, with no hands or feet, only a pair of barely open eyes that lingered for just a moment, unobtrusive, and then departed, leaving no trace. He prayed he was not too late.

Joran's peaceful reverie was shaken by two figures grasping his arms from behind. He sat up abruptly but gave no resistance. They raised him from the cot in silence, prompting him to stand. Joran's head spun as he tried to find his balance on weak legs. How long had it been since he stood? In such a timeless place, he couldn't even begin to guess. With little urging, they walked Joran to the door, their arms linked in his. He now saw everything clearly; the glare had dissolved and the ground responded solidly beneath his feet.

They passed many people, but no one spoke and none of their faces could be seen under their concealing hoods. Joran looked around disinterestedly as they led him through winding corridors of stone, down a wooden ramp, and across an open dirt courtyard to another complex of long walls with rows of inset doors.

Each door had a barred window, and as Joran walked by, he saw within each room a person sitting, unmoving, on a bench against a wall. These wore no robes or hoods; like Joran, they were ordinary people, some young, some old. None met his eyes; they just stared vacantly into space.

Those leading him stopped and opened one of the doors. Without complaint, Joran went inside, and when they had locked him in, he too sat on a bench, contented and comfortable.

From his window he observed a canal on the far side of the courtyard. Water lapped against the sides of the stone causeways, making Joran feel lethargic and serene. A solemn quiet hung in the air. Apart from soft footfalls traversing the yard, Joran heard no voices, no birds, no more sounds of conflict or attack. With a casual glance, he observed his room was empty. Just a stone cubicle with a wooden bench and dirt floor.

From time to time, doors near him opened and people were led out. Through the barred window he watched blankly as the ones in robes directed their charges to long wooden boats tied to posts at the end of the canal. One by one, people were lowered into the boats where they sat on benches, their hands resting in their laps. Once the boats were filled, two robed figures stepped down and stationed themselves at each end, and with long poles they plied their way along the canal, their placid passengers in tow. Joran could not tell from his small window where the canals led, but he didn't care. Once a boat vanished from sight, after many hours another one would appear, empty except for the oarsman, who navigated the craft to the end of the canal where it would wait to be refilled.

Fatigued but determined, the one in hiding kept searching methodically through the fortress. He had looked into every room on the upper and lower levels and now his gaze spread over the courtyard. None of the figures milling about concerned him; none was human. He pressed his hands together and willed his heart on. He refused to be dismayed.

His breath caught in his throat as he spotted the boat floating down the canal loaded with captives. And although he sighed with relief when he searched the faces, his heart bled for the passengers and their fate. He did not know just where the canal led, but its destination held nothing pleasant for those bewitched captives—of that he was certain.

He honed his senses and continued. His mind traveled to the row of doors built into the courtyard wall. One by one he checked, looking in through each barred window, and then, to his surprise and great relief, he found the object of his search.

Wasting no time, the hunched figure, pressed back into the recesses of the storage room, began mustering to himself powers and authority and forces from beyond the walls and the enemy-occupied territory. Silently, his lips moved, his brow fretted, and he called to himself those whom he hoped were still alive, and others he didn't even know. The air around him shimmered and the massive stone foundations began to shake. The gloom surrounding him thickened, became oppressive. He felt a response as a tingle in the back of his mind, then another. He became keenly aware of a shift in attention and surmised he had been discovered.

Quickly, he stood and ran from his cubicle, incanting and summoning as he flew down corridors, bounding off walls as he made for the courtyard. As the thick glare separated before him like a parting of waters, he saw shapes descend upon him, grotesque and dark. He threw off the robe and gloves, freeing his scabbard and hip knife. Others emerged at his side, with swords in hand—not many from what he could tell, but any help was welcome. He raised his voice in a shout, and worlds stopped spinning. Time and seasons fled, the courtyard vanished, and there fell upon him a scourge of evil bent on annihilation.

He slashed fiercely with his sword and knife, plunging into darkness, his steel finding flesh that had no substance in any other realm. His companions rallied alongside him vigorously, but with none of the fury and anguish that fueled him on. And because his fury was spurred by love, his enemies had no chance.

Mayhem followed the sweep of his sword, and his cries alone darkened even the darkest heart attacking him. The easy confidence of his assailants waxed cold in horror at the formidable nemesis ravaging their domain, and those who were not cut asunder imploded in fear. Yet the one fighting did not indulge in the satisfaction of that small victory, for more hordes came, drawn to the unexpected intrusion of power, streaming down from the battlements to provide reinforcement for their evil kin.

What shook Joran was not the earth rumbling underfoot but his awareness rattling free. A shocking chill traveled from head to toe, as if a bucket of cold water had been dumped over his head. A loud commotion exploded outside his cell. He ran over to the door and strained to see out into the courtyard. For the life of him, he could not figure out where he was—this strange place with peculiar light. He grabbed the bars and yanked uselessly. The door handle refused to budge. What was this strange prison?

He traced back through his memory and could only recall fever and misery and pain. Despair flooded him once more, and the realization of what he had done to Charris tore at his gut. Pieces of his captivity rushed into his mind: the terrifying face under the hood, the voice that entered his mind unbidden—and Ruyah's piercing wail!

Ruyah! He knew he must find him and save him! Joran frantically clawed at the door latch again but without success. He was trapped.

Suddenly, lights exploded in the courtyard. Flashes of color burst amid screams and yells. Chaos erupted in a jumble of bodies and dust. Joran was dumbfounded by what he saw.

Like a parchment eaten by fire, the heavens opened up and strange creatures raced down toward someone standing in the center of the yard. Horrible shapes swept through the air, diving and attacking. Joran cringed in terror below the window but peeked out. Other strange bodies fought back from the ground, backlit with a blinding light. Joran could not make out anything clearly; all was a blur before him. For a moment he thought he saw a man, or men, with swords, hacking at their attackers—creatures that changed shape and form as they swarmed. And then he could not believe his eyes!

There was Ruyah—he was certain of it—leaping at his attackers and ripping them with his claws and teeth in wild abandon. The scene before him flickered from bright to dark, as when flashes of lightning streaked the sky. Explosions rocked buildings, toppled towers. Rocks crashed to the courtyard and filled the air with choking dust. One moment he could see the wolf—teeth bared and claws slashing the faces of his attackers—and then he was nowhere to be seen among the men brandishing swords, swinging with terrible purpose.

In the noise and confusion, as Joran stood gripping the bars of the window, the door came ajar and he accidentally pushed it open. Terror overtook him and he stumbled backward into the small room. Someone was coming after him and there was nowhere to hide!

Tucking into a corner, he cowered and hid his head, anticipating his certain death. He covered his ears with his hands to blot out the horrific noise as it grew louder and louder. Rocks tumbled onto his head, causing Joran to look up. The ground shook violently and a huge chunk of stone crashed to the floor only a few feet away, spraying him with grit. If he stayed much longer in his cell he would be smothered alive, yet venturing out into the courtyard would be suicide. What in heaven's name was happening?

Before Joran could decide what to do, someone ran into his cell. Through the dust he saw a hazy figure searching the room, moving in haste and waving his arms like a blind man feeling his way. Joran fell back into his corner and curled up, wishing he could melt into the stones. He steeled his nerve and clenched his teeth, awaiting the slash of a sword or knife. Something grabbed hold of his shirt and he heard a low voice, like a rumble or a growl. Strange sounds filled the room, remarkably clear, pushing all other noise into a muffled background. Whether they were words of a foreign language or animal grumblings, Joran could not tell. The rolling monotone of syllables echoed off the walls and reverberated inside Joran's skull. Yet, in some strange way, they filled him with a sense of peace, sounding strangely familiar and comforting.

Joran lapsed into lethargy, then jerked his head, alert. Whoever held him must be enchanting him, putting him under another spell to dull his mind and control him! Joran kicked and struggled under the tenacious grip, but to no avail. Whatever held him, held him fiercely, and Joran felt like prey in the mouth of a predator.

At that moment a gigantic roar whooshed around him, dissolving his stone prison into powder that a wild wind sucked away. The air crackled and hissed, turned black as night, then lit up with fire and blinding light. Joran felt the wind pull away from him, and watched as visible waves of force billowed out in all directions. Still in the tight grasp of his captor, Joran strained to see the courtyard and the canal, but they were gone, swallowed up.

Suddenly, arms were grabbing at him—other arms—and more

than Joran could count. A mob of creatures encircled him, and the arms were not human! His head spun from the flashing lights and hiss of the air. Joran could not see beyond mere inches from his face—the rest melted into murkiness. But as the one hand kept his grip on Joran, another hand wielded a sword, deftly hacking away at the clamoring and descending mob. Joran screamed as bodies fell on and around him, and what looked like blood spurted onto his face and clothes.

Joran began to black out. As his awareness faltered and his head dropped, he saw the wolf. Ruyah was beside him, and it was Ruyah who stemmed the tide of attackers with teeth and claw. His silver fur shone in the light, matted with blood and dirt. Ruyah's huge body mowed down one attacker after another, never straying far from Joran's side. Howls of passion erupted from the wolf's throat, causing many to hesitate in their attack, and some to flee.

As Joran's eyes closed and he slumped to the ground he heard a loud rip, like a huge curtain being torn in two, and the sound of a million wings beating the air in fright. Then all went silent.

NINETEEN

IS HAND twitched and touched sand. He rubbed the gritty particles between his fingers, then let them fall. His cheek lay pressed against the coolness of the sand and slowly his senses returned to him. Much of his body was numb, the rest bruised and sore.

He opened one eye and saw the starless night spread out across an endless expanse. Wheeling out above the waves, the black bird wove a pattern, strands of moonlight stuffed in its mouth, and Joran watched blankly. On the far horizon, the scalp of the Moon broke through the lid of the sea. Using the woven threads as pulleys, the bird pulled the Moon's heavy weight so she could sit on the ledge of the water. As each wave crashed, Joran felt the vibration through his cheek. But aside from the rhythmic thunder of the rollers coming ashore, the night was unusually peaceful. Never before in this nightmare had Joran known anything other than fear, anger, and trepidation. But for some reason those feelings were absent, and even the Moon's imposing orb did not frighten him.

Joran rolled over and looked up. Every muscle in his body cramped. The sand castle, crumbling with each shudder, loomed above him. Bits of sand, like stardust, floated around him. Spindrift, torn from the cresting waves, lit upon him. The frosted window looked vacantly out to sea, but from Joran's position he could not see Charris's face. The bleeding heart vines tumbled down the cliff, beckoning him to climb. With effort, he sat up. His head reeled and the sky spun. He squeezed his eyes shut and waited for the queasiness to pass. When he reopened his eyes, he found Ruyah sitting still beside him, his silver fur gleaming in the moonlight. In that shimmering light, Joran felt awe at Ruyah's magnificent profile and the nobility that radiated from him.

Always before, when Ruyah joined his dream, he was a shadow, a presence that led or followed him. But this time he was all wolf, from the shiny black nose to his plush sweep of tail. Ruyah's intent gaze studied the water, but when Joran sat up, he turned and cocked his head.

Ruyah! Joran threw his arms around the giant wolf and buried himself in the warmth of his fur. Ruyah, by his side, was a dream come true, and it helped ease his heartache. He thought his heart would burst with joy. Holding him was so tangible, he was amazed. So unlike the shadowy substance of dreams.

I see you are awake.

I thought I was asleep. This is my dream, isn't it?

Ruyah chuckled and Joran felt such joy in that small expression. How much he had missed this wolf—but just how long had he been gone? And *where* had he gone? A sharp awareness of another world intruded and Joran began to shake.

Well, fancy that. I suppose you are *still asleep.*

What am I doing here? And you . . .

Shh, young human. You have been through much. You are exhausted. That is why you are sleeping.

Joran looked deeply into Ruyah's yellow eyes. *But, where was I? What happened? I was . . . somewhere. Now I can't remember, but it was so real, even more real than this dream. And I don't understand.*

Joran sat up taller and looked around. *How are we having this conversation here, like this? How can I be in my dream where I am supposed to be climbing the cliff and trying to save Charris? This is odd . . .*

The wolf lay down beside Joran and watched attentively as the Moon lifted off the ocean's surface. The mottled circle shone brightly but displayed no malice.

Well, you could say that I have put your dream on hold for a bit. It is still here; you know it never goes away. But after your ordeal, you did not need to arrive on this shore in a sea of fear and terror. And you were not ready to awaken. So, here we are.

And you are keeping vigil over me. Joran stroked the wolf's fur and grew quiet. *You saved me, didn't you? From that strange place. There were terrible creatures, and that horrible face—and voice!* He stopped and shivered. *That place was no dream. Now I remember. It was real, yet . . .*

Yes, Joran, it is a real place, but not of this world. You fell into it because you stopped fighting, stopped caring. Ordinary humans are unaffected by the pull it exerts, but, then, you are . . . different. Your powers do not go unnoticed.

Powers? Do you mean my dreaming? I don't understand. And Ruyah, who were all those people, getting into the boats?

They only looked like people, but they were not like you.

Where were they being taken?

Ruyah sighed. *I cannot answer all your questions, Joran. But I will tell you this: had you gotten into one of those boats, any hope of rescue would have been lost.*

Joran grew quiet and listened to the waves pounding the shore below him. He leaned over and saw the beach splattered with shells and blubbery sea lions sleeping on the rocky pinnacles. A mist hugged the ground, softening the shoreline. Salt spray rose up and filled his nostrils and the coolness tingled his face.

Funny, I never noticed how beautiful this place is. I am always too distressed.

The wolf smiled. *Rest, young human; you will need your strength for what lies ahead. Sleep.*

Joran lay on his back and stared at the blackness of night. Just the word *sleep* made his eyelids heavy. Gathering strength for any task at that moment was impossible. As was motivation. *I am so tired. Everything hurts. But you are here, with me, aren't you? I mean, outside my dream.*

Yes, Joran. And I will be beside you when you awake.

Good. Joran sat up and wrapped his arms once more around the wolf. Tears welled up in his eyes. *Thank you, Ruyah. For saving me.*

The wolf leaned his head against Joran's chest and rested in the crook of his arm as Joran lay back and closed his eyes.

Sleep, young human. Sleep.

Why have we seen no towns or people in all this time, Ruyah? Joran shifted the pack on his back. He still hadn't regained all his strength, and walking for hours tired him. When he awoke from his long sleep, he learned that the wolf had carefully hidden his pack still half-full of food and, more importantly, containing his gifts and water skin. What a relief that was! Even in the middle of his hopelessness he felt some consolation in retrieving his gifts; they were reminders of Cielle, Sola, and Noomahh, and the kindnesses shown him. But, the greatest kindness shown him was Ruyah's valiant effort in rescuing him from that forsaken land.

We are not in your part of the world, Joran. There are no humans here. Your search must lead you away from the world of humans and into the realm of your dream. Each step is taking us closer to the sea, and Charris. We are not far now.

Despite Joran's prodding, the wolf would not discuss his capture and rescue. For days Joran pondered in his heart the memories of that place. Little by little the images came back to him:

the silent, robed figures; the fortress of stone; the battle raging all around him. And most of all—the bizarre sense that that world had no real substance or light.

Joran couldn't stop thinking of all the "people" captured, as he had been, and what would be their fate. The simple life he left behind in Tebron was a quiet haven away from these kinds of horrors. He and his neighbors lived from day to day, concerned with their small problems, completely unaware of such a tumultuous life. So what if most of the world lived in peaceful ignorance? If they knew, how would they cope? And how would Joran ever be able to return to a "normal" life again, knowing what he knew?

I don't understand how my dream can lead me to a real place. I must find the sea, for Charris is supposed to be there. But I can only free her in my dream. So why do I have to reach the real sea?

That is just one of life's riddles. It is said among wolves, "God's riddles are more satisfying than the solutions of man."

Joran grunted. *Cielle also said that to me. But I see no satisfaction in riddles, only frustration.*

Another wise wolf said, "Your vision will become clear only when you look into your heart. Who looks outside, dreams. Who looks inside, awakens."

I am sick of talking about dreams and riddles. I am sick of everything.

Joran set down his pack and looked around him. It seemed the farther west they traveled, the more empty the world became. The land mirrored Joran's despondency—gray and uninspiring, a hopeless stretch of scenery void of life. Barren, forlorn, gloomy—it suited Joran's mood. Ruyah had to make him drink and eat. There were no trees or bushes, not even rocks or hills. Nothing. Ruyah found no animals to hunt and not even a fly landed on his face. The air was neither warm nor cool, damp nor dry.

Ruyah shared Joran's water skin, still bulging with cool water. Without it they would die of thirst, for a spring would be unable to bubble up from such hard ground. Once more, time lost all coherence. Joran could not name the time of year or season, if seasons even changed here. Maybe Ruyah had some idea how far they had journeyed, but Joran had no clue, nor did he care. Days, weeks, months were meaningless concepts here. He could only tell the passing of time by the length of his hair and beard, for curls trailed over his shoulders, and his tangled beard worked its way down his throat.

Somehow the wolf knew the way west; some inner compass directed him. Joran was intrigued that animals always seemed to know their way home, even when the sky clouded over, even when they were a thousand leagues from familiar ground. Joran frowned. Humans could not even find their way home if it was just around the corner. And for Joran, even when he was home, he was still lost. It was just as Ruyah had said—that man somehow lost his way in the world and spent his life trying to find his way home. He was finally beginning to see that home was a state of mind and not a location.

Joran's thoughts turned to Charris and his heart sank. Each step was taking him closer to her, but with each step he wanted to flee. He couldn't help thinking he was too late—that she was gone forever. Even if he wasn't too late, he knew Charris would never forgive what he had done to her.

And all the warnings about the Moon terrified Joran. Cielle had told him he would not survive his encounter with her unless he used the moonshell. She had said, "You must put your whole heart into it." For ages Joran had been pondering what that could mean, but to no avail. And Noomahh had given him the silver circlet which would bind something to him, something he would lose. To use only once in dire emergency. All these riddles!

Everywhere he went he sought answers, but all he encountered on this insane journey were riddles upon riddles. Ruyah's words came to mind: *It is no good asking for a simple answer. After all, real things are not simple.*

Joran slumped over in the dirt. The only reason he kept on going was he had nowhere else to go. He had no choice, just as Ruyah said. Though the South Wind had assured him he would find the happiness he sought, he truly doubted he would. Why should he hope for something so elusive?

Joran drank from the water skin, then poured water into his palm for Ruyah to lap up. Even though his heart was weighed down and his mind obsessed with his musings, Joran couldn't help but notice that Ruyah had become more solemn and quiet of late. The wolf did not try to make him laugh, as if the animal's heart was growing heavy. And every so often, when Joran tried to bring up concerns, Ruyah fell silent.

Ruyah, is something bothering you? You have been acting strangely.

The wolf wandered a few steps away from Joran, facing the unknown world before him. Yet it looked to Joran as if he saw something ahead, something that beckoned to him. After a long moment, he turned and looked back.

I am sorry, young human. I do not mean to be distant. I have been preoccupied by things you do not need to concern yourself with. He sidled up to Joran and leaned his head against his shoulder.

Joran stroked Ruyah's silver fur and sighed. *This journey is taking its toll on both of us. I am sorry you have had to go through so much with me. I imagine you regret this "adventure."*

Ruyah looked up at Joran with warmth in his eyes. *No, young human, wolves have no regrets. Our paths have come together for a purpose, and in this I rejoice. We will find the sea, and your wife. And before you know it, you will be back in your cottage in Tebron living happily ever after.*

Joran laughed—the first time in ages. *Now you have regained your sense of humor! Happily ever after is only found in fairy tales, not in real life.*

The wolf lay down with a grunt beside Joran, who looked at the wolf with amusement.

What? No clever sayings to refute me? Joran made his best imitation of the wolf with his smirk of confidence and wisdom. *Well, fancy that!*

Ruyah couldn't help but smile back.

• PART FOUR •
THE UNIMAGINABLE SEA

TWENTY

SOMEONE SHOOK Joran. Yet when he opened his eyes he found himself immersed in the sea, far from land. Small waves smacked against his chest as he bobbed up and down, spinning one way and then the other. The starless canopy above him weighed oppressively on his spirit, and with each moment his despair pulled him down as if his pants cuffs were lined with iron weights. Darkness obscured his sight; he could not make out anything but murky water in all directions. His stomach churned bitterly. He was so very alone.

How many times had he been set adrift in this merciless ocean? Even as he floundered about with his arms, straining to keep his head above water, he wondered why he struggled. He was caught in a never-ending cycle of wandering and dreaming.

Bitter realization sank into his heart. No, this would never end—unless *he* ended it once and for all. He had had enough—more than enough.

As the water pushed him onward he thought about his life. What did it matter? His life and accomplishments amounted to nothing. He only caused pain and suffering to those he loved. And he was fooling himself to think he would rescue Charris and "live happily ever after," as Ruyah had promised.

Joran realized now he would have to do the unthinkable to end it, but his fear still held mastery over him. It should be easy to give up, let the water take him, cover him, swallow him in silence and consolation. Remove him from this dream, this world, as if he had never been born. Just like pulling a warm blanket over his head and falling, gratefully, into an infinite slumber. Every bit of his heart yearned for that release, tempted him with relief. Oh, how much he yearned for that peace!

As he drifted, the Moon peeked out over the edge of the sea, spraying the water with eerie illumination. Joran's skin crawled and his heartbeat quickened. The outline of the Moon on his forehead stung. The seas grew higher and wind skipped across the tops of the waves, forming whitecaps that crested and buckled over him. Water splashed into his mouth as he flailed about. The wind caught him in its grasp and forced him along, but the shore was nowhere in sight. The South Wind's words whistled past his ears: "Hope is the anchor of the soul, to keep you focused and steadfast. Find hope, hang on to it, and set your heart to it like a northern star."

As the sea wrapped around his neck he thought about those words. He swallowed briny water with each wave, and coughed and spit. He chuckled bitterly. Hope was an illusion, a fantasy. Of all the illusions and mirages he had seen on his journey, hope was the most deceiving of all. Hope only led to disappointment—for you, and all those around you. A word concocted by those who had never felt the stab of self-recrimination, those who never knew the pain of betraying the one they loved.

As he mulled these things over, his head drifted under the surface. Joran opened his eyes to a shock of cold, salty water. Although he could see nothing, the depths enticed him. There was something so very quiet and peaceful under the sea. He looked up; a film of moonlight coated the surface like skin and frosted the undulating waves. As he slowly sank down, down, the light grew fainter and he stopped thrashing. His eyes closed and his hands relaxed.

The Moon's laughter invaded his repose. Even under the water he could hear her cackle in triumph. So? She could have him, if that's what she wanted. She had Charris already, why not him as well?

In the obscurity of the sea, Charris's face began to form before him. He took one last look at her features as the depths pulled him down. Her green eyes stared at him with sadness, condemning Joran even more. He would have cried if it were possible, but even the ocean would not be able to contain all his tears. His gaze slowly took in all of her—her black flowing hair, her cheeks, her lips, her chin. He tried so hard to recall how she felt in his arms, her soft skin up against his. A painful sweetness filled his soul; Joran knew his life in this world would end with the memory of her face lingering in his heart.

And then she spoke.

Her words traveled through the thickness of water, but seemed as if whispered directly into his ear. "Joran," she said, looking directly at him. Her expression was absent the fear and confusion he always noted in his dream. "Joran, where are you? I can see you, but you are trapped somewhere." Her eyes continued to look into his, yet they saw deeper, into his heart, where he felt as if a thousand knives struck at him.

He answered, "I am here! Can't you hear me?" The sound of her voice startled him. He reached out his hand to touch her. Instantly a flood of memories assaulted him, memories of Charris beside him, living and laughing with him as they passed their days together.

"Joran, help me! Help me find you!"

Joran wondered at the pleading look he had seen so many times in his dream. The words she always mouthed, but words he never heard. Why did she think it was he who was trapped?

His head grew foggy as darkness settled around him. Charris's face faded. "Joran! Please don't leave me," she cried. Just as her image was nearly gone, he heard her last words: "Joran, I love you."

Joran gasped in suffocation. He tried to breathe and couldn't find air. Frantic, he thrashed at the sea with his arms and kicked with his feet. He felt his chest would explode. He strained to look above him and spotted moonlight growing brighter and brighter as he clawed his way to the surface.

Where had Charris gone? Now he was filled with such need, such longing to find her, he thought he would burst. As his head thrust through the waves and his lungs screamed for air, something grabbed his shirt and hauled him through the water. Sand scraped his back and legs, ripped his clothes. His body felt waterlogged, heavy and bloated like the sea lions perched on the rocks around him. The vast expanse of night spread above him, and off hovering over the horizon was the Moon, huge and full, glaring at him with all her wrath.

Ruyah released his grip from the collar of Joran's shirt, breathing heavily. Joran watched as the drenched wolf collapsed on the sand beside him. A warm wind blew over them as Joran tried to sit up. He coughed and seawater spilled from his mouth.

Ruyah, what is going on? This has never happened in my dream before.

Well, fancy that, young human. You have found the sea. Ruyah's voice was somber as he stood on wobbly legs and shook water from his coat. He lay back down as if too tired to stand.

Then this is not a dream—we are really here.

Well, yes and no.

Ruyah, I saw Charris! She spoke to me! Joran grew anxious. *I must find her right away!*

The wolf did not say anything, only gazed at the Moon. Joran reached over and put his hand on Ruyah's head.

You pulled me out of the water. Why?

You were drowning.

But in my dream the waves always dump me onto the beach.

In your dreams you never give in to despair. Ruyah turned to look at Joran. *What happened to you out there?*

Joran wiped wet hair from his face and thought. *You are right. I gave up. I just couldn't take this anymore. But then Charris called to me. I could actually hear her. And she said she was trying to find me—that I was trapped somewhere. Then she said . . .*

What?

She told me she loved me—and my heart ached.

Ruyah sat quietly for a while. He stood once more and stretched. Moonbeams lit up his fur and Joran was awed anew by his radiance.

Young human, you have finally loosed the second key. I was unsure you would find the strength to do so. The only thing that can beat despair is love. As it is said among wolves, "The way to love anything is to realize that it may be lost." Now that your despair is set loose and sinking to the bottom of the sea, you are free to love.

Joran put his hands on Ruyah's wet shoulders and searched the wolf's eyes. *Ruyah, I love her so much, and I am so afraid she will despise me for what I have done. But, once I heard her voice, heard her plead with me to find her—I couldn't give up. Charris needs me. And I don't know what I can do to rescue her or where to go, but I am not giving up.*

Joran looked around him and saw his pack on the beach, against the cliff. His eyes searched for the sand castle, but he saw only rolling dunes facing the sea.

How do I find her, Ruyah? I must!

Your love will lead you to her. It is an affair of the will.

But Ruyah, if I have just loosed the second key, there is still one more. How will I know what it is? What if I run out of time?

Have faith, young human. You will know when it confronts you.

Joran stood and waited until the spinning subsided. He then

walked to his pack, took out the water skin and drank, clearing his throat of salty brine. He found the wooden bowl and filled it for Ruyah, who came over and lapped his fill.

The wolf sighed. *Joran, it is time.*

Joran put the bowl and skin in his pack and hoisted it to his back. He took a few steps, then stopped and reached down. The sandals he wore were threadbare, and as Joran fussed with them, the straps ripped and fell off. Joran picked up the pieces and looked them over. Without a word he tossed them into the sea, where the waves gobbled them up. His bare feet sank into cool wet sand.

Now he knew he neared the end of his journey. After looking up and down the beach, he knew which way to go. His heart led him, and would lead him to Charris—of this he had no doubt.

TWENTY-ONE

They traveled along the beach for hours, and as they trudged through the sand, the Moon rose higher and higher in the night sky. From time to time the black bird flew overhead, teasing the Moon with its boisterous shrieks. Joran ignored the Moon's harsh stare, even though it beat down on him with heat like the summer sun. The wind pushed them steadily from behind, urging them along as it forced waves upon the beach in loud crashes and flings of salt spray.

Joran and the wolf circled coves filled with jagged rocks, beaches with jumbles of driftwood and seaweed. They climbed over hills when the sea swallowed up the shore, and smelled the dank caves in the cliffs in which the sea echoed and murmured to itself. Joran marched forward, steady and determined, and the wolf kept pace by his side. All the while, the Moon lit their way before them, casting their stretched shadows across the beach that seemed to go on forever.

They spoke little, although at one point, in the gleam of moonlight on the water, Joran could make out creatures rising up from the deep, their sleek backs lifting and tails slapping the water. Joran recalled pictures of these creatures from Sola's massive books, never having imagined he would witness their magnificent rollicking. He and Ruyah watched in wonder as the group of whales moved farther out to sea, leaving the moonlight behind in their wakes. And then, Joran sensed something coming on the wind, causing the hairs on his neck to bristle.

Ruyah's ears perked up. He leaped to his feet and turned to Joran. *There is no time to lose, Joran. Run!*

Joran wasted no time on questions. He tore off down the hill to the shoreline, looking around him as he ran. He could see nothing but the Moon tugging at the waves, but he recognized the disturbing feeling that crawled over him like an army of fire ants. The same sensation he had encountered over and over in his dreams, and the malevolent force that besieged him in the wilderness when he was sick with fever. Just the thought of that fortress with its evil creatures sent Joran into a panic.

He raced as fast as he could but the sand dragged him down. Ruyah kept pace with him, loping close by his side. Far off in the distance, over the ocean, a black cloud gathered, punching an empty hole into the moonlit night. And it headed their way.

Look, Joran! The wolf turned to the cliff, and Joran saw what he saw. Behind him, a tangle of bleeding heart vines trailed down the cliff, and far up on an angled ledge of crumbling sandstone was the sand castle, gleaming under the Moon's harsh glare, almost surreal. Joran looked back at Ruyah, who urged him with his eyes as well as his mindvoice. *Go! Save Charris—quickly!*

A strong wind kicked up, and instead of riding into shore, this wind blustered out to sea in great force, billowing the waves back toward the horizon, toward the gathering cloud amassing near the belly of the Moon, pushing like a wedge against the blackness.

Joran stripped the pack off his back and tossed it on the beach beside Ruyah. As he grasped the vines and dug his toes into the cliff he looked over at the wolf, who stood still on the shore, his head bowed and his lips trembling. His silver fur gleamed and light gathered around him in strange fashion. But Joran had no time to ponder the scene unfolding on the beach. He reached one hand over another, sweat working its way down his face and back. Dizziness and nausea assailed him, but he willed himself on, thinking of Charris and how he longed to hold her again. So many times he had made this climb, and now, exhausted, he pressed himself on, knowing it would be the last time.

Finally, he reached the ledge and dug into the sand with his fingers, trying to heft himself up. Sand gave way and pieces of cliff broke off, but Joran reached again and pulled himself onto the ledge. As he lay there panting, he noticed a swirl of black speeding over the water. The Moon kept laughing as the air began to reverberate with a dull roar.

Joran stood and turned to face the sand castle. Wind spun around him, sending whorls of sand into his eyes and hair, stinging his cheeks. He was at the base of the castle, and all the small imbedded pebbles shone in the moonlight like a thousand forgotten jewels. So often he had stood here, before the window, racked with anger, fear, and trepidation. But now it was ever so much more real, and although he felt fear welling up, his heart burst with love and need.

As he approached the frosted window, the ground trembled. Joran steadied himself from falling and watched as a huge chunk of the sandy ledge toppled slowly to the sea below. He felt more than heard giant waves careening off the side of the cliff and worried for Ruyah. Inching his way to peer over the ledge, Joran carefully eased himself to the ground. Yet when he looked down, the beach was gone; below him the water churned and tossed in great turmoil. Horror grabbed his heart. *Ruyah!*

His eyes searched the water in panic. Just as he readied himself to slide his way down to the water, the wolf nearly collided with him, Joran's pack dragging from his mouth.

Joran again fell to his knees and wrapped his arms around the wolf. *Ruyah, I was so afraid I had lost you!*

I found another way up the cliff. The Moon is harnessing her anger and the foundations of the earth are tearing apart! The wolf looked over at the sea-glass window. *It is time.*

But how do I get her out?

Use your intent, Joran. Focus your love. I know of no other way.

Wave after wave smashed the side of the cliff, causing slides and pulling chunks of rock from their beds into the roiling water in slow motion. Joran stumbled shakily as the rumbling ground tossed him from side to side. He tripped and fell against the window, aware of the ledge giving way just inches from his feet. Through the thick glass he could make out Charris's face, and this time, she was so real, so close, his breath caught in his throat. He rubbed the window hard with his shirt and could tell she was embedded in ice, unable to move, yet her lips were mouthing words. "Joran, save me!"

Joran's heart beat hard, and love infused him with strength and determination. Behind him the dull roar grew to a high-pitched moan, hurting his ears. The thickness of evil carried on the wind hemmed them in and made Joran's head reel. Ruyah, chest hugging the sand, inched up to Joran, who could tell the noise hurt the wolf's ears too. The night sky above became engulfed in ink, and even blotted out the Moon, who kept up her raucous laughter from behind the shroud.

Joran looked around him, picked up a rock, and with both hands smashed it against the window. Charris pulled back, fear racing across her face as cracks formed around her head, cracks that spidered outward and multiplied with each blow.

Over and over Joran smashed the rock against the window. Small pieces of glass shattered and flew out toward his face to be carried off by the wind. Glass turned to ice and ice to water.

Charris's face pleaded with Joran. "Hurry, Joran, hurry!"

Another strike and shards of ice blew out, releasing a spray of chilling water, just as Joran's feet slipped. He looked down.

The sand was siphoning through some giant rift in the ground as through an hourglass. The ledge dissolved and it too became a fluid river of sand drawing down under Joran's feet. All around him the blackness whirled and spun, the noise deafening. Ruyah pushed hard against Joran, who kept pounding away at the window with his rock.

The sand castle began to melt like hot wax before a fire; the turrets sank in a puddle, dripping down the sides of the castle. Joran looked up and saw the entire roof cave in on top of Charris. He focused all his strength and intent, and with one final attack broke through the last vestige of ice, releasing a deluge of sea water that sent Joran and the wolf reeling backward.

What was left of the castle swirled in the torrent around him, foamy and cold. Joran strained forward and reached out his hand. He found Charris and grasped her arm, pulling her with all his might and freeing her from water, ice, and sand. She spilled into his arms.

Above them the sky vanished, and the world whipped around them in a melee of wind and water. Charris wrapped her arms tightly around Joran and buried her face in his chest as the sand kept sucking them down, down toward the violent sea. Her dress was soaked and her feet bare. Even amid the chaos, Joran reveled in having Charris in his arms. He had never thought it possible that he would ever again know this feeling, this unimaginable joy of holding her again. The exhaustion from all the months of journeying to find her—the anguish, confusion, fear—all seemed to melt away along with the sand castle. But Joran knew he could not afford to indulge in even one minute of this joy. He had rescued her only to face losing her at any moment.

Ruyah—where are you? Joran could see nothing in the dark void that swallowed them up. He flailed his arms, feeling for fur as sand bit his eyes. Charris gripped tighter as they slid, the sand drawing them down into the sea. She yelled something incoherent to Joran; the waves pounded louder and louder as the two continued to slip and slide, and as the world dissolved around them.

I am right here, Joran, by your side! Ruyah poked Joran's leg with his nose. *Here is your pack. Quickly, take out the moonshell, the sunstone, and the silver circlet! You must use them to save Charris and yourself!*

Joran felt blindly for the pack. He fished around inside and withdrew the gifts given him by Cielle, Sola, and Noomahh. He stuffed the shell and stone into his pocket and grasped the circlet with one hand. The Moon, hidden behind the maelstrom, laughed again, sending a chill of fear through Joran's bones. The wind roared and a cold frost gathered at his toes. In the gloom he watched his half-buried feet—and Charris's feet—quickly becoming coated with frost. He reached down to feel for Ruyah, and the wolf looked up at him, white ice coating his fur.

In the midst of the horror, Joran startled at Ruyah's calm expression, his face radiating peace and serenity. Joran, holding the circlet loosely in his hand, gaped in wonder at the wolf. The silver loop glowed dully and began to vibrate.

Ruyah, what is it? What do I do? How do I stop this madness?

The wolf spoke reassuringly. *Joran, my young human, it is time to loose the last key. You have to open the lock.*

How? How do I do this?

The heart is the key. Ruyah looked deeply into Joran's eyes. *It is always the key to opening every difficult lock.*

What are you saying?

Charris looked at Joran, displaying her terror. "Joran, what is happening? We are going to drown!" She grabbed him tighter as they continued slipping. The churning sea was only a few feet below them, and there was nowhere to go but down into the dark, foreboding water. Joran tried to find his balance as he rocked back and forth, slipping, slipping down. He found it hard to focus on the wolf's words over the din of the whirlwind.

The moonshell. Remember Cielle told you the only way to stop the Moon was to put your whole heart into it.

Yes, but I don't understand!

Joran, pull out your knife.

Joran did what the wolf ordered, but he did not like where this was leading.

Joran, you must trust me. Now—this is what you must do. Unclasp the circlet.

Joran pulled the circlet apart. Sparks snapped and crackled from the silver, and wind gathered around them, expectantly. He held the knife in his other hand. The black cloud withdrew a bit, hovering in anticipation. Charris stared wide-eyed as if seeing the wolf for the first time. She yelled over the drone of the wind.

"Joran, that is a wolf! What is it doing here?"

"Please Charris, he is my friend and has helped me rescue you."

"Rescue me? From what?"

"I will have to explain later." Charris leaned her face into Joran's shoulder, holding tightly to his arm as the wind whipped at her hair and clothing.

Ruyah came in front of Joran and sat back on his haunches. *Look at me, Joran.*

Joran turned and focused on Ruyah. Wind lashed hair into his face as he strained to listen. *Now you must kill me. Take the circlet and tighten it around my neck.*

What! Are you crazy? Joran threw the silver circlet to the sand as if it were hot to touch. Water hissed and splattered as it began to sink.

Joran, trust me. This is the only way. Or we will all die.

No, I will not do this thing!

You must. You have no other choice.

Joran shook—every muscle in his body rebelled. What the wolf was asking him was insane! He looked around him and saw the last mound of sand slipping under their feet. Water began to foam around them and the icy shock of it sent Charris screaming.

"Joran! Do something!"

Ruyah looked calmly at Joran. *Young human, it is time. Remember how you cut my paw, to release me from the trap?* Joran nodded vacantly. *Now you must take the circlet and strangle me. Once I am dead, use your knife and cut out my heart. Place it in the moonshell. Hurry.*

No! The Moon told me to put my *whole heart into it! Not yours!*

But Joran, the wolf said, a rush of love filling his eyes, *I am* your *heart.*

Joran could not move. Horror flooded him, like the waters rising up his legs. Now he knew he was truly drowning.

Joran, you must loose your fear and trust me.

But Ruyah, how can I kill you? I love you so much! I don't want to lose you!

The wolf smiled. *It is said among wolves, "To be trusted is a greater compliment than to be loved." Will you honor me with your trust? Noomahh told you whatever you bind with the cord, you will lose. But that which you lose you will bind forever to yourself. Joran, this is the only way to save Charris and yourself. But, by doing this, I will be bound to you forever.*

How? How can you be bound to me if you are dead?! Joran's voice reflected the hysteria he felt. Tears poured down his face and he thought his heart would break. Water surged on all sides and Charris squeezed Joran tighter. Now their knees were immersed, and the force of the waves swayed them, threatening to lift them up off the sand as the silver coil floated ominously before them. Water rose up to the wolf's haunches, but he still did not move.

Joran looked deeply into the wolf's yellow eyes and a sudden, strange feeling washed over him. If he could name it, he would have called it understanding, and for a timeless moment Joran experienced a deep longing, a recognition and sadness that also contained boundless joy. Coating his fear, his horror, this surge of peace enveloped him like a warm blanket, and all the turmoil and mayhem was blotted out. Love filled him and expanded like the endless sea, and his spirit soared.

Steadily, without another thought, Joran picked up the circlet and fastened it around Ruyah's thick neck. His hands stopped shaking and a stillness came over him as Charris looked on aghast. He pressed his forehead against Ruyah's for a brief moment. The chaotic wind around him grew strangely silent as time stopped, and all Joran could hear in that hidden space was the pulse of his blood pounding in his ears.

Ruyah, forgive me!

With a sharp yank he strangled the wolf, who, without a sound or struggle, fell limp into the water. The silver circlet dissolved with a hiss and the wind around them quickly abated.

Wielding his knife, he worked quickly and efficiently, cutting open the wolf's chest and finding the heart. Blood turned the water red as Joran, weeping uncontrollably, reached in and severed the heart, still warm in his hands. As the sea rose to their waists, Joran pinned the wolf's lifeless body between his knees as it bobbed on the waves. Charris clung to Joran, too shocked to speak. With his free hand he pulled the large scalloped moonshell from his pocket.

The moment he set the wolf's heart into the shell, he heard the Moon gasp. In an instant, the black cloud of night sped off, the sound of a million bat wings racing toward the horizon where the Moon huddled in fear. The turbulent water grew calm and the waves subsided, draining away from Joran and Charris as if someone had pulled a plug.

Joran noticed his feet stood on the firm sand once more. The stars returned in multitude above them, shimmering like diamonds. A calm fell upon them, heavy with the enormous weight of the world. Charris still held fast, shaking and cold. Ruyah's limp body lay on the sand, his silver fur dull and soaked. Joran looked at him and grief overtook him. He collapsed to his knees, setting the shell—with the wolf's heart in the bowl of the shell—gently on the beach.

All around them the sea lapped their tiny island, but where was their escape? As far as Joran could see, the ocean went on forever, and he was still in the endless night of his dream. The Moon stayed on the rim of the horizon, unusually quiet, a dim, impotent presence. Both he and Charris shivered with cold, and his pack had been swept away.

Why had Ruyah asked him to do such a mad deed? What had been the use of killing the wolf? The evil cloud had left, but now they were doomed to die—without food, water, or warmth—trapped in his dream. He would much rather have drowned along with Ruyah than face this end! Why, oh, why had Ruyah insisted Joran kill him?

As Joran stroked the wolf's coat, Charris kneeled by his side. Her eyes questioned him, but her touch was meant to comfort. She put her arm around Joran and lay her head on his shoulder. She spoke softly. "You really loved that wolf, didn't you?"

Joran looked at her, wiping his eyes. He could think of nothing to say in reply. He just nodded and wept.

After a while he lifted his head and turned to Charris. Words snagged in his throat. "Charris, I am so sorry. What I did to you. Sending you away."

Charris stopped his lips with her fingers. "Shh. It's all right, Jor. I am just so glad you are safe. I dreamed you were trapped. I could see you through a window, and I kept calling out to you, trying to find you, but you always faded out of sight." Charris wrapped her arms around her knees, trying to warm herself. Joran embraced her. "How did we end up here, Jor? And where are we?"

"It will take a long time to explain. Charris, I have been trying to find you for an eternity. You disappeared one night; it was my fault. I thought you had been . . . unfaithful to me." He hung his head in shame. "Will you ever be able to forgive me?"

Charris didn't answer, but she lifted Joran's chin with her hand and kissed him tenderly. Joran sighed and lost himself in her embrace. Whatever happened now didn't matter. Now he felt peace, the peace he longed for, even though it appeared that that peace would be short-lived and laced with sorrow. He looked at the moonshell resting on the sand. *Ruyah! Why?*

Something curious caught his attention; he leaned over to observe the shell more closely. What? he wondered. Surely his eyes were fooling him. The heart lay in the scoop of the shell—but it moved!

Joran's mouth dropped open. The wolf's heart pulsed with a barely perceptible rhythm. Charris came over and, taking Joran's hand in hers, watched alongside him. With each beat the shell grew wider and taller, and as the shell grew, the heart beat stronger. Joran and Charris stepped back, the night settling quietly around them until the only sound puncturing the air was the steady thump of Ruyah's heart.

Larger and larger the shell grew, its creamy sides changing shape gradually, stretching and forming until, before them, resting on the sand, was a sleek boat the pale shade of the Moon. The prow curved upward in a curl, like a snail shell, and it glowed softly as if made of moonlight. Joran touched the hull and jumped back. Rather than hard and smooth, the surface of the boat was soft and warm, like skin. And the oddest thing was that the heart was nowhere to be found, yet the boat itself throbbed with a small, steady pulse as if alive.

Joran walked around the boat. Swirling designs of waves mimicked the moonshell's pattern. The inside of the boat was completely smooth, but the bottom was lined with what Joran could only describe as fur. He shook his head in wonder, then took Charris's hand once more. They pushed the boat—surprisingly light—over into the water, and Joran helped Charris climb in. He gathered Ruyah's cold, stiff body into his arms and, stumbling under the weight, carried it over to the boat and gently set it on the floor.

As he collapsed on the bottom of the boat next to Charris, across the sea, at the end of the world, the Moon cast a final glare and fell over the rim, disappearing from sight. The stars returned in force, glittering in brilliance and illuminating the placid water, which reflected back the heavenly multitude in breathtaking radiance. A sudden warm wind lifted them and pressed them out to sea, across water slick as glass, the prow of the boat scattering stars in its wake. Warm wind dried their clothes, soothed their aches, and calmed their hearts.

Joran let the wind carry him and his cares far into the night as he rested one hand on the body of the wolf and finally, at last, awoke from his dream.

TWENTY-TWO

Charris slept in the crook of Joran's arm as the night stars traversed the stretch of sky. On the eastern horizon, light danced, chasing the last lingering stars from their beds. A warm, calm morning dawned, with a light so pure and cleansing that Joran's skin tingled. He had no memory of the last time he had seen a true morning, with the Sun floating into the world like a dandelion seed on the wind. Perhaps the Sun really did burn with anger each day, but Joran sensed no rage, no harsh judgment cast down on the world of men. This was the first morning, born anew with healing on its wings, and although Joran had saved Charris, his journey was not over. As much as Joran wanted to feel happy, the brightness of the day was dulled by a heart laden with the loss of his friend.

He took comfort in the warm wind's presence, but where they were headed was a mystery. Would the ocean ever end and, if it did, where would they land? How would they ever be able to find their way back to Tebron?

Through the night they had slept a hard, exhausted sleep in the bottom of the boat. The soft floor and comforting heartbeat chased away nightmares; Joran had slept a sleep of death, awaking in rebirth to the realization that never again would he be haunted by those fearsome images. Charris was no longer trapped and his anger seemed a distant memory. The world gradually became tangible, colors returned to normal, the natural cycles of the earth were restored. Yet, here he and Charris were, in a magical boat; there was nothing normal about that.

He looked over at the wolf's body. Ruyah, his dearest friend, was truly dead. There was no getting around that fact either, even if the boat did pulse from his heart. Ironic, Joran mused bitterly, that Ruyah's heart was somehow still beating strong, while his own heart was surely breaking.

As the Sun rose higher, Charris began to stir. She opened her eyes and brushed the hair from her face. Joran leaned over and kissed her.

"Good morning." He smiled at her sleepy face, at the love in her eyes, and tried to console himself. At least his wife was now safe—and back in his arms. Something precious had been salvaged from the shipwreck of his life.

"Someone needs a haircut and a shave! Look at this wild head of hair you have—and I've never seen you with a beard. Makes you look . . . older."

"I feel older, much older."

"And where did you get this?" she asked, touching the moon on his forehead.

Joran sighed. "That's a long story."

She sat up and squinted at the brilliant day, at the calm water spread out around them. "I was dreaming. Such a strange dream too." She rubbed her eyes. "We were in a storm, and something was coming after us. I was so scared. We were slipping into a huge sea of water, about to drown—and you rescued me. And somehow, I can't remember, we escaped." Her eyes fell onto the wolf and she became quiet.

"Joran, that was no dream, was it?"

Joran shook his head.

"How did I get from Tebron to that place? I have no memory . . ."

Joran shrugged. "It's complicated."

His stomach growled, reminding him how long it had been since he'd eaten anything. If only he had been able to save his pack, they would have had food and water. Now, if they did not find land soon, they would be in trouble once more.

Charris leaned back into Joran's arms. She sighed. "Well, I am just glad to be with you, wherever we are. But I really want to go home."

"So do I."

Home. The word filled him with images of Tebron, and the memories of that place came rushing at him full force. A longing in him rose so forcefully he nearly cried, and at the same moment, the wind increased and pressed the boat quickly, skimming it through the water like a knife through soft butter. Joran's attention snagged on something in the distant sky, riding on the wind's current, coming toward them. A flock of colorful birds swooped down on them, dropping fruit into their laps and filling the bottom of the boat with more than they could eat for weeks. Joran recognized the elegant plumage of the birds from the South Wind's cave, and the fruit they delivered came from her trees. He watched as the feathered contingent turned around and winged their way back. Charris's jaw dropped as she watched them fly away and melt like a vapor into the ribbons of clouds.

"Joran, look at them. They are so beautiful—where do they come from?"

"The South Wind sent them. She is the one directing our boat."

"The South Wind? Who is she? How do you know this?" Charris took a bite from a large green fruit. "Oh, this is delicious—I've never tasted anything like it."

Joran reached for a dark red plum. He took a bite and the juice dribbled down his chin. Sweetness exploded in his mouth and refreshed his soul. "There is so much to tell you, I don't know where to begin."

"Then start at the beginning," she said, wiping plum juice off his beard with a chuckle.

Joran looked down at the wolf and his heart ached. With the knowledge that the Wind watched over them, he relaxed. Maybe, as she had promised him, he would return home and live a happy, peaceful life. But, with Ruyah gone, there was an ache in his chest he knew nothing could ever fill. He felt his own heart had been cut out. Why did Ruyah have to die? And how had he known his sacrifice would save them?

Joran thought back to the moment in the cave when he and the wolf had stood before Noomahh. How the South Wind and the wolf had spoken to each other, and how Ruyah had grown solemn. *"You have a tricky path ahead of you, Ruyah. You risk much to gain all."* Joran frowned. Well, it seemed that Ruyah had risked everything and lost all. He lost his life—so what had he gained? And if by losing the wolf, Joran had bound him forever to him, what did that matter now? Ruyah was dead. What comfort was there in that? Tears streamed down his face as he stroked the wolf's head. Just another stupid riddle; he thought he was done with riddles.

They followed a steady course west, with the Sun rising the next morning and the wind pushing them relentlessly. He and Charris ate the fruit and soaked up the sun, and Joran told her of his adventures—from the day he left Tebron until arriving at the sea. Charris bombarded him with questions and was amazed at his tales; they were so fabulous even Joran wondered if they had truly happened.

That night brought another splattering of stars, but the Moon never made an appearance. From time to time Joran caught sight of a large black bird winging above them, and again he slept a dreamless sleep—until the morning of the third day, when he awoke abruptly as the boat ran aground on the shore of a nameless beach. Backed up against the sky were towering mountains that looked remarkably like the Sawtooth Ridge embracing the forest of Tebron.

Charris and Joran jumped out onto the shore, marveling at the scenery. After pulling the boat up onto the beach, Joran looked around him. The air smelled fresh, of forest and mountain, but the warm wind that had guided them along thinned and died, leaving a brisk, cold morning. They had landed in a crescent cove, with spindly trees growing close to the water's edge. Apart from a few small birds pecking the sand, the beach was desolate. Snow glistened on the tops of the mountains, and the distinct chill of winter permeated the air. The place was somehow familiar, but Joran had never seen the ocean until his dreams. Yet he sensed he had been here before.

Charris cuddled up next to Joran in an attempt to get warm. He looked down at her bare feet, tinged blue from the cold. "Now what?" she asked.

Joran had no idea. Just where were they? And with no extra clothes or means to make a fire, Joran wondered why the South Wind had led them there. Had she just deposited them on the closest beach? How long could they last without warmth and shelter?

Before he could tackle any of these problems, there was one thing Joran had to do. He would bury Ruyah, and if he could not find a stick or useful rock with which to dig a grave, he would dig with his bare hands. He could not fathom the thought of leaving the wolf's body to rot on the beach, or to be carried away into the sea to be feasted upon by some creature of the deep.

"Charris, would you help me? I need to get Ruyah out of the boat."

They grasped Ruyah's heavy body and, tipping the boat to its side, dragged it out along the beach. Charris remained quiet while Joran bent over the wolf, and, unable to control himself, wept his heart out. Great sobs shook his chest and his throat closed tight. A steady stream of tears fell onto the wolf's muzzle and glistened on his fur like pearls. Joran stroked the wolf's silver fur and leaned over and kissed his nose. Quietly, he said good-bye.

Ruyah, my sweet and wonderful friend. I will miss you. More than you will ever know. You are truly bound up in my heart, and I will never let you loose. Why, oh, why have you left me?

Just as he thought these words he felt a trembling underneath him. The wolf's body began to move and shimmer. Joran pulled back in surprise. He watched in shock as a transformation took place. The wolf faded, but something else began to appear. Charris hurried over to Joran's side and they both gawked as, gradually, the wolf's body completely vanished and in its place stood a man.

Joran had never before seen anyone like him. With silver hair and a short, neat beard, he stood proud and tall. His contagious smile—a smile that showed an ageless, timeless face—filled Joran with unspeakable happiness. He was dressed in fine clothes, but it was his stature, not his attire, that bespoke royalty. And he radiated a glory so powerful that the beach lit up around them; even the sea sparkled in gold. The air hummed with a vibrant energy, causing even the birds along the water's edge to stop and stare. As Joran looked at him, the man's eyes met his, and Joran gasped.

They were deep brown, not yellow—but they were Ruyah's eyes. He had looked into the wolf's face so many times he knew this beyond a doubt. And the man before him saw that look of recognition and smiled warmly. Joran glanced down and noticed the last two fingers on one of the man's hands were missing.

Joran cried, helpless to hold back the flood streaming down his face. The man walked over to Joran and wiped the tears from his face. "It is all right to cry, Joran." The timbre of the man's voice was deep, coming from a faraway place, full of timeless comfort that bespoke wisdom and truth. It was a familiar voice, like the one Joran often heard speaking in his heart in the quiet hours late in the night.

Looking up, Joran saw the man's eyes fill with tears. He wrapped his arms around Joran, and for a very long time neither of them spoke. Charris watched in amazement.

"Thank you, Joran, for trusting me. You set loose the third key—your fear, letting go of your need for control, for answers. You had to lose something you loved, and that is not an easy thing. What you did was difficult beyond imagining, and I know it caused you great pain." The man rested his hand on Joran's shoulder and looked deeply into his eyes. Joran wiped his face and found his voice. "I don't understand! Why did I have to kill you? And how is it you are a man and not a wolf?"

"Look, Joran!"

Joran followed the man's eyes and saw a small cottage tucked neatly under a rock ledge. A wisp of smoke rose from the chimney and fallen leaves draped the rocks outside. Over a ridge, coming down from one of the Sawtooths, was the man, a great wizard and king, weary and injured from battle. Joran rummaged through the wizard's thoughts and memories and a larger picture began to gel in his mind. Centuries of battling evil, other worlds, other realms where he struggled with these powers. This wizard had existed from the beginning of time.

And then the chill crept up his neck. Joran knew this blackness and horror all too well. He gasped as the wizard ran into the cottage, watched as evil attacked and smothered, as the wizard reached out for his wife and then lost her. Then he held his breath as he saw the wizard race into another softly lit room and throw himself over a small bed. He heard the spoken spells and saw the black cloud skulk away, carried off in the wind. And then the wizard reached down and picked up—his son!

In that instant everything Joran had ever pondered fell into place. He knew, so clearly, so easily, that he was that infant. A strange stirring of power filled him as he connected all the pieces of his life together: how he had never fit into his family, how he had looked and behaved differently than everyone around him, why he was able to speak with animals and wield power in his dreams, trapping Charris with his anger. All made sense in that moment of revelation. He was a wizard's son!

Now Joran watched as his father fastened him to a large bear, and he followed the bear with his gaze as she worked her way down the mountainside into the forest of Tebron and to—the goose woman's house!

Joran gasped again. There was the goose woman, looking just as old and shabby as Joran remembered her, standing outside her shack. She was untying the cloth from the bear's chest and carefully removing the baby. She muttered her words to the bear.

You brought me a little cub. She looked at Anya and nodded. *Ah, this is the wizard's son. I cannot care for him, but I know who will.*

The bear stood by as the woman disappeared into her shack and shortly returned. Joran recognized the woven birch basket, the one on the sill at his mother's house. Shyra had said to him, "Joran. You go in there. With the eggs."

The woman carried the basket carefully down the steps, balancing with her staff, a bundle tucked under blankets and eggs all around. With a nod, Anya shuffled back into the cover of trees. Draped in fog, the old woman waddled slowly down the trail to the cart road leading to the village of Tebron.

Joran stared in surprise as the door to his village home opened and Oreb stood there, leaning down to hear what the goose woman said to him. Shyra joined him on the stoop, and behind them, Joran could make out three small boys, running and chasing each other boisterously through the living room. Oreb and Shyra conferred with the woman for a time, and then Shyra reached into the basket and pulled back the blanket. Her face lit up, so young and alert that Joran's chest throbbed with pain at the simple beauty he saw there. Shyra looked at Oreb, who paused, then nodded his head. As Oreb lifted the basket and brought it into the house, the goose woman turned back to face the closed door and spoke quietly, chuckling to herself.

"Good-bye, little cub. You will be safe here." She then hobbled down the steps, back through the village, and lost herself in fog.

Joran's vision returned to the wizard's cottage, half-buried in rock and draped with an ominous cloak of quietness. The wizard stood before the house and wove a deep spell, muttering words and gathering invisibility. Soon the house was gone and only rock remained. Then, with another string of phrases, the man became wolf and trotted off down the ridge, never looking back. The vision faded, and Joran stood immobile.

The wizard spoke quietly. "Joran, you have seen this evil. I did not want to give you away, but if I'd kept you, I would have lost you as I'd lost Rhianne. I bided my time, watching over you as you grew, and living a life of solitude and secrecy."

"Rhianne—your wife. My mother." Joran let that realization sink in. "But, you came with me on this journey." A look of understanding lit up his eyes. "You made sure I would find you and befriend you."

The wizard nodded at Charris. "When you trapped your wife, I had to help. No one in Tebron would know how to lead you to her. And you had many things to learn about your powers before you could face the Moon and rescue Charris."

He laughed. "I also had such joy in being with you, this time as your friend and companion, instead of watching you from afar. How often I wanted to tell you the truth, but there is a time for everything. And there is one other thing."

The wizard gestured to them to sit. So they sat on the beach and listened, riveted by the wizard's words.

"I also needed the sunstone. I had learned of them ages ago, long before you were born. Yet I had no way of getting one of the stones on my own. I learned they came from the palace of the Sun, but, as you well know, one does not just walk into that place. So I waited many cycles, watched you to make sure you were safe from forces of evil as you grew to manhood. When you began your journey, I knew it was time."

The sunstone! Joran remembered and reached into his pocket. He pulled out the stone and handed it to his father. In the wizard's palm it began to glow.

"Can you use it—to fight this dark power?"

The wizard laughed deeply, and the sound made Joran's heart sing for joy. "Because of you, yes."

"But I thought Sola said only one with a pure heart can wield its power, a heart with no darkness."

"And you cut out my heart, Joran. All human hearts have some part of darkness in them, but since mine was forfeited, I was given a new heart, one that is pure. I, too, had to lose something to gain the sunstone. I had to give up the small vestige of humanity I had, and for that I was granted a new, wonderful name."

"But this evil power—who is he and what does he want? Why is he capturing people and taking them away on boats?"

The wizard took Charris's and Joran's hands in his own. He leaned closer and said, "Let me tell you about good and evil.

"The evil in the world is not a person, or an evil wizard. Evil is a composite of all the stolen pieces of each person's name throughout time. It is said among . . . wizards"—with that he smiled—". . . that 'evil is a parasite, not an original thing. All things that enable a bad man to be effectively bad are in themselves good things—resolution, cleverness, intelligence, will.' Evil steals the piece that makes men remember who and what they are. The part that would bring them into harmony with the law of nature in all things. That is why men never feel complete—because they are missing a piece of their name. And that is why I have been given a new name—one without any darkness—a perfect, complete name.

"This evil is very ancient, and in a way, the saying is true: 'The danger is not in man's environment, but in man.' In one sense, humans create this evil, yet it is a momentum that gathers to itself like a rolling thundercloud. For eons evil has trapped and enveloped many, has empowered the weak and greedy, and used creatures for its own dark purposes. Yet, it cannot survive in the harsh glare of light. With the sunstone:

Light will shine in the darkness, and darkness will flee.
It will be a day of liberation as the captives go free.

Joran thought of his mother, Rhianne, and how hard it must have been for Ruyah to be patient and do nothing. And now, Joran guessed, Ruyah would have the power to free her and so many others. Joran's head reeled with so many new truths. He had a true father and mother. What was his mother like and would he meet her soon? Did he have brothers and sisters? Would he learn to live as a wizard's son, and not just be a simple blacksmith in Tebron? Maybe his riddles had now been answered, but they had been replaced by an avalanche of questions. One question came foremost to his mind.

"Is your name really Ruyah? Or is that your wolf name?"

The wizard laughed and leaned over to ruffle his son's hair. "It is one of my many names, and you can use it if you wish. I did give you my name to keep, remember? Yet I would be pleased if you called me 'Father.' "

Joran chuckled and embraced Charris, pulling her close. He met his father's eyes with tears in his own and, shaking his head in wonder, said, "Well, fancy that!"

· PART FIVE ·
THE SHORTEST WAY HOME

TWENTY-THREE

JORAN KNEW he should be tired, but his joy buoyed him along as if this time he were afloat on a different sea, one of happiness. He and Charris had watched in wonder as the wizard stood on the beach and wove spells, creating whorls of light and pulling textures from the air. Now they were clothed in warm attire—thick woolen shirts and trousers, comfortable lined boots, and heavy woolen cloaks. On Joran's back was a pack filled with food and a bulging water skin. He and Charris had watched in silence as wave after wave broke gently against the beached boat, eating away at it, just as the crumbling sand castle had dissolved, until all that lay on the beach was a large creamy shell. The wizard picked up the moonshell and handed it to Joran. Cielle's words came to mind as he weighed it in his hand. A souvenir, indeed.

Now his father walked before them with a steady stride, leading them up through the brush along a trail as the morning sun traveled in an arc overhead. The chill of the day burned off, and they stopped to rest at a clearing that overlooked the cove below them. Joran held Charris's hand as they took a long last look at the unimaginable sea—the sea that went on forever, just as the South Wind had described.

Joran smirked, thinking of all the tales he had heard of the sea—how it was filled with giant creatures, how it was smooth as glass, how it was turbulent and swallowed men like fish. How it was all those things—and more. Now Joran could add his own tale of the sea, but he knew, like all other tales, his would hardly be believed either, and would end up a matter of jest over ale in the tavern.

As they walked, the wizard told Joran amazing things about his world, and about many other worlds. And he grew excited speaking of Rhianne and so many others he missed and hoped to be reunited with. Much Joran did not understand, but he thrilled at listening to his father's voice. The sound of that voice was the most beautiful music he had ever heard. His was the soothing voice he had heard while forsaken in the cell in the fortress, when he huddled in terror on the floor. And it was also Ruyah's voice, the wise and kind voice that spoke directly to his heart.

The wizard halted and turned to his son. "Joran, I will always be near you. All you have to do is call. You have my name."

Joran's heart was so full of love and gratitude that words failed him. He wrapped his arms tightly around the wizard. "Father, how can I leave you now?"

"I will come to you shortly. But, as you know, I have a task to complete, whereas your task is finished."

"Joran—look!" Charris pointed up the trail. He released his father and watched curiously as a large, dark shape plodded toward them from a coppice of birches, bending branches and scattering the few clinging leaves.

The wizard chuckled as the huge bear lumbered along, her heavy bulk swaying from side to side. She lowered her head as she approached the wizard, burying her nose in his chest. "This is Anya." He stroked her plush auburn head.

Joran's face filled with wonder. "The bear you called that day. She took me to Tebron."

Anya turned and looked Joran over, sniffing his neck. *You have grown big, little cub. You have your mother's face—under all that hair.*

Joran smiled and stroked the bear, who yawned sleepily.

"She will lead you back to Tebron, back to your home," the wizard said.

"How can that be?" Charris asked, reaching out to touch Anya's head. "Tebron is nowhere near the sea."

Joran turned to her. "I suppose you could say that distance is an affair of the will." He saw his father smile, tears welling up in his eyes.

"Go. Anya will keep you safe. Go in my love and with my blessing. We will be together again soon, my young human."

Charris gave the wizard a warm embrace and lowered her head respectfully. "Thank you, thank you so much for saving us. You have brought Joran such joy and peace." She added, "I don't know anything about wizards or how to live among them, but I suppose I shall learn, since I seem to be married to one."

The wizard chuckled and kissed the crown of her head. Charris's cheeks flushed.

The wizard embraced his son one last time, and soon they were both in tears, laughing the same laugh. Joran and Charris followed the bear up the trail and into a crevice between steep rocks. Joran stopped and looked back to where his father had stood, but he was gone. All that remained was a brilliant light casting a gleam on the trees alongside the trail. Not quite sunlight or moonlight, but more like the essence of light itself—like liquid joy, Joran mused.

Only minutes after they had passed through the crevice, they emerged onto a rocky outcropping overlooking a wide vale, with a ribbon of river winding through it. And further down they saw a forest of giant trees, their tops scraping the sky—a thick forest hugging the walls of the mountain that encircled the vale.

"Joran—there's Tebron!"

From the heights they spotted the small village and the thatched roofs of the shops and houses. Joran thought he could see his own cottage just outside town. A winter frost coated the fields below, and when Joran listened hard enough he could hear the sound of the river wafting up the side of the mountain. A wave of homesickness filled his heart. Thoughts of returning to his simple life energized him. He felt as if he could run all the way back to Tebron.

He laughed, and the laugh was a healing to his heart. He had surely taken the long way 'round to find his way home. As his heart soared, a familiar voice found its way into his mind, laced with a hint of humor.

It is said among wolves, "And the end of all our exploring will be to arrive where we started and know the place for the first time."

Joran smiled and squeezed Charris's hand. "Let's run!"

Charris laughed and chased after Joran, the big bear frolicking at her heels as they bounded down the hill. Before they knew it, they were in the field behind their cottage, where they said good-bye to Anya. They held each other as they watched her pad her way back up the slope and into the woods beyond their sight.

A strange sensation came over Joran as he gingerly opened the door to their cottage. He half expected to find it covered in dust and cobwebs, or even occupied by someone else. Surely, since they had been gone for so long, something would have looked different, and yet—Joran's eyes were drawn to the kitchen table. The note he had written to Callen was still there, propped up against the lantern. Curious, Joran picked it up, and the parchment had not yellowed at all.

"Well, this is odd."

"What is it, Jor?" Charris looked around her. "Hey, there are my drawings—the new pattern I was working on." She immediately sat down at the table and shuffled through her sketches.

"I left this note for Callen, but he never came by. Wait, I'll be right back." He rushed out the door, leaving Charris poring over her birds and flowers.

As soon as he threw open the barn door, he saw the goat out in her pen. Charris's horse was in the back pasture nibbling grass.

Well, did you change your mind? I suppose you felt bad about sending me off to some strange farm.

Joran walked over to the goat. *Didn't the Agrens pick you up? What are you doing here?*

The goat grunted and chewed her cud. *I live here, remember? And you just left a short while ago. You said they were picking me up* tonight. *Does it look like night yet?* With a huff, she turned her back on Joran and wandered out into the pasture, mumbling to herself.

Joran was confused. He felt his beard, then touched the moon etched on his forehead—just to be certain. On the bench in the barn sat the wooden nail box, alongside the dish of half-eaten bird seed. He smiled. He hoped Bryp was happy now that she had found a home.

Joran went back inside his cottage and found Charris engrossed in her work. Her hand held a paintbrush, and she made wide, sweeping strokes on a large parchment. She didn't even look up when Joran came to her side. He looked at her design: one of the elegant green birds from the cave of the South Wind, with a frill of plumage trailing from her back. Surrounding the bird was the emerald sea, with frothing waves curling in a circular frame around the bird. He watched, intrigued, as her brush swirled, forming a chain of moonshells woven through the waves. She dipped her brush in a jar of water, then dabbed it in white paint. With a smooth flair of her wrist, she added a small, creamy moon off in the distance, hanging over the water, silent and unobtrusive.

Joran gently kissed the top of Charris's head—she never missed a stroke—and went to light the stove to brew her a cup of tea.

"You look young again—without all that hair." Charris reached over and stroked Joran's smooth chin as they walked down the cart road toward town. She had given him a haircut and a shave, and for the first time in a while, he could feel the cool air on his neck. The Sun dropped behind the ridge of mountains, casting an orange glow on the winter sky. The air tingled with a promise of snow.

"Your brothers are going to wonder about that moon on your forehead."

Joran smiled and nodded. All the hard, soapy scrubbing hadn't erased one line from his skin. The Moon may have marked him, but she had failed to triumph over him. He could live with that reminder.

As they traveled down the road, Joran looked up toward the ridge where he had so often seen the wolf watching him. There was no wolf there now, although Joran knew someday he would see him again, in one form or another. He thought of the wolf's proud stature, his beautiful silver fur, his quirky sense of humor. He missed his wolf.

Charris nudged him.

Coming up the road was a small figure, hunched over a walking stick. Joran stopped abruptly. He waited as the goose woman wobbled her way over to him, her scarf tight around her head and her wooden shoes clacking against the gravelly ground with each step. She halted in front of him and strained to look up into his face. Her smile spread, revealing her rotting teeth, then she grasped Joran's collar and pulled him close.

"Well, back so soon, little cub? I see you found your missing wife."

"I did. Thank you." He gave her a kiss on the top of her head and she jumped back, surprised. Joran chuckled.

"Well, now, did you find that nasty, tricky Moon? I hope she didn't give you too much trouble." The woman coughed and wheezed, then caught her breath. "But then, we guessed you would find her." She shook her head and smiled as if in conspiracy. Her eyes narrowed. "Ah, you found someone else too, didn't you?"

Before Joran could answer, she turned off toward a trail that led through the salmonberry bushes. She stopped and studied Joran from his head to his feet.

"New boots. Nice." With that she vanished into the forest.

Charris looked at Joran and they both erupted in laughter. They continued down the road until they came upon the old Baylor farm. Joran's breath caught in his throat. All his jealousy and anger, his trapping Charris, and his resultant long, long journey, were because of what he had seen there—at the rundown barn next to the water-wheel. While they had floated along in the boat, Joran had told Charris his tale, yet purposely omitted this part. He had been too embarrassed and ashamed to voice what he had seen and assumed so readily. Even now his shame accused him and he grew silent. He dropped his gaze and hurried his step. But Charris stopped.

She waved at someone. He looked over at the barn and there was the woman from his vision! She wore a pale woolen dress—draped with Charris's shawl around her shoulders—and loaded a bale of hay onto a cart. Her dark hair splayed down her back and Joran marveled at how similar she looked to his own wife. Similar, but different.

"Hi, Charris!" she called over, then pulled the cart into the barn.

Joran found his voice. "Who is that?"

"That's Jena. She and Raold just got married."

"She's wearing your shawl."

"She works with me at the mill. She's always admired it, so I gave it to her—for a wedding present. Doesn't it look wonderful on her?"

"I thought that was your favorite."

"It is. But I can always make another, Jor. She could never afford one like it. And it's made her so happy." Charris smiled and started skipping down the road.

Joran shook his head from the irony of it all. For one person that shawl had brought great happiness and, for him, it had brought misery. But how could he despise the sequence of events that shawl had set in motion? It had led Joran to truth, to finding his true identity and his father, and—he also had to admit it—adventure.

Charris turned back to Joran and waved him on. "Come on, Jor. We'll be late!"

"Well, Charris, how was your trip home?" Felas spooned a huge portion of steaming beans onto his plate. He passed the bowl to Callen, who did the same. Platters and bowls of food covered every inch of the wooden table. Dishes and silverware rang in the flurry of serving and eating. Malka busied herself in a kitchen steamy and warm. Bela stood next to the baby's chair, forcing a spoon into his mouth while he fussed.

"Easy, Bela, you'll break the only two teeth he has," warned Malka from the next room.

Charris thought for a moment between bites. "It was an adventure." She threw a glance at Joran, who was cutting up some meat on his mother's plate. He smiled back.

Felas answered. "Well, we're glad you made it back before this bad storm blows in." Outside the window the wind moaned, and a chill air whistled through the cracks.

Shyra looked out at the dark night. "I think someone needs to prune those trees before the wind breaks the branches."

Maylon stirred a pot over the stove and called over to his mother. "Mum, the trees are fine. Enjoy your meal."

Callen sat across from Joran and stared at him. "Tell me again how you got that moon on your forehead. Who dared you to have that thing printed on your face?"

Bela chimed in. "I think it's cute, Uncle Jor! Papa, may I have one too?"

Maylon came into the dining room and set a bowl of potatoes at his daughter's place at the table. "No."

"Potatoes!" Bela put down the spoon and jumped into her chair. Malka scooped a heap onto Bela's plate.

Callen spoke again. "You look different, Jor. I can't put my finger on it."

"Charris gave me a haircut today."

Callen shook his head. "That's not it. You look—older. Years older."

Joran shrugged and tucked into his dinner.

Felas, next to him, tousled his hair affectionately. "See what marriage will do to you? Still looks like a young pup to me. Talk to any animals lately?" Felas reached across the table and grabbed the bowl of potatoes. He slopped some on his plate and then spooned a small dab on his mother's. Shyra ate slowly, methodically, as food appeared before her.

"At least her appetite is still good," Joran noted.

"Bela!" Malka yelled.

Bela had taken to decorating the baby with potatoes, with a potato hat and a smear of potato above his eyes. She quickly drew her finger in a circle on the baby's forehead before her mother grabbed her hand forcefully.

"See, Uncle Jor—nice moon!"

Everyone laughed, even Shyra, who looked over at Joran and spoke quietly.

"Did you find them, Joran?"

The table grew quiet as Joran's brothers marveled at the sudden lucidity of their mother. Malka came in and quietly wiped potatoes off the baby's head with a wet rag.

"Find what, Mum?" he answered.

"The eggs, little cub." Her face showed concern.

Felas chuckled. "Little cub. She must think you're a bear."

"Hush, Felas!" Malka chastened. She went over to Shyra and set down a glass of water. "You finished, Mum? Or do you want some more?"

Malka waited but Shyra didn't answer her. She kept looking at Joran, questions swimming in her eyes.

"Yes, Mum," Joran replied, taking her hand in his. "I found the eggs."

Shyra sighed deeply, relief returning to her face. "Good," she said. "Very good."

Charris linked her arm through Joran's as they leaned against the back fence, the night sky above them speckled with stars. Joran watched his family through the living room window; his brothers teased each other and laughed. The room, warmly lit by firelight, was a small shoal of happiness in the night. Outside, where he and Charris stood, the quiet settled thick and permeating. It coated them—their love and satisfaction—like a quilt, making Joran feel warm and safe. Joran watched in amusement as Bela tumbled with the baby. From time to time he heard laughter trickle out of the house and into the night air, and the sound comforted his heart.

From the backyard of his family home, Joran could just make out the tops of the mountains rising up behind the great forest. He thought about Ruyah—his father—and of so many of the things he had told him during their journey together. Joran had returned to the real world of shoeing horses, of baking bread—his world— and it suited him well, just like the new clothes Ruyah had made him. Sure, he now understood there was much more to the world, forces of evil and great battles drawn out over time. And maybe someday he would be called to take part in a life that was bigger than the one he lived in Tebron. But for now, he was content to be home.

Ruyah had told him his task was finished, but Joran sensed it was not. For the wolf had taught him that the perfect happiness of humans was a perilous balance, that there were an infinite number of angles at which a man may fall, but only one at which he could stand.

The South Wind had told him happiness could not be found by looking for it; only by searching for truth could it be discovered. Joran had searched for truth and, to his surprise, he had found happiness along with it. But just because he was standing today didn't mean he wouldn't fall tomorrow.

He thought bitterly of the day he walked past the Baylor farm and saw the man embracing a woman he assumed was Charris. In just one quick moment he had fallen—and look what that fall had wrought! He vowed in his heart, as he held Charris close, that he would work hard at this perfect happiness and do nothing to threaten it, for as strong as love seemed, it was also fragile as glass. And that was what made it so precious.

Suddenly, Joran felt the ground tremble. Far up the mountain, from behind the Sawtooth Ridge, a huge explosion of light burst into the sky. Charris gasped and they both shielded their eyes, for the light shooting out into the darkness was brilliant, like the light of a thousand suns. The world around them lit up like lightning streaking from the east to the west.

In the harsh, blinding glare, Joran watched his brothers come running out of the house, followed by Malka and Shyra. They stood in the middle of the apple orchard with hands raised and mouths opened in wonder. Out of the sky, jewels of light, like diamonds, rained down upon them, twinkling in the air as they fell. Like sparks, they crackled and exploded in tiny spurts as they hit the ground. A myriad of shooting stars descended upon the earth, bathing them all in brilliance.

Joran squinted as he looked up above the mountaintops. White, pure light, pulsed like a silent beacon into the night—and that is just how Joran saw it. A beacon welcoming him home, calling the world of men to stop wandering lost and come home. Calling humans to embrace their place in the universe bound by the perfect law of freedom.

Ruyah had told him, *the center of man's existence is a dream.* During his journey to the Moon, the Sun, the South Wind, and the sea, Joran had lived in a dream. He had come home to discover he had never left. Throughout his journey, he had looked outside—to find peace, to find Charris, to find his place in the world. Yet, Ruyah had rightly told him, *Who looks outside, dreams. Who looks inside, awakens.*

A surge of peace and joy filled him—from the crown of his head down to the tips of his toes, shaking him awake as if he'd been asleep his entire life. He put his arm around Charris and drew her close while he watched the pulsing light, which beat synchronously with his heartbeat. Now he understood how he could be both the dreamer and the dreamed—and that he could dream while wide awake.

And that made all the difference.

THE END

ENDNOTES

Elements from "The Enchanted Pig" (*Grimm's Fairy Tales*) provided the inspiration for the story.

Quotations in the book are from the following sources:

C. S. Lewis (mostly from *Mere Christianity*), G. K. Chesterton (mostly from *Orthodoxy*), Emily Dickinson, Carl Jung, T. S. Elliot, Friedrich Nietzsche, William Wordsworth, George MacDonald.

The Scriptures alluded to by Sola and Ruyah are found in the Holy Bible in John chapters 1 and 4; Matthew 8:20; James 1:25; and Hebrews 4:12, 13; 6:19.

The song sung by the bard comes from a Robert Burns poem: "A Red, Red, Rose" (1796), as adapted for the movie *Fly Away Home*, entitled "10,000 Miles," sung by Mary Chapin Carpenter.

ACKNOWLEDGMENTS

A big hug of gratitude for my readers, critiquers, encouragers, and prayer partners. I couldn't walk this path without holding your hands and having your shoulders to cry on. Your prayers lift me up and buoy me on the journey. A special thanks to Kathy Ide, Renae Brumbaugh, Catherine Leggitt, Ann Miller—you are each a godsend—my four legs of support.

And thanks to so many others who read, advise, and encourage me in my writing journey: Jim Bell, Elisabeth Pajara, Stephanie Morris, Jessica Dotta, Nancy Ellis, Pola Muzyka, Jeanette Morris, Rachel Williams, Kimberly Bass, Cheryl Ricker, Nick Harrison, Tina Dee, Sophia Yamas, Sharon Hinck, and the gals in the San Jose Christian Writers' Group and the Santa Cruz Writers' Group. Sometimes just a kind word at the right moment was all it took.

I have great appreciation for all those at AMG Publishers—for their enthusiasm, deep faith and reliance on God, and their dedication to their authors. I am very blessed to partner with you. Thanks to Rick, Trevor, Dale, and John for your encouragement and sharing my vision. And thanks to my agent, Susan Schulman, for encouraging me.

And most of all, thanks to my husband, Lee Miller, who is a constant support and fountain of encouragement. I love you beyond words and am so grateful to God for you. Thank you for the gift of time you give me to write and pursue my dream. And thanks to my daughters, Megan and Amara. You are so amazing and inspiring. These books could not have been written without all your great ideas, input, tough criticisms, and wild imaginations. You are God's greatest gift to me in this world.

DISCUSSION OF
THE WOLF OF TEBRON

I WROTE *The Wolf of Tebron* in order to portray God in a way that captures his love and devotion to our personal growth and salvation. God is both a God far away and a God close by (Jer. 23:23), and my aim was to dramatize a relationship that brought God into every aspect of our lives. Ruyah, the wolf, is not just a random companion, but shows what a true friend God is by providing for all Joran's physical, spiritual, and emotional needs. Each book in this collection of fairy tales aims to bring the reader to a better understanding of our Creator by using allegory and metaphor, drawing from traditional fairy tale elements along with Scripture.

I also wanted to explore the writings and themes of the famous Christian apologists G. K. Chesterton and C. S. Lewis, and so researched their books to glean wisdom that helped support the themes of my book. In addition to quotations from Chesterton and Lewis, this fairy tale pulls from great philosophers, and poets and writers of literature. Although *The Wolf of Tebron* could be classified as a "literary" fairy tale, the whimsical story and powerful allegories contained within are presented in a style that should appeal to young and old. What resounds from the pages of the book, overall, is God's great sacrifice, demonstrated in Ruyah's choice to give his life so Joran may live.

While this book quotes little from the Bible, the allegory of redemption underlies the story. We learn that Ruyah is not really a wolf but a wizard and king from ages past, and that in sacrificing his human life he receives a new name and the power to destroy evil. His intent is not just to save his son, Joran, but to save all humanity from wandering forever lost, out of harmony with all creation.

I have provided below a discussion of the literary and scriptural references found in *The Wolf of Tebron* that can be used in book club discussions and in high school and homeschool environments. With its rich vocabulary, array of metaphors and allegory, and literary content, this book makes a wonderful resource to be used in high school English classes.

1) The element of evil is portrayed in the book as a dark, nebulous force that appears first in the attack against the wizard, which forces him to go into hiding as a wolf. We learn the wizard has been fighting this evil for eons. Throughout the book, this presence of evil keeps reappearing in Joran's dreams, and whisks him away as captive to another realm. What does the wizard tell Joran about this evil and its source? How does the Bible refer to evil as darkness? (Read Eph. 6:12). What other things does darkness symbolize in the Bible? (Compare John 1:5; 12:46; Rom. 13:12; 2 Cor. 6:14; Col. 1:13; Rev. 16:10.)

2) The Moon is a symbol of lunacy in the book, but she is also portrayed as a vicious enemy who is holding Joran's wife captive. G. K. Chesterton is quoted in the book by

Ruyah: "The Moon is the mother of lunatics and has given to them all her name." The word *lunatic* is derived from *luna,* or "moon," as some long ago believed the moon caused madness, and even today the tidal pull of the moon is thought by some to influence moods. How does Joran battle with the Moon and what does he have to "loose" to conquer? Cielle also hums and sings songs that have moon themes. Can you identify any of the songs, poems, or nursery rhymes?

3) The goose woman calls Joran "little cub," and even his mother uses that appellation in addressing him. Why do you think they call him that?

4) The goose woman tells Joran he has trapped Charris with his anger. What did she mean? What does Joran learn about his anger and how to contain it? In the book, Joran must loose three keys before he can rescue his wife. How does this compare with the way God transforms our "old selves" into new creations made in the image of his Son?

5) The book is full of metaphors about dreaming. Carl Jung, the famous psychologist, said, "Who looks outside, dreams. Who looks inside, awakens." Waking and dreaming are motifs woven throughout the book. Joran is plagued by his dream; he searches the world for Charris, often feeling he is in a dream. And it is in his dream where he must find Charris to finally "wake up." Ruyah says, "The center of man's existence is a dream" (Chesterton). What do you think Chesterton meant by that? Ruyah tells Joran that humans are walking about as in

a dream, forgetting their names and who they are (also Chesterton). Wordsworth said, "Our birth is but a sleep and a forgetting." How do those verses aptly describe humanity's state today, and what is Ruyah's hope for mankind in the future?

6) Another thought about dreams: At the end of the book, Joran realizes he is both the dreamer and the dreamed. Earlier, Ruyah tells him that the Creator is the great dreamer, having dreamed the world into existence. Joran finally realizes he can dream while wide awake, "and that made all the difference." What do you think he means by that?

7) One of the themes of the book involves honor. The animal world follows an honor code, faithful to the perfect law of freedom. What is that perfect law and do humans follow it? The phrase is taken from James 1:25, a verse that implies that God's law results in freedom. Jesus said by following him, one would be truly free (John 8:31–36). What does he mean when he says, "If the son makes you free, you shall be free indeed"? Explain what Ruyah means when he says the law of nature binds, but also frees?

8) When Joran complains about being confused, Ruyah quotes Chesterton: "The world does not explain itself." He then quotes C. S. Lewis: "It is no good looking for a simple answer; after all, real things are not simple." What is the wisdom in adopting that point of view as we go through life? In what way are real things *not* simple? Chesterton seemed to feel mysteries in life are a good

thing, and implied that God allows mysteries when he said, "The riddles of God are more satisfying than the solutions of man." What do you think he meant by that?

9) Chesterton, in a sense, encourages us to be mystics. Just what is a mystic? Ruyah quotes him: "The mystic allows one thing to be mysterious and everything else becomes lucid." If one allows for mystery in God, how does that belief make everything in the world lucid?

10) Ruyah says (quoting Chesterton): "The vision is always solid and reliable. The vision is always a fact. It is reality that is often a fraud." Chesterton spoke of this in the context of comparing imagination and fantasy with what is considered in society to be practical, logical reality. Chesterton was told when he was young that, when he grew up, he would give up all those abstract, imaginary dreams and get down to reality, which meant leaving his dreams behind. But he felt that point of view was wrong, and that treasuring imagination and "vision" was vital in life. How are the things "seen" in this world often the fraud, whereas the "unseen" things are more solid? (Compare 2 Cor. 4:18).

11) Ruyah quotes Chesterton's words: "The perfect happiness of man . . . is an exact and perilous balance; like that of a desperate romance. Man must have just enough faith in himself to have adventures, and just enough doubt to enjoy them." This is a huge underlying theme of the book, as Joran seeks to find perfect happiness. C. S. Lewis said (paraphrased by Noomah): "In man's life, as in everything else, happiness is the one thing you cannot

get by looking for it. If you look for truth, you may find happiness in the end. But if you look for comfort, you will not get either comfort or truth—only wishful thinking and, in the end, despair." What qualities must we bring to a search for happiness, and why might we not find it by looking for it? What does the Bible say will bring true happiness?

12) C. S. Lewis said, "The longest way 'round is the shortest way home" (possibly quoting from an Irish proverb). How did Joran take "the long way 'round" to get right back where he started? How does this imply that our life journey may take some wrong turns before we arrive at our final destination? And why is a long road sometimes the best?

13) How does Ruyah show his love for Joran? How does his sacrifice mirror God's as he gives his life to save Joran? Joran is instructed to put his heart in the moonshell, but Ruyah insists his own heart (Ruyah's) must be used instead. What does Ruyah mean when he tells Joran, "But, I am your heart"?

14) Discuss the allegories of Ruyah compared with Christ in: his sacrifice, his position of power, his resurrection and transformation, and his authority over evil.

15) Joran is told that love is an affair of the will (Lewis). What does that mean? Can you love someone you don't like, and how does this kind of love reflect God's love for humanity? How is love demonstrated by action? (John 3:16; Matt. 5:43–48).

C. S. Lakin welcomes comments, ideas, and impressions

at her Web sites: **www.cslakin.com** and

www.**gatesofheavenseries.com**.

Look for *The Map Across Time*—the next book in

The Gates of Heaven series, releasing spring 2011

Coming Soon from Living Ink Books

THE MAP ACROSS TIME

C. S. Lakin

ISBN-13: 978-0-89957-889-7

An ancient curse plagues the kingdom of Sherbourne, and unless it is stopped, all will fall to ruin. The King, obsessed with greed, cannot see the danger. But his teenage twin children, Aletha and Adin, know they must act. A hermit leads Adin to a magical map that will send him back in time to discover the origin of the curse. Once back, Adin must find the Keeper, who protects the Gate of Heaven, but all he has is a symbol as a clue to guide him. Unbeknown to Adin, Aletha follows her brother, but they both arrive in Sherbourne's past at the precipice of a great war, and there is little time to discover how to counteract the curse.

For more information visit

www.LivingInkBooks.com

or call 800-266-4977

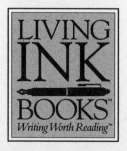

Other Releases from Living Ink Books

SWORD IN THE STARS

Wayne Thomas Batson

ISBN-13: 978-0-89957-877-4

Haunted by memories of a violent past, Alastair Coldhollow wagers his life on the hope that a sword will appear in the stars and the foretold Halfainin, the Pathwalker, would come. Meanwhile, tensions simmer between Anglinore and the murderous Gorrack Nation, threatening war on a cataclysmic scale. The fate of all could rest on an abandoned child and the decisions of those who desperately seek to identify him. *Sword in the Stars* is the first release in **The Dark Sea Annals** series.

For more information visit

www.LivingInkBooks.com

or call 800-266-4977

Other Releases from Living Ink Books

MASTERS AND SLAYERS

Bryan Davis

ISBN-13: 978-0-89957-884-2

Expert swordsman Adrian Masters attempts a dangerous journey to another world to rescue human captives who have been enslaved there by dragons. He is accompanied by Marcelle, a sword maiden of amazing skill whose ideas about how the operation should be carried out conflict with his own. Since the slaves have been in bonds for generations, they have no memory of their origins, making them reluctant to believe the two would-be rescuers. Set on two worlds separated by a mystical portal, *Masters and Slayers* is packed with action, mystery, and emotional turmoil, a tale of heart and life that is sure to inspire. Book 1 of the new **Tales of Starlight** series!

For more information visit

www.LivingInkBooks.com

or call 800-266-4977

The **Dragons in our Midst®** and **Oracles of Fire®** collection
by **Bryan Davis**:

RAISING DRAGONS

ISBN-13: 978-089957170-6

The journey begins! Two teens learn of their dragon heritage and flee a deadly slayer who has stalked their ancestors.

THE CANDLESTONE

ISBN-13: 978-089957171-3

Time is running out for Billy as he tries to rescue Bonnie from the Candlestone, a prison that saps their energy.

CIRCLES OF SEVEN

ISBN-13: 978-089957172-0

Billy's final test lies in the heart of Hades, seven circles where he and Bonnie must rescue prisoners and face great dangers.

TEARS OF A DRAGON

ISBN-13: 978-089957173-7

The sorceress Morgan springs a trap designed to enslave the world, and only Billy, Bonnie, and the dragons can stop her.

EYE OF THE ORACLE

ISBN-13: 978-089957870-5

The prequel to *Raising Dragons*. Beginning just before the great flood, this action-packed story relates the tales of the dragons.

ENOCH'S GHOST

ISBN-13: 978-089957871-2

Walter and Ashley travel to worlds where only the power of love and sacrifice can stop the greatest of catastrophes.

LAST OF THE NEPHILIM

ISBN-13: 978-089957872-9

Giants come to Second Eden to prepare for battle against the villagers. Only Dragons and a great sacrifice can stop them.

THE BONES OF MAKAIDOS

ISBN-13: 978-089957874-3

Billy and Bonnie return to help the dragons fight the forces that threaten Heaven itself.

Published by Living Ink Books, an imprint of AMG Publishers
www.livinginkbooks.com ✦ www.amgpublishers.com ✦ 800-266-4977